The Breaking Dawn

BOOK ONE
THE KINGDOM OF MERCIA

JAYNE CASTEL

Historical romances by Jayne Castel

DARK AGES BRITAIN

The Kingdom of the East Angles series
Night Shadows (prequel novella)
Dark Under the Cover of Night (Book One)
Nightfall till Daybreak (Book Two)
The Deepening Night (Book Three)
The Kingdom of the East Angles: The Complete Series

The Kingdom of Mercia series
The Breaking Dawn (Book One)
Darkest before Dawn (Book Two)
Dawn of Wolves (Book Three)
The Kingdom of Mercia: The Complete Series

The Kingdom of Northumbria series
The Whispering Wind (Book One)
Wind Song (Book Two)
Lord of the North Wind (Book Three)
The Kingdom of Northumbria: The Complete Series

DARK AGES SCOTLAND

The Warrior Brothers of Skye series
Blood Feud (Book One)
Barbarian Slave (Book Two)
Battle Eagle (Book Three)
The Warrior Brothers of Skye: The Complete Series

The Pict Wars series
Warrior's Heart (Book One)

Novellas
Winter's Promise

MEDIEVAL SCOTLAND

The Brides of Skye series
The Beast's Bride (Book One)
The Outlaw's Bride (Book Two)

Epic Fantasy Romances by Jayne Castel

Light and Darkness series
Ruled by Shadows (Book One)
The Lost Swallow (Book Two)

All characters and situations in this publication are fictitious and any resemblance to living persons is purely coincidental.

The Breaking Dawn by Jayne Castel

Edited by Tim Burton.

Cover photography courtesy of www.istockphotos.com.

Maps courtesy of Wikipedia.

Excerpt from the poem 'Marwnad Cynddylan' (Canu Heledd).

Visit Jayne's website and blog: www.jaynecastel.com

Follow Jayne on Twitter at: @JayneCastel

***

For Celia – Hoghatch Lane won't be the same without you.

And for Tim. With love.

***

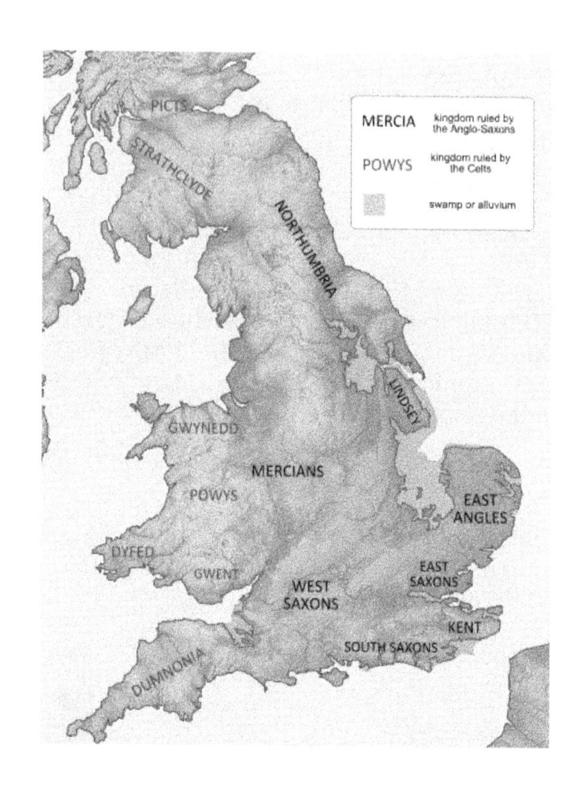
PICTS
STRATHCLYDE
NORTHUMBRIA
LINDSEY
GWYNEDD
MERCIANS
POWYS
EAST
ANGLES
DYFED
GWENT
EAST
SAXONS
WEST
SAXONS
KENT
SOUTH SAXONS
DUMNONIA
MERCIA
kingdom ruled by
the Anglo-Saxons
POWYS
kingdom ruled by
the Celts
swamp or alluvium

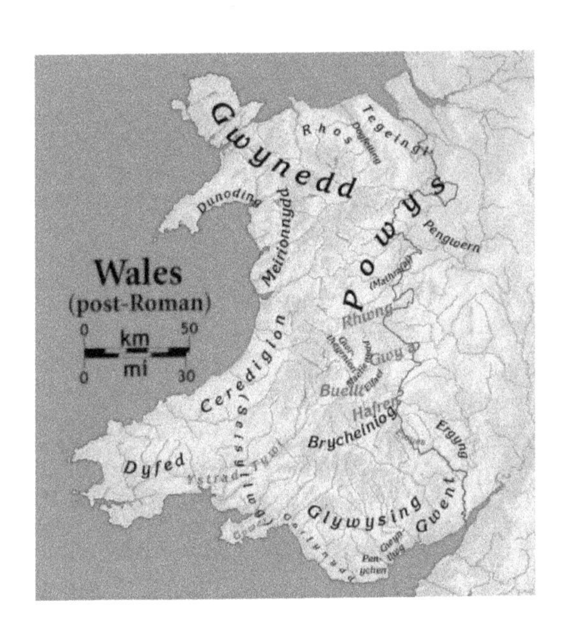
Wales
(post-Roman)
0 km 50
0 mi 30
Gwynedd
Rhos
Tegeingl
Dunoding
Meirionnydd
Powys
Pengwern
Ceredigion
Brycheiniog
Dyfed
Glywysing
Gwent
Ergyng
Buellt
Hafren
Rhwng
Gwy
Ystrad Tywi

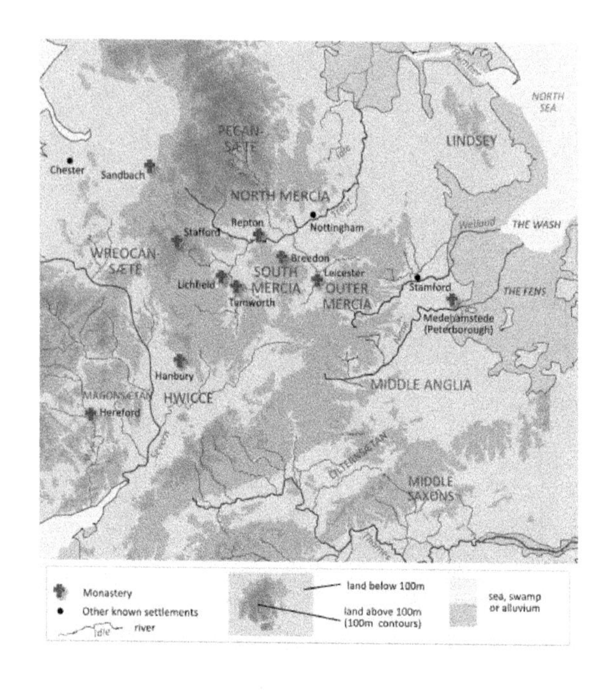
NORTH SEA
PECAN-SÆTE
LINDSEY
Chester
Sandbach
NORTH MERCIA
Repton
Nottingham
Stafford
THE WASH
WREOCAN-SÆTE
Breedon
SOUTH MERCIA
Leicester
OUTER MERCIA
Lichfield
Tamworth
Stamford
THE FENS
Medehamstede (Peterborough)
Hanbury
MIDDLE ANGLIA
HWICCE
Hereford
MIDDLE SAXONS
Monastery
Other known settlements
river
land below 100m
land above 100m (100m contours)
sea, swamp or alluvium

Historical background for *The Breaking Dawn*

Although you don't need to be a history buff in order to enjoy *The Breaking Dawn*, I thought a little historical background might help set the scene.

In the 7th Century, England was not as we know it today.

The Anglo-Saxon period lasted from the departure of the Romans, in around 430 AD, to the Norman invasion in 1066 AD.

My novels currently focus on the period from 600-700 AD. This is a significant century, sandwiched between the departure of the Romans, and the first Viking invasion in 793 AD—a period in which Anglo-Saxon culture flourished. The British Isles were named Britannia (a legacy of the Roman colonization) and split into rival kingdoms.

In this novel, we focus on two of them: The Kingdoms of Mercia and Powys. The Kingdoms of Northumbria and the East Angles are also mentioned.

Glossary of Old English and Welsh words (in alphabetical order)

The words below are all explained, as you encounter them, throughout the story. However, I have included a list, for reference.

beth – What (Welsh)
cariad – darling (Welsh)
Cymraeg – Welsh (language)
Cymry – Welsh (people)

ealdorman – earl
Englisc – English (language)
fæder – father
Fy arglwydd – My Lord (Welsh)
fyrd – a king's army, gathered for war
geburs – peasants
handfasted – married
heah-setl – high seat (later called a 'dais') for the king and queen
hōre – whore
Hwaet? – What?
Maes Cogwy – the Welsh name for Maserfield, location of a famous battle
mōder – mother
Nithhogg – a fire-breathing dragon that lived in the underworld
Powys – Wales
thegn – a king's retainer
theow – a slave
thrymsas – Anglo-Saxon gold shillings
Thunor – Thor
wealca – a tube linen dress with shoulder straps attached with brooches
Wes hāl – 'greetings' in old English
Winterfyllth – Anglo-Saxon Halloween
Woden – the Anglo-Saxon father of the gods (Viking: Odin)
Wyrd – fate

Cast of characters

Merwenna – young Mercian woman
Beorn – Merwenna's betrothed
Seward and Aeaba – Merwenna's brother and sister
Cynewyn (pronounced *Sinwin*) and **Wilfrid** – Merwenna's parents

Cynddylan (pronounced *Sindylan*) – Welsh prince
Gwyn – captain of Cynddylan's army
Owain – Welsh warrior
Penda – King of Mercia
Cyneswide (pronounced *Sinesweed*) – Queen of Mercia
Cyneburh (pronounced *Sinber*) and **Cyneswith** (pronounced *Sineswith*) – Penda's daughters
Paeda (pronounced *Peda*), **Wulfhere** and **Aethelred** – Penda's sons
Rodor – Penda's right-hand-man
Caedmon – Mercian warrior
Drefan of Chester – cloth merchant
Heledd – Cynddylan's sister
Morfael – Cynddylan's brother
Elfan – Cynddylan's uncle

However long the night,
The dawn will break.

African proverb

Prologue

The Promise

The village of Weyham, Kingdom of Mercia—Britannia

Spring 641 AD

"Will you marry me?"

Merwenna's breath caught. Had she heard correctly—had he really uttered those words?

"Excuse me?"

"Merwenna." Beorn stepped close to her, his gaze longing, his voice tender. "Will you be my wife?"

The young couple stood alone in the woods surrounded by skeleton trees.

Warmth had not returned to the world although it was early spring, and nature still lay dormant. They had both donned heavy fur cloaks for their walk, as the morning air held winter's bite—yet Merwenna did not feel the morning's chill. Joy bathed her in warmth as if she stood next to a roaring fire.

A smile broke across her face, and she flung herself into his arms. She had not been dreaming. The moment she had longed for had finally come.

"Of course I will!"

Beorn laughed, his relief evident. His arms tightened around her, and he pulled her close. "Thank Woden—for a moment there, I thought you would refuse me."

The feel of his young, strong body against hers made her pulse quicken.

Beorn pulled back slightly and met her gaze. As always, she was struck by the blueness of his eyes, and the beauty of his chiseled features.

"Refuse you?" Merwenna stared at him, incredulous. It had taken her nearly three years of gentle encouragement to reach this point. "I was beginning to think you would never ask!"

Beorn flushed slightly, embarrassed, and looked away. They both knew he valued his freedom highly. Like her father, Beorn served Weyham's ealdorman. They were warriors who farmed the land around the village by day, but would ride to war with the ealdorman, if commanded. However, unlike her father, who had lived a warrior's life for many years before wedding her mother—Beorn was young, and chafed at the thought of spending the rest of his days in Weyham.

Merwenna gazed at her betrothed, drinking him in. Wavy blond hair fell over his shoulders, and since autumn he had worn a short beard, which suited him.

She waited for him to say something else. She expected an excuse for making her wait so long. Yet he remained silent.

"Beorn?" she said finally, realizing that he was still avoiding her gaze. "Is something the matter?"

The young man looked up and shook his head. "The thing is . . ." he began hesitantly, "the handfasting itself will have to wait."

A chill stole over Merwenna at these words, and her joy dimmed.

"Hwaet?"

"The king is gathering a fyrd," Beorn continued, the words rushing out as he gained momentum. "He intends to march north and face King Oswald of Northumbria. I've decided to join his army."

Merwenna stared at him. Her shock turning to upset.

When she did not respond, Beorn's face grew serious. "Merwenna?"

"You ask me to marry you," Merwenna replied, her voice quivering as she struggled to stop herself from crying, "and then in the next breath announce that you are going to war. Why did you even bother to propose?"

"Because I love you." Beorn took hold of her hands and squeezed gently, his gaze earnest. "I want us to be married. It's just that we shall have to wait a little."

Merwenna took a deep breath, cursing the tears that stung her eyelids. She always cried too easily; it made her look feeble. "And I love you," she answered, blinking furiously. "But, I have just passed my twentieth winter. At this rate, I shall be an old maid before we wed."

"Just a little longer," Beorn replied, squeezing her hands once more. "I will return to Weyham and we shall be handfasted. I promise."

"You're going to war." Merwenna's tears spilled over as desperation seized her. "You can't make that promise!"

She ripped her hands from Beorn's. Then she turned, her cloak billowing, and started to run in the direction of Weyham. Dead leaves squelched underfoot, and the chill air burned her lungs, but Merwenna paid it no mind. She had almost reached the outskirts of the village when Beorn caught up with her.

"Merwenna, wait!' He grabbed her arm and pulled her up short.

She turned, tears streaming down her face, and tried to shrug him off. "Let me be!"

"I made you a promise, and I intend to keep it," Beorn insisted, his gaze imploring. "I will return to you!"

Merwenna's tears flowed without restraint now. Sobs welled up, and she had to choke them back. "You don't know that."

"Yes, I do." He set his jaw stubbornly.

"Men die in battle," she reminded him, "and when two king's armies meet there will be a great slaughter, surely you realize the danger."

"Penda's the greatest king Britannia has ever known," Beorn countered with the supreme confidence that only young men possess. "His fyrd will be mighty. The Prince of Powys is also sending a large company of warriors to join our army. The Northumbrians won't withstand our combined might."

Merwenna wiped away her tears and shook her head wordlessly. She cared not if the whole of Britannia was rallying at Penda's side. The thought that Beorn would go off to battle and might never return made her feel as if she was being buried alive.

"Penda is a mighty king," Beorn insisted, staring down at her with fire in his eyes. "He will be victorious."

Merwenna stared back at him. Her cheeks stung from the salt of her tears, and it took all her self-control not to start sobbing uncontrollably. This was folly—why could he not see it? However, it was clear Beorn's mind was made up.

"When will you leave?" she asked, her voice barely above a whisper.

"Tomorrow morning."

Merwenna stared at him. If he had punched her in the belly, it would have hurt less. Suddenly, her world was crumbling around her. Just moments ago, her heart had been bursting with joy. Now, her future looked bleak.

The man she loved was riding to war, and there was nothing she could do to prevent it.

***

Beorn of Weyham struggled to tighten the saddle's girth. He nudged his shaggy pony in the belly with his knee, until the stubborn beast exhaled. Then he tightened the girth another notch. The last of his preparations dealt with, Beorn turned to the small group of kin and well-wishers who had gathered to see him off.

He had not been looking forward to this. Good-byes were not something he had a lot of experience in. His mother and sisters were all weeping, a sight which upset him. His father, at least, was stoic.

"Serve the king well, my son." Horace stepped forward and clasped Beorn in a bear-hug. "Make me proud."

"I will, fæder."

Behind him, Beorn could hear the other warriors gathering: the low rumble of their voices, the snort of their horses. It was just after dawn. A light frost covered the ground, and the lightening sky promised a day of good weather ahead. They stood in Weyham's common, a stretch of grass in the center of the village. A collection of squat, wattle and daub homes with thatched roofs surrounded them. It was the only home he had ever known, and shortly he would be leaving it—perhaps for a long time.

Beorn stepped back from his father and took a deep breath. He was anxious to be off. Saying goodbye was harder than he had anticipated.

Yet first, he had to see Merwenna.

She stood a few yards away, patiently waiting. When he turned to her, Merwenna stepped forward to speak to him. Her eyes were red-rimmed, but that did not detract from her loveliness. In her build and coloring, she resembled her winsome mother—small and brown haired with startling blue eyes. However, there was a seriousness to her face that gave her some of her father's look. One of her most startling features was her beautifully molded, rose-bud mouth.

Beorn had always been captivated by her lips and her breasts, which were impressively full for such a small female. They gave her a womanly look on an otherwise girlish frame.

"Farewell, my love," Merwenna spoke, her voice quivering from the effort it was taking her to hold back tears. Despite that she was swathed from neck to shin in a heavy rabbit-skin cloak, he could see she was trembling. Suddenly, Beorn felt as if his heart had lodged in his throat. She was not making this any easier.

Although Beorn was eager to ride south-east to Tamworth and join the king's fyrd, he was also sorry that he and Merwenna could not be handfasted first. He longed to bed her, to tear the clothes off that delicious body. He could have wed her before leaving, but she deserved better. When he returned to Weyham, victorious, their joining would be all the sweeter. He wanted to make her proud of him; he wanted to come back to Weyham sporting silver and gold arm rings, prizes from the king for his valor. He wanted to be worthy of her.

"Goodbye, sweet Merwenna." He pulled her against him and hugged her tightly. "Wait for me. I shall return."

Drawing back from his betrothed, Beorn cupped her face with his hands and stooped to kiss her, not caring that half the village was looking on.

"I must go," he murmured. "Wait for me, my love."

"I will," she whispered back, her eyes huge on her heart-shaped face.

Beorn moved over to his pony and prepared to mount it. He was too big for the beast, but fortunately the pony was sturdy, and it had been the only horse his family could spare. Frankly, he was fortunate to be riding at all—most of the kings' fyrd would arrive inTamworth on foot.

His mother started wailing then. She broke free from her daughters' embrace and rushed toward her son. Beorn enfolded her in his arms as she sobbed.

"My boy! Don't go—I'll never see you again!"

"Enough, Arwyn!" Horace hauled his wife back. "You're embarrassing the lad. Control yourself!"

"Farewell, mōder," Beorn said hoarsely, struggling to hold back tears of his own. He had never seen his mother so upset. "Don't worry—you *will* see me again."

His assurances only made his mother sob even louder. Turning away from his parents, Beorn mounted his pony and quickly adjusted the stirrups. He rode away feeling wretched; his mother's heart-rending wailing was almost more than he could bear.

It was a relief when he could no longer hear her.

Beorn joined the throng of men leaving Weyham, glad to be finally on his way. His hamlet sat on the heavily wooded western fringes of the Kingdom of Mercia. It was nestled at the end of a long valley, in the shadow of dark hills that rose to meet the sky. Beorn rode through his village, passing the ealdorman's timbered hall along the way. He listened to the crunch of frozen leaves underfoot, the creaking of leather and jangling of horses' bridles, and felt his skin prickle with excitement.

A warrior had to be able to say goodbye without shedding tears. He had done well this morning, yet it was nothing compared to what lay ahead. He rode toward battle and glory—toward his future.

BOOK ONE

Mercia

Chapter One

Battle Lords

Maes Cogwy—in the territory of north-eastern Powys—Britannia

Three months later . . .

The young man lay on his back, an axe buried in his gut.

Prince Cynddylan ap Cyndrwyn of Powys stared down at the corpse. The dead man's face was a grimace, his blue eyes staring up at the heavens. He looked disbelieving, angry even, that his end had come.

"Did you know him?" Gwyn, captain of Cynddylan's army, stopped next to his prince and glanced down at the warrior.

Cynddylan – 'Dylan' as he was known to those closest to him—nodded. "Mercian lad. Followed Penda around like a puppy and begged him to let him fight in the shield wall," he replied. "Hard to forget a man who does that."

Gwyn snorted. "Fools always die young."

Dylan gave a grim smile in response, his gaze remaining upon the dead warrior. "Yes, they do."

Dylan had spoken to the young man a few times on the journey north-west from Tamworth. Now, he struggled to remember his name. Beorn—that was it. Not that his name mattered now.

He was carrion for crows, nothing else.

Beorn's corpse was just one of hundreds that littered the battlefield. Dylan and Gwyn stood at the center of a wide, marshy field fringed by forest on all sides. Dusk was settling, creating a haze over the surrounding woodland. They were in Powys, Dylan's domain, where Northumbria had met Mercia and Powys in battle.

The Northumbrians had lost.

The victors combed the battlefield, killing any of the enemy who had not died from their wounds and stripping them of their weapons and arm-rings—the spoils of war.

Dylan straightened up. His shoulders and arms burned from exertion, and the mail shirt he wore felt as if it was filled with rocks. His fine purple cloak was ripped and stained with blood. Yet apart from a few bruises and superficial cuts, he was unhurt.

The thrill of victory made Dylan cast aside his battle-weariness. This was a great moment for his people. He had done his father proud; if only the old king had been alive to see it. He had now earned the crown his father had worn.

Upon his return to Pengwern, he too would be king.

The prince glanced over at Gwyn. His captain's thick dark hair had come loose from its leather thong at his nape and was now a tangled halo around his heavy-featured face. He was covered in thick leather armor, making his tall, muscular form look even more intimidating than usual. However, Gwyn's left thigh was slick with dark blood.

"You're injured," Dylan frowned.

The warrior grunted in response, brushing his concern aside. "Just a nick—those northerners are skilled with a spear."

Dylan nodded. Gwyn's observation was an understatement; it had been the hardest battle he had ever fought. They had sacrificed a lot of men in order to bring the Northumbrians to their knees. He had come here with over seven-hundred men, but he would leave Maes Cogwy with less than half that number.

"Get that leg seen to," he told Gwyn. "I've got a king to find."

"Which one?" the warrior raised a dark eyebrow.

"The one who still has his head attached to his shoulders."

Gwyn gave another snort, turned and limped off, leaving the Prince of Powys alone.

Dylan turned his attention to the other side of the battlefield—where his and Penda's men were dismembering the Northumbrian king.

Fortunately, for Oswald, Penda had killed him first.

He had delivered a fatal blow to the neck with his legendary sword—*Aethelfrith's Bane*. The sword had once belonged to another Northumbrian king—Aethelfrith—slain by King Raedwald of the East Angles many years earlier.

The King of Mercia stood now watching his men at work on King Oswald. Penda was an imposing figure, clad in mail and leather, an iron helm obscuring his face. He looked on while his men hacked at the Northumbrian king's corpse with axes.

One of the Mercian warriors hauled Oswald's severed head up by the hair and impaled it upon a pike. Then, with a victory roar, the warrior strode through the battlefield, brandishing his grisly prize.

Dylan halted a few yards from Penda and waited for the Mercian to acknowledge him. However, the Prince of Powys did not sheath his sword. Instead, he wisely kept hold of it in his right hand. Its blade was dark with Northumbrian blood; he would not put it away until he was sure that Penda would not betray him.

"Prince of Powys," Penda rumbled, tearing his gaze from Oswald's final humiliation. He looked then, upon the man he had allied himself with. "Well fought, Cynddylan son of Cyndrwyn."

Dylan nodded curtly. "And you, Lord Penda."

The Mercian King reached up and removed his helm, revealing an austere face that had once been handsome. He had pale blue eyes and a mane of white-blond hair. Penda was in his early forties but appeared to have the strength of a man half his age. Dylan's impression of the man before him was of coldness, and of calculation. He had never liked Penda—few did—but he had a grudging respect for him nonetheless.

"That is a fine sword," Penda nodded at the weapon that Dylan still held. "And you know how to wield it."

Dylan nodded, acknowledging the compliment. "It was my father's."

Penda's cool gaze shifted from Dylan then and swept over the battlefield behind him. "A great triumph for Mercia. Long has Oswald been a thorn in my side." His gaze settled upon the head of the Northumbrian king that was making its way around the field. "But no more."

Coarse laughter reached them. Dylan glanced across the battlefield at where the warriors had removed Oswald's head from the pike. He and Penda looked on as the men hung the Northumbrian king's head and hands in a tree; a gnarled elm on the edge of the marshy field.

It was done. The enemy was defeated, they had won. The Prince of Powys shifted his gaze from Oswald's remains, instead taking in the wide field, the surrounding trees, and the darkening sky. Maes Cogwy would forever be a sacred spot for his people. Mercia and Powys were now allies. Songs would be sung around the fire for generations about their victory here.

But now, it was time to go home.

***

The village of Weyham—the Kingdom of Mercia

"Hurry, Merwenna. If we are going, it must be now!"

"I am hurrying!" Merwenna gasped, hiking her skirts and clambering up the mossy bank after her brother. "Wait for me!"

The sun was rising over the edge of the trees to the east, and the sky was a pale, chalky blue, promising a warm day ahead. Brother and sister had been sent out to Weyham's market to buy two milking goats. Little Aeaba had wanted to join them, but Merwenna had insisted she stay behind—much to her younger sister's upset.

Merwenna and Seward had crossed the village, nearly running in their haste to leave Weyham without being waylaid. Seward carried a leather pouch containing a few thrymsas—the money they had been given for the goats. Merwenna carried a jute sack, slung across her front, containing some provisions she had taken from the family store. Their parents were busy with their morning chores but would expect Merwenna and Seward back shortly.

It was late summer, and the first day of the harvest. Many days of hard work lay ahead while food was collected, preserved, and stored for the coming winter. It was the most crucial time of year; a family could starve on account of a failed harvest.

It was the worst time of year to run away.

Merwenna broke into a sweat thinking about her parents' reaction. Even so, she quickened her pace and followed Seward into the trees. It was selfish of them both, to leave right when they were needed most, but Merwenna had thought long and hard before making her decision.

She had not been able to wait in Weyham any longer.

Three long months had passed since Beorn's departure, and since then no word had been heard. She did not even know if Mercia had been victorious against Northumbria.

She had to know if Beorn lived—every waking moment was spent worrying about his fate. With each passing day, she grew increasingly agitated. Her mother had told her to wait, and she had tried, but now with the end of summer approaching, she could bide her time no longer.

When she had asked Seward to accompany her to Tamworth, she had expected him to refuse. Even worse, she had feared he would go to their parents about it.

She need not have worried.

Seward was restless, with a longing to visit new places and meet new people. At eighteen winters, he was old enough to go to battle but his father had forbidden it. Seward was needed at home to help farm the fields and feed the family. Her brother had chafed at his father's decision. He was eager to know of the world beyond Weyham, and he had jumped at the chance of a journey to the King's Hall.

He strode off ahead, not bothering to check if his sister was keeping up. Like his father, he was not overly tall, but strongly built, with short brown hair and hazel eyes. Despite that Seward was ignoring her now, Merwenna felt safe and protected in his presence. She would never have embarked on this journey alone. The road was good, but it was at least five days to Tamworth from Weyham. Seward would make sure they reached their destination safely.

Then, I will know of Beorn's fate, Merwenna thought, her belly twisting with worry. *I will bring him home.*

Life had been colorless and joyless for Merwenna since Beorn's departure. Now, for the first time in weeks, there was a lightness in her stride. The cool morning breeze on her skin sharpened her senses, and she breathed in the scent of wild-flowers, damp earth, and grass.

Finally, she was doing something. With every step she drew closer to Beorn. The lump of dread that had settled in her belly the day he had left, began to ease.

Once they left Weyham behind, Seward broke into a slow jog, covering the ground quickly. They kept out of sight of the road although Seward made sure they followed its course south-east. Merwenna ran behind him, the sack containing their supplies banging against her hip as she did so. It was not long before a stitch in her side caused her to call out to her brother.

"Slow down," she gasped. "I can't keep running like this."

Seward slowed and looked back over his shoulder, his exasperation evident.

"I'm just trying to make sure we distance ourselves from home," he called back. "The faster we do that, the better."

"I know, but I'm not used to running long distances. Can we walk for a bit?"

Seward sighed and slowed to a walk, allowing his sister to catch up.

Above, the sun had cleared the treetops and warmed their faces.

"They will know we've gone by now," Merwenna said eventually.

Seward nodded, but did not reply.

"Are you sure *fæder* won't come after us?"

"As sure as I can be—he can't leave mōder and Aeaba alone with the harvest."

"He will be furious."

Seward shrugged, as if he had already considered and dismissed the notion. "You knew that when you made the decision to leave. However, we are both grown and must make our own decisions. If we had asked, fæder would only have denied us. You saw how he was when I asked to go to battle?"

'He was only trying to protect you."

"And he'd only be trying to protect us now. No, Merwenna. You wanted to know Beorn's fate—this is the only way. Unless you'd prefer to return to Weyham and wait till the king sends word?"

Merwenna shook her head, setting her jaw into a stubborn line.

"I thought not," Seward laughed, throwing his arm around her shoulders. "Come—the road is long, and we've barely started along it. Catch me if you can!"

And with that, Seward released her and sprang forward. He sprinted through the trees like a deer.

With a groan, her legs still protesting from her earlier run, Merwenna took off after him.

Chapter Two

A Meeting at Market

Tamworth, Kingdom of Mercia—Britannia

Merwenna's first glimpse of Tamworth was of the great tower, rising against a windswept sky.

She had never seen a dwelling made of stone before, nor had she ever seen such a tall structure. She literally gaped before reaching for her brother, plucking at his tunic to get his attention.

"Seward—look!"

Seward twisted and gazed up at the massive tower thrusting into the heavens above the tree tops. Like his sister, he had never seen anything like it. The tower was made of a dull-grey rock, and even from this distance, Merwenna could make out the patches of lichen that encrusted it.

The Great Tower of Tamworth, Merwenna gazed at it, excitement leaping in her breast. *We've made it.*

The five days, most of it on foot, it had taken them to reach Mercia's capital, had been exciting for them both. As Seward had predicted, their father had not come after them. Two days out from Weyham they had decided to risk traveling on the road, and those they had met on the way had been friendly. At dawn this morning, they had met a cloth merchant on his way to Tamworth—and they had spent the last stretch, perching on the back of his wagon, amongst bolts of linen.

The wagon bounced along the rutted track, between rows of magnificent horse chestnuts, before emerging into the gentle hills around the base of Tamworth. Merwenna watched with interest the folk laboring in the fields around the town. They were geburs—peasants bonded to the Mercian king—giving their labor in return for his complete protection. The geburs were gathering a bountiful harvest of cabbages, turnips, carrots, and onions that would see Tamworth through the long winter to come.

The sight of the folk working the fields reminded Merwenna that her parents and Aeaba would be working alone this year, and much harder than usual—all because of her and Seward's departure. Still, upon finally reaching their destination, Merwenna's guilt was short-lived.

As the wagon trundled toward Tamworth's gates, Merwenna stared up at the stone walls of the Great Tower of Tamworth and took a deep breath. Perhaps Beorn was already here—waiting for her. The thought made her pulse quicken.

The cloth merchant—a stout, balding man of around forty winters—flicked the reins. He urged the two heavy-set ponies that pulled his wagon, through the gates and into the town itself.

Merwenna perched upon a bolt of linen and gazed at her surroundings. Thoughts of Beorn were momentarily cast aside as a wall of noise and smells assaulted her senses. She saw street vendors hawking hot pies and freshly roasted rabbit; the aroma of their wares made her stomach rumble. She heard the wailing of a babe somewhere in the crowd, and the excited shouts of children who ran amongst the throng of folk going about their daily business.

The wagon trundled along dirt-packed streets, in-between tightly packed wattle and daub houses and workshops. They passed an iron-monger's and breathed in the tang of hot iron as the smith beat out a blade on his anvil. They passed the baker's and caught the aroma of hot oat-cakes, fresh out of the oven.

Further on, they rumbled by the town's mead hall; a long, low-slung, and windowless structure. Here, Merwenna caught the unmistakable whiff of fermentation. She made a note of the hall's position, for they would need to retrace their steps back to it; hopefully, it would be able to accommodate them for a few days. They would sleep on the floor with others visiting Tamworth.

Eventually, the cloth merchant brought his wagon to a halt in the middle of a crowded market place. It lay not far from the wooden perimeter that divided the Great Tower from the rest of Tamworth. Here, Merwenna and Seward clambered down from the wagon, their limbs stiff and aching. Despite the discomfort, the ride had saved them over half a day's journey, and Merwenna had been grateful to rest her blistered feet.

"Thank you," Seward shook the cloth merchant's hand. "We are grateful for the ride."

"I'm sure you are," the man gave Seward a sly look before casting a glance in Merwenna's direction. "You didn't think I'd let you travel for free, do you?"

Seward released the merchant's hand and stepped back, his smile fading. His hazel-eyes narrowed as he took the measure of the cloth merchant for the first time.

"We have no gold," he said finally.

This was not strictly true. They carried the leather purse with them although they only had enough for food and lodgings to sustain them for the few days they would stay in Tamworth—nothing more.

"How unfortunate for you," the merchant's gaze gleamed as he spoke. "Yet I expect payment all the same."

"But we have nothing to pay you with," Merwenna spoke up, only to receive a quelling look from Seward. He was in charge here.

"Really?" the merchant grinned, enjoying himself now. Around them, the crowd jostled; merchants, farmers, and traders were all vying for the townsfolk's attention. Merwenna was not used to being surrounded by so many people—and she felt her chest constrict.

This was not how she had envisaged arriving at Tamworth. There was something in the merchant's leer that frightened her.

"If it's payment you require, we can help you at market today." Seward offered evenly. "You have much cloth to sell—you could do with our help."

"I can sell my wares without your assistance," the merchant replied with a shake of his head. His gaze then shifted back to Merwenna. "However, your sister is a comely wench. If you give her to me for this night, I shall consider your debt paid."

A deathly silence followed his words.

Seward stared at the merchant, his face turning hard. Merwenna watched her brother flex his fists, the muscles in his bare arms bunching as he did so.

"You want to lie with my sister?" he asked, enunciating each word as if he could not believe he had heard correctly.

"That's right, lad," the merchant grinned. "And if you give her to me, our debt is settled."

"I'm not lying with you—foul goat!" Merwenna exploded before Seward could reply. "I'd die first!"

The merchant's grin faded at her insult. "A debt is a debt," he growled.

"The price you ask is too high," Seward growled back. His face had gone red, and he stepped menacingly toward the merchant. Like his father, Seward was slow to anger. However, when roused he was not lightly crossed. Merwenna could see her brother's rage kindle like a Winterfyllth bonfire. She longed for his patience to snap—she wanted him to lash out and break this letch's jaw.

"If you will not accept our offer of assisting you sell your wares, we will be off," Seward told the merchant. "You will not lay a hand on my sister."

"You must pay!" the merchant thrust his chin out pugnaciously. "Gold or your sister—you decide!"

He made a grab for Merwenna—a rash and foolish move, for Seward's fist lashed out and connected with the man's jaw. The merchant sprawled back against the bolts of cloth.

The crowd suddenly hushed around them. Folk had finally noticed that an altercation had exploded between the two young travelers and the balding man.

"Fool," the merchant spat blood onto the dirt and hauled himself to his feet. Then he drew a hunting knife from around his waist. "I'll cut you up for that."

Merwenna's breath caught in her throat. Seward was unarmed and suddenly out of his depth. She could see the mean glint in the merchant's eyes; he was much older and slower than her brother. Yet she realized, with a sickening jolt, that this man had killed befor—and could do so easily again.

"Leave him be!" Merwenna stepped in front of Seward, holding her hands up in supplication. "Please don't kill him."

"Merwenna!" Seward grabbed her around the waist and hauled her back from the merchant. She could hear the rage in his voice and knew this situation was just moments away from spiraling out of control.

"You want to save your brother?" the merchant advanced toward Seward, knife raised. "Then you know what you must do, you little whore."

"Wait!"

A woman's voice, cultured and gentle, cut through the crowd.

"I will pay for them. Do not harm him."

Merwenna glanced around, searching for the woman who had spoken. A moment later, the crowd parted and a blonde woman of around forty winters stepped forward. She was finely dressed in a long, sleeveless blue tunic with a silk trim. Her slender arms were bare, adorned only with bronze arm-rings, and a heavy belt studded with amber sat low on her hips. Her golden hair was braided and wrapped around the crown of her head.

Merwenna stared at the woman. She had always thought of her mother as comely, easily the finest-looking woman in Weyham, but this woman outshone her. She had never seen a woman so beautiful.

The woman approached them, her skirts rustling as she did so. She walked with regal grace. The cloth merchant's attitude transformed the moment he set eyes on the woman.

"Milady," his face went slack with shock. He lowered his knife, before bowing his head respectfully. Around him, the crowd grew tense.

Merwenna spotted four warriors following the woman. They were all big men, clad in tunics of fine cloth and gleaming leather. Each man carried a heavy ash spear, their expressions formidable. Merwenna's stomach somersaulted as she realized who the newcomer was.

Only one woman in Tamworth could command others. Only one woman would walk about town with an armed escort.

Cyneswide, Queen of Mercia, stood before them.

Chapter Three

The Queen's Guests

"My Queen," Merwenna blurted, her face flaming "I'm sorry. We did not realize this man wanted payment for assisting us. We would never have accepted his help, had we known."

Merwenna curtsied low and, out of the corner of her eye, saw Seward bow reverently. Like her, he looked stunned. Never had they imagined the Queen of Mercia would ever bandy words with them, let alone come to their aid.

"I was only demanding what I was due," the merchant blustered, finding his tongue once more.

"What is your name?" Cyneswide asked.

"Drefan, Milady. Drefan of Chester."

"How much do they owe you, Drefan of Chester?" Cyneswide asked, her gentle manner not slipping an inch as she met the man's eye.

"Two thrymsas," he muttered, his face reddening.

This utterance caused a few gasps amongst the crowd. Two gold coins—thrymsas—was an exorbitant fee. However, the queen did not flinch. Instead, she turned to the warrior to her right. He was a huge man with shaggy brown hair and a wintry gaze.

"Pay him, Rodor, if you please."

The warrior nodded, before retrieving a leather pouch. He extracted two gold pieces and handed them to the merchant.

Merwenna watched the transaction, relief flooding through her. This woman's kindness easily matched her beauty.

"Thank you, Milady," she murmured, "I am so sorry to have caused this much trouble."

"It was no trouble at all," Queen Cyneswide fixed her with a calm, blue-eyed gaze. "You and your brother are not from Tamworth, are you?"

Merwenna shook her head.

"What are your names?"

"I am Merwenna, and this is my brother, Seward, of Weyham, Milady."

The queen nodded. "And what is your business here?"

Merwenna took a deep breath and cast a glance at her brother. Seward seemed to have swallowed his tongue in the presence of the beautiful queen. He wore a slightly stunned look as he gazed upon Cyneswide.

"My brother has escorted me here," Merwenna replied hesitantly, her voice barely above a whisper. "I have come to seek my betrothed."

"Your betrothed?" Queen Cyneswide's fair brow creased into a frown.

"He rode to war with the king," Merwenna explained. "I have had no word in three months—I had to come and look for him. I have to know if he lives."

"Have you had any news of the battle, Milady?" Seward finally spoke up.

"I have," the queen smiled at Seward. "Good news. We have defeated the Northumbrians—Mercia is victorious."

The wave of relief that slammed against Merwenna then, made her feel light-headed. Seeing his sister's reaction, Seward stepped close to Merwenna and placed a protective arm about her shoulders. Merwenna sagged against him, her legs suddenly weak.

"The king and his fyrd ride toward Tamworth as we speak," the queen continued, with a warm smile. "I dearly hope your betrothed is among them. Your loyalty deserves reward."

Merwenna dropped her chin, embarrassed. Tears stung her eyelids, and she frantically blinked, trying to hold them back. "Thank you, Milady."

"Where are you lodging?" Cyneswide turned her attention to Seward once more.

"Nowhere, as yet, Milady," he replied. "We will see if there is space for us at the mead hall."

Merwenna, regaining control of herself, and managing to stem the threatening tears, watched the queen pause a moment.

"There is no need for that. You may stay in the King's Hall while you await your betrothed."

Merwenna stared at the queen, her mouth opening in shock.

"M . . . Milady," she stuttered. "That is too generous an offer."

It was indeed, for the queen's proclamation had caused murmurs to ripple through the amassed crowd. Some whispered eagerly to each other, darting keen glances at the brother and sister who stood before the queen. Others stared at them with ill-concealed envy.

Drefan of Chester—the cloth merchant—looked as if he had just supped on sour milk. He glared at Merwenna, his eyes glittering under heavy lids.

"Perhaps," the queen gave an enigmatic smile, "but it's mine to make."

Merwenna smiled and cast a glance at Seward; her brother was grinning ear-to-ear.

"Come," Cyneswide held out her arm to Merwenna. "Escort me back to the Great Tower."

Merwenna took the queen's proffered arm, while Seward took up the rear, alongside the queen's escort. The brother and sister traveled light, carrying nothing more than leather satchels slung across their fronts. As such, there was no need to return to the cloth merchant's cart.

As they moved away, the cloth merchant stepped forward.

"Milady," he called out. "Do you not wish to buy some cloth? I have the finest linen, and even a bolt of blue silk that matches your eyes."

Cyneswide turned back, her gentle gaze suddenly hardening.

"I think not," she replied. "I do not buy from men who would bully a maid into giving away her virtue. You will receive no purchase from me today—or any day."

Merwenna followed the queen out of the market place. However, as she moved away, she made the mistake of glancing back at the cloth merchant.

Drefan's gaze seized hers for an instant, and what she saw there made her step falter. She had made an enemy—and she knew he would never forget it.

***

"Mead, Milady?"

A man approached Queen Cyneswide and her two guests, as they sat near the fire pit. He was young and slender with haunted eyes. The iron collar about his neck marked him as a theow—a slave. The sight of him fascinated Merwenna; there were no slaves in Weyham.

"Yes, thank you," the queen replied, "and pour some for my guests as well."

The slave poured their clay cups to the brim, avoiding their gazes as he did so. Merwenna took a sip of mead and had to stop herself from wrinkling her nose; it was not a drink she was used to. Instead of taking another sip, she let her gaze travel around their surroundings.

It was all she could do not to gawp. Tamworth's Great Hall was vast. Damp stone walls that emanated a chill, despite that it was late summer and still warm outside, ringed a massive open space. A thick layer of rushes covered the floor, and two hearths roared at either end. To the right of the space, wooden steps led up to a private platform. Merwenna craned her neck to look up at the rafters high above. They were blackened, with a hole in the center to let out smoke from the fire pits.

The hall was a hive of activity. Servants and slaves moved across it as they went about their chores, while others worked at a long table that ran along the wall, preparing the evening meal.

There were few men about, as most had gone to war with their king, but those who remained to guard the Great Tower were indolent this eve; they sat drinking and exchanging riddles around the second fire pit, or playing knucklebones at one of the long tables. In contrast, the high-born ladies, most of them ealdormen's wives, sat at the far end of the hall, bent over looms or industriously winding wool onto wooden distaffs.

Merwenna saw two girls among the high born ladies. They had fine blonde hair and delicate features, bearing a startling resemblance to Cyneswide. Seward had also noticed the two beauties and was finding it difficult to ignore them. The queen saw him looking and smiled.

"They are my daughters—Cyneburh and Cyneswith."

Seward, who had been caught blatantly staring, flushed and looked away.

Cyneswide's smile faded and she focused her attention upon Merwenna. "Soon they will marry and leave this hall; when they do I will be surrounded almost entirely by men. I have three sons as well . . . here are the trouble-makers now."

Merwenna followed the queen's gaze across the hall to where three boys had just entered. They were dressed in fine linen tunics and leggings. The two youngest, who were both blond, playfully cuffed each other before ending up in a noisy wrestle on the rush-matting, amongst the dogs. The oldest of the three, a darker-haired lad, cast them a disdainful look and continued on his way across the hall toward his mother.

"Wulfhere, Aethelred—enough!" Cyneswide called out. The boys ignored her, and a moment later their mother was forced to call to them once more. "Boys—if you don't stop this instant your father will hear of this upon his return."

The lads sprang apart, as if doused with cold water. They climbed to their feet, dusted themselves off, and approached their mother, stopping next to their brother. The eldest boy was staring at Merwenna, as if he had never before seen a woman.

Cyneswide noted the direction of his gaze and smiled.

"This is Paeda, my eldest son—and these are his younger brothers, Wulfhere and Aethelred. Boys, this is Merwenna, and her brother Seward. They will be our guests for the next few days."

All three boys nodded, their gazes curious. Merwenna observed them in kind; the brothers were all tall for their age and handsome.

"What have you been up to all afternoon?" the queen asked, before reaching out and ruffling Wulfhere's hair.

"Out searching for frogs," the boy replied. Merwenna could see much of his mother in his face, however his pale blue eyes and white-blond hair must have come from his father. "Paeda caught ten but I made him let them go."

"Wulfhere's a big baby," the dark-haired boy sneered at his brother. "I told him I was going to bake a frog pie and make him eat it—and he believed me."

Wulfhere glowered at Paeda in response but said nothing. The youngest, a boy barely older than seven, started laughing, only to receive a cuff across the ear from Wulfhere.

"Enough boys—go and play knuckle bones with the men," Cyneswide waved them away with a tired smile. "We will eat soon—and I promise, no frog pie."

The boys went off, jostling each other as they did so. The queen turned back to Merwenna with a tired smile. "My sons exhaust me with their boundless energy. My girls were much less trouble at the same age."

"I suppose they will calm down once the king returns," Merwenna replied.

"They will," Cyneswide sighed, her smile suddenly brittle, "but for now, let us enjoy this evening. Come, tell me of Weyham—I have never traveled that far west."

Merwenna took a mouthful of pottage and glanced worriedly at Seward.

Her brother was at ease in the King's Hall, too much so in her opinion. He had downed three large cups of mead and was now starting on his fourth. The mead was far stronger than the brew he drank at home. Seward was now merrier than she had ever seen him.

The mead had also loosened his tongue. He laughed and joked with three other youths seated near him; their laughter rang across the table, echoing high amongst the rafters.

Merwenna gave Seward a pointed look, willing him to keep his voice down. Fortunately, they did not sit at the 'king's table'. The royal family and highest-ranking men and women sat on the other side of the hall.

However, the queen's absence from their side had made some of the warriors bold. Two of them were staring rudely at Merwenna now. Seward was oblivious as he regaled his new friends with his latest hunting exploits.

A female slave passed by, carrying a large tureen of pottage. She was winsome and curvaceous with thick dark hair and green eyes.

"Wes hāl, my beauty," Seward leaned back to admire the girl as she refilled his trencher. Her rough homespun tunic could not hide her luscious curves.

Merwenna gritted her teeth. Her brother did not usually behave so boldly with women—yet this evening he appeared to have forgotten himself. The slave girl gave him a shy smile in response and moved away, continuing down the table, her hips swaying. Seward's gaze lingered on her until the girl had moved out of his line of sight.

Merwenna stared down at her pottage and bit her tongue to stop herself from reprimanding her brother.

Drunken oaf.

They were guests here. After this afternoon's incident, she thought Seward would have been more careful. The queen had bestowed a great honor upon them, but her brother hardly seemed to care.

Merwenna pushed her half-eaten trencher aside and tried not to notice that Seward was filling up his cup—again.

Chapter Four

Awake in the Night

Seward smiled at the slave girl, and looked deep into her emerald eyes.

Woden, she's comely.

The mead he had consumed had made him feel invincible. His limbs were weightless, and his senses, which should have been dulled, felt heightened.

Here he was, a lad from a backwater village, drinking in the King's Hall. Not only that—but this dark-haired beauty had been favoring him with lusty looks all night long. His breeches were growing tighter by the second, and the sight of the girl's slightly parted lips, as she cleared the table in front of him, caused lust to knife through his groin.

Weyham had no girls that compared to this wench—and no woman had ever given him such a melting stare. Earlier in the evening, he had noticed that she wore an iron band around her neck, marking her as one of the king's slaves, but that had only heightened his desire for her.

Wait until I tell my friends about this, he congratulated himself. *They'll never believe me.*

"What's your name, lass?" he murmured in her ear.

"Cerwen," she replied, her voice a gentle purr. Her lilting Cymry accent caressed him, making his manhood swell even harder.

Gods, how he wanted her.

It was getting late. Seward had moved to the far end of the hall. He was now seated at a table, where a group of men had continued drinking and swapping stories long after the evening meal had ended. Two pitch torches hung from the wall, casting a flickering orange light over the table.

Beyond, many residents had laid out their cloaks upon the rushes and stretched out for the night. Merwenna, who had been glaring at him all evening, had finally given up and taken herself off to bed. The princesses had retired to their bower, cloaked from view by a tapestry, and the queen had climbed up to her quarters on the platform above.

There were few folk about to witness Seward's boldness as he reached out and squeezed the girl's rounded rear. The others at the table were so drunk, they did not appear to notice, or care.

The girl squealed, her eyes teasing in the torchlight. "Milord!"

'Milord'—I like the sound of that.

Seward could get used to living in the Great Hall of Tamworth.

***

Merwenna awoke to the feel of cold, damp stone against her back, and tried to ignore her protesting bladder.

She had used the privy before retiring for the night—but now she needed to go, again.

She lay next to the wall, inside the Great Hall, far from the glowing hearths. Around her, she could hear the rustle of breathing, and a chorus of gentle snores.

She was warm under her cloak, and loath to struggle outside to relieve herself.

Merwenna lay there for a while and mulled over the day's events. She ruminated over her brother's drunkenness. His behavior this evening had drawn far too much attention to them; she would have to speak with him of it on the morrow.

Then, her thoughts returned—as they often did—to her betrothed.

Mercia had beaten Northumbria—Beorn was coming home. Tears of relief stung her eyelids as she relived the moment the queen had informed them of Penda's victory. She clasped her hands to her breast under her cloak and whispered thanks to the gods, and prayed that Thor had watched over her love.

Yet her prayers could not distract her from the fact she needed to use the privy.

Merwenna reluctantly pushed her cloak aside and rose to her feet. Then she carefully edged her way around the room, stepping over the slumbering bodies of men, women, children, and dogs. She reached the door that led out into the Great Tower's entranceway and stepped out into a long, narrow antechamber, lit by flickering torches. Corridors led off it, to the left and right, to storerooms. There were great oaken doors at one end—the way outside.

The privies lay through those doors, in the yard beyond the hall. Merwenna hurried toward the doors. She was half-way across the space, when a sudden noise made her pause. It was a muffled groan—and it was coming from one of the narrow corridors that led down to the tower's store rooms.

She swiveled toward the sound and looked into the shadowed passageway to her right.

What she saw there froze her to the spot.

Seward and the slave girl he had flirted with earlier in the evening were coupling in a frenzy. Her brother had the girl up against the wall and was thrusting into her. The slave's skirts were hiked up around her hips, her shapely legs clasped around him.

Merwenna stared, her shock turning to horror.

What, for the love of the gods, are you doing?

What should she do? Part of her wanted to shout at him—to make him stop—whereas the rest of her just wanted to turn tail and run.

Had Seward completely lost his wits?

At this precise moment, the young man did not appear to care about the consequences of his actions. Instead, his mouth devoured the girl's. His hand's clasped her buttocks as he rammed into her.

Merwenna could watch no more. She was too mortified to say anything. She did not want him to know that she had witnessed this. It was best if she slipped away quietly; best if she continued on her way to the privy and pretended she had seen nothing.

She backed up two steps and collided with a hard wall of muscle and leather. She cried out in alarm and tried to side-step the obstacle—but an arm clamped around her torso in an iron band. She looked up and saw the stone-hewn face of Rodor, the warrior who had led the queen's guard earlier in the day.

Rodor ignored her. Instead, his cold gaze was riveted on the couple entwined in the shadows just yards away.

Chapter Five

Seward's Shame

"I am truly sorry, Milady," Seward repeated, his voice low.

Merwenna glared at the back of his head and fought the urge to kick him. It was a bit late for apologies.

The queen regarded Seward impassively. Her two daughters and three sons had gathered behind her, looking on wide-eyed at the young man who had just given an account of himself.

A poor one, in Merwenna's opinion.

Dawn had just broken over the Great Tower of Tamworth. Pale light filtered in from the narrow windows high up in the tower, illuminating the dust motes that drifted in the air. Inside the hall, the mood was somber. Servants moved gingerly about the edges, preparing griddle bread and rousing the glowing embers in the fire pits. Many were distracted in their work; their gazes flicked constantly to the small group that stood before Queen Cyneswide.

Merwenna waited behind Seward, her cheeks burning in humiliation. The slave girl stood next to Seward. Her head was bowed; her hair a dark curtain shielding her face. The girl's shoulders were slumped in defeat, trembling slightly as she wept. Ever since Rodor had interrupted the lovers, the girl had not uttered a word.

"I know you come from an isolated village, Seward," the queen spoke eventually, "and perhaps you are ignorant of the ways of others. Yet I cannot believe that you did not know that to touch a king's slave is forbidden."

Merwenna's stomach twisted at these words. Cyneswide spoke calmly although there was no mistaking the flinty edge to her voice.

"Please forgive me," Seward bowed his head and Merwenna caught the sincere regret in his voice. "I never meant to give offence. I'm a fool."

"Indeed you are," the queen sighed, exasperated. "You do realize that if this girl bears your child, the king will deal with her harshly."

Seward looked up and glanced over at where the slave stood, her head still bowed.

Merwenna caught a glimpse of his face, and the purple bruise that was forming around his left eye. After hauling Seward off the girl, Rodor had hit him so hard that Seward had fallen, senseless, to the ground. The warrior stood now, a grim sentinel, to Seward's right, awaiting the queen's orders.

"I d . . . did not think," Seward stammered. "Please don't punish Cerwen for my mistake."

Rodor suddenly lashed out, striking Seward across the face. Her brother staggered backward and collided with Merwenna.

"Slaves don't have names!" he growled.

"Rodor, please," Queen Cyneswide interrupted, her voice still gentle. "That's enough."

Merwenna noted that the queen had not even flinched during the exchange. This woman had probably seen many men slain before her in this hall. The awareness made Merwenna's legs start to tremble.

Cyneswide turned her attention back to Seward, her gaze narrowing. "You are both responsible," she replied gently. "Cerwen knew what she was doing."

Merwenna looked down at her feet, wretched. Seward could lose his life for one impulsive act. At that moment, she saw no way out of the mess he had got them into.

"It is fortunate for you that my husband is not here," Queen Cyneswide continued. "He would make an example of both of you. Still, I cannot let this go unpunished. You will both be whipped this morning. After that, you must leave Tamworth, Seward, never to return. Cerwen will remain here, and I only hope that you have not planted a seed in her womb."

The slave girl gave a muffled sob and looked up, her emerald eyes pleading. Next to her, Seward's body went rigid; Merwenna could see from the set of his shoulders that he was outraged.

"But Milady," he burst out, "we did not . . ."

"I remind you again," Cyneswide interrupted him. "Had you come before my husband, you would be dead now—your head on a pike outside the town walls—as a reminder of what happens to those who abuse the king's hospitality. I would advise you to hold your tongue. For your own good, it's best if you are far from Tamworth when the king returns."

Merwenna felt danger in the air around them; Seward was close to crossing an invisible line. She hated the thought of him being whipped, but if it meant that he would walk out of Tamworth alive, then he would have to suffer his punishment.

"Merwenna," Queen Cyneswide turned her attention from Seward then. "Come forward."

Merwenna did as bid, keeping her gaze downcast. She could feel stares boring into her and felt her cheeks burn hotter still.

"If you wish it, you may stay on here and await your betrothed's return."

Merwenna looked up, shocked by this offer. She had not wanted to leave Tamworth without knowing of Beorn's fate. How could she remain here after what Seward had done?

"Milady," she gasped. "You are kind—but I should leave with my brother. We have caused enough upset here."

Queen Cyneswide smiled, the anger that had flared while addressing Seward vanishing.

"You are not to blame for your brother's behavior."

"But I can't stay here without his protection," Merwenna replied. "I cannot travel home alone."

"I will ensure you come to no harm here," the queen promised her. "And if your love does not return, I will have the king's men escort you home."

Merwenna stared at the queen, momentarily struck speechless by the offer. She was desperate to know that Beorn was safe, but she had to stay with her brother. She turned to Seward then and discovered he was glaring at her. His hazel eyes—so like his father's—were almost green; a sure sign he was furious.

"What will you do?" he asked, his voice flat.

His manner made Merwenna draw back.

She was willing to go with him and abandon her search for Beorn. Yet he was staring at her as if she had betrayed him. It was not her fault the queen had made her that offer. It was not she who had shamed the pair of them. She had been worrying about him, while he was only too ready to think the worst of her.

Merwenna had been about to tell Seward that she would return home with him, but now she hesitated.

"What should I do?" she asked him, deliberately keeping her tone neutral.

"You can't stay here—not without my protection."

"But the queen has guaranteed that I will be safe here and escorted home if Beorn doesn't return."

Seward's gaze narrowed. "You would let them cast me out and not follow? I only came here because you begged me to!"

Merwenna stared back at him and felt her own anger rise. It was an odd sensation—both hot and cold. It made her reckless.

"I'm staying here, Seward," she snapped. "Travel home without me."

Merwenna stepped back from her brother. Her brief flare of anger faded when she saw the hurt in his eyes. They had always been close, but she had now driven a wedge between them. Merwenna felt sick to her stomach as she turned back to Cyneswide and gave the queen a brittle smile.

"Thank you, Milady. I shall stay."

Queen Cyneswide nodded and turned to Rodor.

"Take Seward and Cerwen outside and give them each ten lashes of the whip."

The warrior nodded, his mouth thinning with satisfaction.

"Very well, Milady."

Merwenna watched, horrified, as two warriors hauled the slave girl across the rushes toward the doors. Cerwen struggled, her tears drying as she realized that the queen would show her no mercy. Instead, she started cursing in a tongue that Merwenna recognized as Cymraeg. She had seen a few of the Cymry in Weyham over the years, traveling over the borderlands between Powys and Mercia. Like Cerwen, many were raven-haired and blue or green eyed.

Rodor turned to Seward and gave him a slow, dark look, as if challenging him to make a similar scene. Instead, Seward stared back—the light-hearted mood of the day before a now distant memory. Then his gaze shifted to his sister.

Merwenna stared back, tears suddenly welling. She was so sorry it had come to this—yet pride would not let her back down.

"Good-bye dear sister," he said, his voice harsher than she had heard it. "We shall meet again in Weyham."

The words sounded more like a threat than a promise. It was as if she did not know him at all. Her free-spirited brother had turned into a cold stranger.

Seward turned and let Rodor lead him from the hall, without a backward glance.

Chapter Six

The King's Return

Merwenna wiped sweat off her forehead with the back of her wrist and squinted down at the tunic she was mending. It was unbearably stuffy here inside the Great Hall. The air was so close that it made her feel light-headed. It was difficult to concentrate on the task at hand.

The aroma of baking bread mingled with the odor of stewing cabbage and onion, and that of stale sweat. Despite that it was one of the hottest afternoons of the summer outside, the two fire pits within the hall smoldered. Slaves were baking griddle bread over one of the fire pits—placing thin discs of dough on a hot iron plate. A simmering cauldron of pottage cooked over the second fire pit.

She sat with the other women, opposite where the two princesses, Cyneburh and Cyneswith, embroidered pieces for a new banner. It bore the Mercian crest—pale gold with a wyvern—a two-legged dragon with spread wings—at its center. The banner was to be a gift to their father for his victory, and it was nearly finished. The princesses had both proved to be haughty and unfriendly toward Merwenna, in stark contrast to their mother's warmth.

Queen Cyneswide perched at a huge loom, not far from her daughters, where she and two ealdormen's wives worked at a tapestry. It was half-finished, but Merwenna could see that it was to be a panorama of green hills and verdant forest, with a great tower in its center—Tamworth.

Merwenna looked down at her mending and tried to swallow the nausea that had plagued her ever since she had watched her brother walk outside to be whipped that morning. She was already regretting her decision—only now it was too late to put things right. Without Seward's reassuring presence, she felt vulnerable in the king's hall.

Despite Cyneswide's graciousness, the other women here were not welcoming. Merwenna had caught them whispering and could only imagine it was about her. Once or twice, she had caught some of the women staring—and their gazes had not been friendly.

Merwenna did not belong here. She was a village girl and by rights should not have been sitting with the high born ladies. Her father had once served Raedwald of the East Angles many years earlier, but now he was of lesser rank. These days, he served Weyham's ealdorman. Merwenna had been proud of her father's rank at home, but here she realized that he would have been treated as a landless peasant among folk such as these. It was only the queen's generosity that allowed her to remain here, and everyone present knew the truth of it.

Merwenna's gaze traveled then to Cerwen. The slave was sweeping food scraps away from the hearth. The girl's pretty face was pale, her eyes hollowed. Merwenna's gaze shifted to the collar about Cerwen's neck, and she felt her own throat constrict. She had not been among the eager crowd that had followed the lovers outside, clamoring to witness their whipping. Still, from inside the hall, she had heard Cerwen's screams. From her brother, she had heard nothing.

Suddenly, Merwenna could not stand to be inside the Great Hall a moment longer. She felt as if the walls were closing in on her. The sharp glances from the other women were like boning knifes, stabbing and twisting till she could bear it no more. She needed air.

"Excuse me," Merwenna put her mending aside and rose to her feet. "I must visit the privy. I shall be back soon."

Whispers followed her, as she crossed the floor. She could feel the weight of their stares pressing between her shoulder blades.

Merwenna let out a long breath of relief as she stepped beyond the doors. Outside, the afternoon sun slanted onto the wide yard, cooking the hard-packed dirt. It was so hot that the dogs that usually prowled the space had taken refuge in the shade, tongues lolling. The sun was a white orb in a hard blue sky. Yet despite the heat, Merwenna's breathing steadied. At least here, she was not scrutinized.

She made her way down the stone steps to the yard and moved into the shade, near one of the panting dogs. The beast paid her no mind; it was too intent on snapping at flies that buzzed too close.

Although she was lightly dressed, in her best green wealca—a tube linen dress with shoulder straps attached with brooches—she felt sweat begin to slide down her spine. There were few folk about on this unusually hot late summer's afternoon. Merwenna spied two warriors, sweating in boiled leather, guarding the gates leading into the yard.

"What are you doing out here on your own, girl?"

A rough male voice sounded behind Merwenna, causing her to start. She whirled to see Rodor standing a couple of feet behind her, his cold gaze fixed upon her. His sleeveless tunic was dark with sweat, and he smelled of horses.

"Just taking some air," Merwenna replied nervously. There was something about Rodor that put her nerves on edge—that and the fact he had been the one to whip her brother. Rodor said little but thought a lot; she could see it in those gimlet eyes. There was also cruelty in the lines of his face.

"Careful," he smiled. "Wandering off alone makes you look as if you're looking for the same kind of trouble as your brother."

Rodor looked her up and down speculatively. "Perhaps you are."

Merwenna was horrified by his words, but tried her best not to show it.

"It was too hot in the hall," she replied, pretending that she had not understood.

Rodor's gaze flicked to the pole that stood in the center of the yard.

"Your brother wept like a maid while I whipped him," he murmured. "I'd wager you would have whimpered less."

Merwenna felt the sweat that coated her skin turn cold. Her stomach balled in sudden anger. Not for the first time in her twenty winters, she wished she had been born a man. She would have punched that leer off his face.

She was saved having to respond, when one of the guards at the gate turned and waved to Rodor.

"The King returns!" he shouted. "His fyrd approaches!"

Rodor strode forward, Merwenna forgotten. "Open the gates," he ordered. "Let them in!"

The ground started to tremble, and Merwenna heard the thunder of the approaching army. Her heart leaped.

Beorn!

Moments later, a stream of lathered horses and sweat-soaked, armored men poured into the yard. Merwenna stayed put, her back against the sun-warmed stone, as to run out to greet them would be to risk being trampled. Her gaze frantically searched the faces of the men that surged into the yard, filling the wide space.

Where is he?

The din was incredible. The horses kicked up clouds of dust, and the stillness of the sultry afternoon shattered. Merwenna imagined that this was only a fraction of the king's army—the rest of his fyrd would stretch down the street outside and beyond to the market square.

Merwenna's chest ached with longing as she continued to search the crowd for Beorn's handsome face. Next to her, the dogs had risen from their slumber and were standing, eager-eyed, their tails wagging.

How will I find him in this crowd?

Eventually, Merwenna realized that it was unlikely that Beorn would be here. She would not find him at the head of the fyrd, amongst the king's ealdormen and thegns.

She was just about to dive into the crowd of milling men and horses, in search of her betrothed, when her gaze was drawn to an imposing figure that could only be the King of Mercia himself.

She had heard many tales of Penda of Mercia. Throughout the kingdom he was a god amongst men: tall, blond, and merciless.

The tales did not exaggerate.

A man that towered above all around him swung down from a grey stallion. He was finely dressed in leather, mail, and a thick blue cloak. His face was shielded by an iron helm and when he removed it, the face underneath was no softer.

A cruelly handsome face, and eyes the color of a winter's sky, surveyed the yard. Long ice-blond hair, streaked with grey, streamed over his broad shoulders. Penda of Mercia was indeed striking, as would be his sons when grown. Merwenna instinctively feared him.

The king threw his reins to a slave and cast a cool glance about him.

Merwenna looked away from the king and squared her shoulders. The thought of combing Tamworth in search for Beorn frightened her, but she would do it nonetheless. This was why she had come here; this was why she had not left with her brother. Merwenna crossed the yard, ducking out of the way of a horse that kicked out as she passed behind it.

That was close. Merwenna's heart started to hammer against her ribs but she pressed on.

She would search the king's army, from one end to the other, until she found her betrothed.

***

The Prince of Powys watched the slave pour his cup full of mead. She was a dark-haired wench that he would wager was of Cymry blood. Her pretty face was pinched and drawn, and she avoided his gaze as she went about her task.

Dylan watched her go, before his gaze shifted to the huge platters of food that slaves and servants were laying out on the long tables lining either side of the Great Hall's fire pits.

After days of travel and a frugal diet of stale seed cakes and hard cheese, his belly growled at the sight of the feast before him. Spit-roasted wild boar dominated the table, surrounded by apples roasted with walnuts and honey. There were platters of braised leeks and buttered carrots, and tureens of rich mutton stew—all accompanied by mountains of griddle bread.

Beside Dylan, Gwyn gave a grunt of pleasure and started helping himself to the roast boar and apples.

"A good feast this," he acknowledged with his mouth full. "Penda has fine cooks."

Dylan gave a shrug before filling the trencher before him with mutton stew. "It is impressive. Let us hope that Penda is as generous with his gifts, as he is with his stores."

Gwyn nodded, his eyes glinting at Dylan's meaning. Powys had made a pact with Mercia before Dylan marched his men to war, but Penda had yet to honor it. Still, now that they had reached Tamworth, there would be plenty of time to talk of such things. This eve, Dylan was in no hurry.

Dylan's gaze shifted to the other end of the table, where the king and queen dined together. Their offspring—a fine looking brood—flanked them, the two adolescent girls to the right and the three boys on the other side.

The king and queen spoke little, but Dylan noticed the ease between them; the frequency with which their gazes met. Queen Cyneswide was entering her fourth decade, but she was still a beautiful woman. Dylan could see, by the softness of her face every time she looked in Penda's direction, that she plainly adored her husband.

No accounting for taste.

Dylan took a draught of mead and turned his attention back to the feast. He sampled a bit of everything, and was beginning to feel uncomfortably full when servants brought honey cakes, plum tarts, and apple pies to the table. The feasters fell upon the sweets, as if they had not already consumed a king's share of food, drizzling the cakes with thick cream.

It was then, as Dylan sat considering whether it was prudent to eat anything else, that one of the girls serving the sweets, caught his attention.

It was uncomfortably hot in the hall and the young woman's face and arms gleamed with sweat. She wore a pretty green wealca that hugged her lissome form. She was small and slender but with a swelling bosom that made her look ripe and womanly. Her thick mane of brown hair was tied back, revealing a long neck. When she turned in Dylan's direction, he saw the girl had a plump, rosebud mouth and startling blue eyes.

Desire lanced through Dylan, making him catch his breath.

Months without a woman made him suddenly hungry for one. A night with such a girl would definitely put a smile on a man's face. The slave he had been admiring earlier was forgotten as his gaze devoured the lovely serving wench. Consumed by lustful thoughts, Dylan looked away and held out his cup to be filled by a passing slave.

When he looked back in the girl's direction, she had gone.

Chapter Seven

Ill-tidings

"Let the dancing begin!"

The feasting had ended, and the mountains of food scraps tidied away. Servants had pushed the long feasting tables back against the walls, to make way for the musicians—two playing bone whistles, and one on a lyre—and the throng of dancers.

The king and his family looked down upon the revelry from the heah-setl—high seat—at the far end of the hall, watching as the ealdormen and thegns led their wives out onto the center of the floor to dance.

Merwenna leaned over a water barrel at the opposite end of the hall and sipped from a long-handled ladle. She drank thirstily. The water tasted stale but was a balm in the airless heat of Penda's Great Hall.

The musicians had struck up a lively tune. Men and women whirled around the center of the hall. Merwenna stepped back from the water barrel and let her gaze travel over them. There was joy and revelry on their faces—but she could not share their gaiety. She would not rejoice for Mercia's victory until she found Beorn.

Merwenna's vision blurred with tears of frustration. She had spent the afternoon scouring Tamworth for her betrothed but had not found him. She had asked many men if they had seen Beorn, or knew him, but none had. Some of the men she had asked had been rude to her, others lecherous and frightening. Merwenna had returned to the tower, weary and tearful, only to have an ealdorman's wife—a bossy, shrill woman named Hild—inform her that she could earn her keep by serving at the evening's feast.

Merwenna had not minded the task; it kept her busy and stopped her worrying about Beorn. However, as the evening progressed, anxiety wove itself into a tight ball in the pit of her belly.

I must speak to the king, she finally decided. Her worry was eating her up inside; she had to take action. *Only he can help me. How else will I know if Beorn has survived?*

Straightening her back with resolve, Merwenna stepped away from the wall and started to make her way around the edge of the hall. It was slow progress. The Great Hall heaved with the press of sweating bodies. It was so hot in here that Merwenna started to feel light-headed.

She longed to escape into the cool evening, to breathe fresh air—but first she had to speak to the king.

Through the press, she caught glimpses of the king and his entourage. Now that the feast had ended, and the tables had been shifted, Penda's most favored ealdormen sat at the foot of the high seat—as did a striking dark-haired man.

The stranger was dressed in a mail vest and leather breeches. A plush purple cloak hung from his broad shoulders. The man stood out from those seated around him. He had chiseled features, a lithe build, and raven hair—marking him as one of the Cymry. He lounged back on cushions, watching the dancing, his expression slightly bored.

This must be Cynddylan son of Cyndrwyn of Powys—the man who had brought his army to aid the Mercians in their victory.

The prince looked as if he would have rather been elsewhere than in this hall full of noisy, high born Mercians. Merwenna was about to refocus her attention upon King Penda, when Cynddylan's gaze met hers.

She gasped, her step faltering, and was grateful when the swirling dancers obscured his view of her. No man had ever looked at her like that, not even Beorn. The heat of this stranger's gaze had made her body prickle as if she stood naked in a draft. The sensation was unnerving.

Refocusing her thoughts, Merwenna edged closer to the high seat. She would not be distracted; there was too much at stake.

I must find Beorn. The king will help me.

She gathered her courage as she went and mentally rehearsed the request she would make before the king. The dancers moved aside, and Merwenna once more had a view of the royal family. She reached the foot of the high seat and, not hesitating—lest her nerve fail her—she stepped up to address the king.

"My Lord, Penda," she addressed him tremulously, curtsying low. "Please, may I have a moment of your time?"

Penda looked up from where he had quietly been conversing with his wife. His gaze focused upon Merwenna, and then narrowed.

"What is it wench? Why do you interrupt your king?"

"I apologize," Merwenna bowed her head, "but there is something I must ask. There was a young warrior named Beorn who rode with you to war—Beorn of Weyham. Do you know of his fate?"

The king's gaze narrowed further.

"Bold wench," he addressed her coldly. "How did you gain entrance to my hall? How dare you badger me? Be gone before I give you to my men."

"Penda," Cyneswide interjected gently, placing a restraining hand on her husband's forearm. "Merwenna is my guest. She should not have approached you so boldly, but she is plainly desperate to know the fate of her betrothed."

The king inclined his head and gave his wife a bemused look.

"Your guest?"

Cyneswide nodded, flushing slightly. "Please help her, for my sake."

Penda glanced back at Merwenna, his gaze hewn from stone. "I know not if your betrothed survived the battle or not," he admitted. "Thousands of men serve me. I do not know the names of most of them, let alone this *Berthun*."

"*Beorn*, Milord. He was tall and blond, with a short beard. He had blue eyes."

"That description could fit many of my warriors," Penda's mouth twisted in scorn. "Stop wasting my time."

"Beorn of Weyham did serve you, Penda."

A man's voice, deep and lightly accented, sounded behind her. Merwenna swiveled, and her gaze met that of the Prince of Powys once more. Cynddylan ap Cyndrwyn remained seated, lying back indolently on cushions.

Merwenna stiffened. Prince or not, he should rise to his feet when addressing Penda.

As if thinking upon the same lines, the King of Mercia's cruelly handsome face grew harder still. His gaze upon the Prince of Powys was wintry.

"Do you not remember him?" Cynddylan asked, seemingly unmoved by the king's cold stare. "The lad who followed you around for days before the battle. The one who personally asked to fight in the shield wall to show his loyalty to you."

Penda's gaze narrowed as if taking the measure of the man seated below him.

Merwenna glanced from the King of Mercia's face, to that of the Prince of Powys. She was aware of the tension between them that had nothing to do with her presence. There was an unspoken challenge in Cynddylan's eyes.

"Perhaps," Penda's gaze flicked back to Merwenna. "Blond, bearded, and handsome, you say?"

Merwenna nodded, feeling sick to the stomach.

"Then I do remember him. The Prince of Powys speaks true. The lad was eager to please. A young warrior who thought war was a game. After I told him he could fight in the shield wall, I never saw him again. I know not if he lives."

"He does not," Cynddylan's words echoed in the sudden hush.

Merwenna was aware that the music and dancing had stopped and that many were staring at her. She turned to meet the Prince of Powys' gaze. There was pity in his moss-green eyes that made her legs start to tremble.

Suddenly, she did not want to hear any more.

"How do you know this?" she finally managed, her voice hoarse with the effort it was taking for her to keep her composure.

"I saw his body among the dead, after the battle," he replied, his tone gentling. "Your betrothed died with honor, fighting for his people—for his king."

Chapter Eight

Nón-mete

Not again.

Merwenna stared down at the hem she was embroidering and watched her tears drop onto the linen.

Blinking furiously, she swallowed the rising sobs and took deep, steady breaths. Eventually, her tears stemmed, and she picked up her bone needle to resume her work, keeping her gaze downcast lest anyone attempt to make eye-contact with her.

Two days had passed since the king's return. The two longest days of Merwenna's life.

She had received news of Beorn's death so publically, for Cynddylan's interruption had drawn the attention of all. However, grief had overridden embarrassment and, after the Prince of Powys had told her of her betrothed's end on the battlefield, she had dissolved into tears and fled the hall.

No one had come after her, and Merwenna was glad for it. Away from prying eyes, she had curled up in the shadow of one of the outbuildings and wept until exhaustion. Alone, she nursed her pain in the long twilight. Suddenly, she wanted the comfort of her family around her. For the first time since leaving Weyham, she longed for her mother's embrace.

Beorn. Every time she thought of him, the tears flowed afresh. He had been so young, so earnest—so brave. She had tried to warn him that war was not like in the songs that the older men sang around the fire pit, but he had merely humored her.

Now she would never hear his voice, look into his eyes, or kiss him—ever again.

Merwenna could not think upon Beorn without raging against fate. The likes of Penda and Cynddylan lived, so why could not have Beorn?

Merwenna stabbed her bone needle into the linen and did a quick, neat stitch.

Anger was so much easier to tolerate than grief.

As always, it had been a lonely morning sitting apart from the other women as she worked. She was a guest in the King's Hall but even so was expected to earn her keep. This did not bother Merwenna. Industry kept her sadness at bay.

Even so, it was time to leave Tamworth.

She felt much stronger today. Ever since the news of Beorn's death, she had hidden from the world. Yet this morning she could see beyond the cloak of grief. She needed to go home, to face her parents—and Seward—and to help bring in the last of the harvest.

The aroma of mutton pie reached Merwenna then, causing her belly to growl. She looked up to see the inhabitants of the Great Hall were taking their places at the long tables for nón-mete—'noon meat'. Merwenna put aside her embroidery, rose to her feet, and moved to join them.

I will speak to the queen this afternoon, she made herself a silent promise as she took a seat on one of the low benches. *I will ask her for an escort home tomorrow*.

Merwenna had just taken a seat, when she felt someone's gaze upon her. She glanced up and looked straight into the eyes of the Prince of Powys. He was walking past, on his way further up the table, to where he would take his seat.

The prince gave her a slow smile in greeting.

Flustered, Merwenna looked away. She did not look up again until he had moved on. She was not sure why, but there was something about that man that unnerved her. Part of her hated Cynddylan for revealing that Beorn was dead. His blunt words had crushed any hope.

Meanwhile, at the other end of the table, the royal family took their places.

Penda and Cyneswide sat at the head, flanked by their children to the left and Penda's most trusted ealdormen down the right. The three boys had pushed and shoved their way to the table, elbowing each other for the chance to sit next to their father. However, one quelling look from Penda calmed them. Giving his younger brothers a superior look, Paeda took his place closest to the king.

Servants circulated the hall, filling cups with milk, ale, or mead; or placing wooden platters of braised leeks on the table. The mutton pie arrived, and Merwenna's mouth watered at the sight of it. She was just beginning her slice, tearing into the crumbly pastry with her fingers, when she heard one of the princes—the middle one, Wulfhere—address his father.

"Fæder," the boy began, his handsome face earnest with purpose. "One of the town smiths has a litter of pups he is giving away. They're hunting dogs. May I have one?"

Penda swallowed a mouthful of pie and washed it down with a gulp of ale, before answering. "We have plenty of dogs in the tower, Wulfhere. Choose one of them."

"But they're all grown—and they all belong to others," Wulfhere insisted, his voice quavering slightly as he sought to control his nervousness. Merwenna did not blame him. Penda's mere presence was enough to chill the blood. "I promise I will look after it, fæder," the lad finished, his face hopeful.

"No," Penda's tone was dismissive as he turned back to his meal. "You'll have a dog of your own to train when you're grown—when you've earned it. I have enough beasts skulking about the hall as it is without a whelp under my feet."

"But, fæder," Wulfhere did not back down. He stared at his father, his eyes glittering. "I promise it wouldn't be any trouble. I would . . ."

"Enough," the word came out in a low growl, but its menace caused Penda's son to pale. "You whine like a maid. One more word, and I'll take my belt to you."

Merwenna watched the lad hang his head, hiding his expression under a cascade of white-blond hair. To his left, the eldest brother, Paeda, smirked; while to his right, the youngest, Aethelred, sniggered.

Merwenna, who had always not only felt her own emotions deeply, but also those of others, longed to go to the boy and comfort him. Her gaze flicked to Cyneswide—and she was surprised to find the queen's expression composed. But, when she looked more closely, Merwenna caught the flicker of sadness in her eyes.

Glancing back at Prince Wulfhere's stricken face, Merwenna counted herself lucky that she had not been born into such a family.

Further up the table, Dylan also watched the exchange between father and son.

He remembered that at the same age as Wulfhere, he too had pestered his father for a dog. Unlike Penda of Mercia, Cyndrwyn of Powys had eventually relented. That pup—a tiny creature that had once fitted in the palm of his hand—had grown into a huge, shaggy beast.

They had grown up together. *Taranau*—'thunder' in his tongue—had become his shadow, his friend.

Dylan's father, who had died the winter before, had been a stern, inflexible man in many ways. Yet seeing Penda's treatment of his son, made Dylan see his own father in a new light.

He will make his sons the image of him, Dylan thought wryly.

Dylan turned his attention back to his pie. Like the rest of the fare that Penda's cooks prepared, it was delicious. Now that the weariness of the journey back from Maes Cogwy had abated, Dylan was too restless to enjoy it.

He pushed aside the remnants of his meal, took a deep draught of mead, and cast another glance in Penda's direction.

Enough. The battle was done. The Northumbrians had been defeated, and yet Penda continued to deflect any talk of compensating his allies for their losses. He had been a guest under Penda's roof for over two days—long enough, in his opinion—and was eager to begin the march back to Powys.

He had a kingdom to rule, and would be crowned upon his return to Pengwern, the capital of Powys. Dylan and his men were guests in Tamworth, but Penda's hospitality was a thin veneer. Last night, there had been a brawl outside the mead hall, between Dylan's men and Mercian warriors. If they stayed much longer, the truce between Powys and Mercia would be at an end.

Penda, it's time for us to talk.

Chapter Nine

Cyneswide's Word

Merwenna approached the group of high born women. They were working industriously at their distaffs and looms. The queen was among them, seated at her loom, and flanked either side by her daughters. She looked up as Merwenna approached, as did Cyneburh and Cyneswith.

Merwenna ignored the girls' haughty stares. Instead she focused upon the queen, who at least was smiling at her.

"Good afternoon, Merwenna. I have not seen you all day. Are you well?"

"Yes, Milady," Merwenna returned the smile and dipped into a low curtsey. Then she took a deep breath and pushed on, before she lost her nerve. "I am well, but anxious to return to my kin. Now that I know Beorn's fate, I cannot remain here."

Cyneswide nodded her blue eyes clouding slightly. "You are grieving. I am sorry your betrothed did not survive the battle—I had so hoped he would."

"Thank you," Merwenna dropped her gaze to the floor, feeling her throat tighten at Beorn's name. "You are most kind."

She paused then, struggling to compose herself, while aware that the other women all watched her. Some of them enjoyed seeing her grief, especially after the dishonor that Seward had brought upon her.

Taking a deep breath, Merwenna looked up and met Cyneswide's gaze.

"Milady, you promised me an escort home, when I was ready. I would like to depart tomorrow. Can you provide me with one?"

Even as she spoke these words, Merwenna was painfully aware of her boldness. She knew that the queen had made a promise. Yet to actually stand before her and demand she make good on it, was another thing entirely.

The queen held her gaze for a moment before her smile faded. Her expression changed to one of regret.

"I'm sorry," she said softly. "I have tried to speak to the king about you, but he will not hear of sparing one of his men to escort you home."

But you promised!

Merwenna choked back the words, panic flaring in her breast, her palms breaking out into a cold sweat.

"Perhaps you can ask at the market?" the queen continued gently. "There are bound to be merchants traveling in the direction of your village. Perhaps you can journey with one of them?"

One like Drefan of Chester, Milady?

Anger surged within Merwenna's breast. Queen or not, this woman had given her word. While her husband had been absent, Cyneswide had been strong, capable, and decisive. Now that Penda had returned, she was but a shadow of that woman.

Merwenna managed a sickly smile although inside she was in turmoil. She was so annoyed that she had to clench her fists to stop it from showing on her face.

"Thank you for at least trying on my behalf," she eventually replied, hoping her ingratitude was not showing on her face, "and for your hospitality. I shall take my leave now."

The queen's eyes widened. "There's no need to rush off, Merwenna," she admonished. "You can wait till morning at least."

Merwenna shook her head. Then she stepped back, curtsying once more as she did so.

"No," she said firmly. "I'm going home today."

Merwenna crossed the Great Hall to the small bower she had been sharing with the princesses for the last few nights. It had been an uncomfortable spot, lying pressed up against the damp stone wall, but ever since Seward's departure, the queen had deemed it the safest place for her young guest to sleep.

Inside, she retrieved her satchel and stuffed her traveling cloak into it. Then, slinging it across her front, she emerged back into the hall.

The hall was in chaos. Slaves wove their way through the mass of leather-clad warriors, in last-moment preparations for the meal. The rumble of men's voices echoed like thunder in the lofty space.

It was nearing meal time and the king's men, rowdy and high-spirited as usual, flooded the hall. They were an intimidating group—tall, broad, and loud. They groped the serving girls, kicked dogs out of their way and strode toward the long tables either side of the two fire pits, roaring for cups of mead as they went. The victory had put Penda's men in good spirits, but it had also made them insufferable. Merwenna was wary of them.

Fortunately, no one paid her any mind as she edged her way around the wall and slipped out the doors.

Outside, despite that it was not yet near dusk, the light had faded considerably, for dark clouds had rolled in from the north. The air crackled with the promise of an approaching storm. *Thunor* was preparing to ride his chariot, drawn by his two goats—Gap-tooth and Gnasher—across the sky.

Merwenna took a deep breath of the humid air, squared her shoulders, and stalked away from the Great Tower of Tamworth. She crossed the yard, passed under the stone arch, and stepped out into the pot-holed street beyond.

Despite her purposeful stride, Merwenna's stomach felt twisted in knots. Anger had propelled her out of the Great Hall and into Tamworth, but now the reality of matters hit her.

She was about to face a five-day journey alone.

Tamworth stank of urine, rotting food, and animal droppings; and Merwenna's memory of the incident in the market square was still fresh in her mind. She breathed shallowly and kept her gaze downcast as she hurried through the network of narrow streets.

She had to hurry. Soon, the town gates would be closing for the night. She wanted to make sure she was outside Tamworth's walls when they did.

***

"Storm's brewing," Gwyn muttered, as he and Dylan crossed the stable yard.

The Prince of Powys glanced up at the sky and felt the first drops of cool rain splatter onto his upturned face. "A violent one by the looks of it," he replied.

They had spent most of the afternoon with their men, who were camped outside Tamworth's walls, checking on those who were injured and readying the others for their imminent departure. With a tempest on its way, it was time to return inside.

Impatience had needled at Dylan for most of the day; this eve, he planned to remind Penda of his oaths.

Most of the king's men were already seated when Dylan and Gwyn entered the Great Hall. As always, there was a great deal of activity and noise inside. A pall of greasy smoke hung in the air.

Letting Gwyn go on ahead, Dylan paused on the threshold. His gaze swept the hall and rested upon where Penda had just taken a seat at the head of the king's table.

The Prince of Powys set off across the hall toward him.

Rodor had been about to take his place at the king's right, when Dylan slid onto the bench next to Penda. Taken aback by the prince's sudden appearance, Rodor cursed under his breath and stood threateningly over him. He clearly expected Dylan to rise and give him back his place.

Dylan glanced up and met Rodor's glare. "I'm feasting here this eve," he informed him. "Find somewhere else to sit."

With that, Dylan turned to face the king, dismissing Rodor. He could feel the warrior's glare blister him between the shoulder blades. Dylan ignored him although he felt his own anger rising.

Rodor would pester him again at his peril.

Penda regarded Dylan with thinly veiled amusement. The Mercian King had just taken a sip from a large bronze goblet studded with amber and garnets. Next to him, his queen was daintily picking at a leg of marsh hen. She glanced Dylan's way and favored him with a gentle smile.

Dylan acknowledged her with an answering smile. "Milady."

"Good evening, Cynddylan," Penda rumbled. "It appears you are eager to speak to me. Rodor looks displeased. I'd warn you against annoying him too greatly, for he has a long memory."

Dylan shrugged, fixing Penda in a level gaze. "The day I shall concern myself with Rodor, is the day I return to my mother's tit. I am seated here to talk of more kingly matters. It is time we spoke of the alliance between our kingdoms."

Penda raised his eyebrows at that before taking another draught of mead. "Speak your piece then."

"You remember the agreement," Dylan regarded Penda coolly. "If Powys helped Mercia win the battle against the Northumbrians, you would grant us rule over the area east of our current border. Do I have your word that this land is now ours?"

Penda's face went still, as cold and hard as one of the statues the Romans had left behind. Only his eyes showed any response, glittering coldly in the firelight.

"That land belongs to me."

"It belongs to whomever earns it."

Penda's gaze narrowed slightly, before his mouth curved into a tight smile.

"Very well," he drawled, finally. "You can have as far east as Hanbury."

Dylan took a deep breath, controlling the anger that flared in the pit of his belly. The king's offer was an insult, and everyone within earshot knew it.

Penda knew the Prince of Powys had a fiery temper. He wanted Dylan to lose control, to lash out. He was counting on it.

"Hanbury lies barely a morning's ride from our eastern border," Dylan said, making sure to keep his voice even and emotionless. "That is no prize for the deaths of fine Cymry warriors. Give us as far east as Lichfield, and we will be content."

"Lichfield," Penda ground out the name like a curse. "You demand much."

"I demand only our due," Dylan replied. "The promise our alliance was founded upon. Powys is a great ally for Mercia. We rallied to your side against the Northumbrians, and we would do so again. However, you must recompense our losses or next time your neighbors march on your borders you will fight them alone."

They were strong words—but they had the desired effect. The rumble of conversation around them had died, and Dylan was aware of gazes, many of them hostile, upon him. He paid them no heed, his own gaze riveted upon the King of Mercia's face.

Much depended on Penda's next words.

Penda's fist clenched around the stem of his goblet. His face, however, gave nothing away. A long pause stretched between them before the king finally spoke.

"Very well—you may have the land."

A thrill of victory surged through Dylan although he was careful to keep his face neutral. He was aware of the aura of danger that suddenly crackled around him. Penda had agreed to his terms but he felt as if he were standing in the center of a frozen lake, upon very thin ice. One misstep and he would plunge to his death.

"Thank you, Lord Penda," he nodded, rising to his feet to find Rodor still standing behind him.

If the king looked coldly furious, Rodor looked fit to explode. His face was contorted with rage, his cheeks flushed.

"Your man may have his place back," Dylan smiled at Rodor, showing him his teeth. "Now that I have my answer, I will abuse your hospitality no longer. I shall ready my warriors to leave with the breaking dawn."

Dylan moved away from the long table, but had only distanced himself a couple of yards when Penda's cold voice hailed him.

"Lord Cynddylan."

Dylan turned. "Yes?"

"You have the land as far east as Lichfield for now, but do not think it will belong to Powys forever. There will come a day when Mercia will reclaim its territory—remember that."

Dylan inclined his head, and returned Penda's gaze. "And there will come a day when Powys does not answer Mercia's call—remember that."

Dylan turned from the Mercian King then and strode from the hall without a backward glance. His hand itched to reach for his sword, but it awaited him in the entrance way beyond the doors. All the same, he could feel Mercian stares knifing him between the shoulder blades and hoped Gwyn was watching his back.

It was done. He had received the gift he had been waiting for—now it was time to be gone from Tamworth.

Chapter Ten

Rodor Makes a Pledge

"The Prince of Powys and his men have departed."

Rodor stopped before the heah-setl and fixed the king with a penetrating stare.

The king grunted, but did not bother to look his way.

Penda leisurely reclined in his high-back wooden chair, watching his sons play-fight with wooden swords. It was a magnificent throne—with arm-rests that had been elaborately carved to resemble two dragon heads.

"Milord," Rodor began again. "Are you just going to let Cynddylan leave?"

Penda ignored him. His gaze remained upon Paeda and Wulfhere. The boys were sparring, and the play-fight had suddenly turned serious. Wulfhere, a year younger than Paeda, was starting to gain the upper-hand—a move which had caused his older brother to snarl insults at him.

"Arse-licking little shit," Paeda spat, his face red with the effort to keep his brother at bay. "You seek to ingratiate yourself with fæder. I'll beat you senseless for this later."

"Not if I get you first!' Wulfhere snarled back, before clubbing his brother on the side of the head with the blade of his wooden sword.

Paeda's howls echoed up into the rafters.

The queen rose to her feet, sweeping down from the high seat to prevent the fight from deteriorating into a bloody brawl.

"My Lord Penda," Rodor's patience had reached breaking-point. "Cynddylan insulted you, before your entire hall. Will you let that lie?"

Those words drew the king's attention. As Rodor has suspected, Penda was out of sorts this morning. His face grew taut and his head swiveled to his thegn.

"You forget your place, Rodor," he rumbled. "If he had truly insulted me, his head would be on a pike outside Tamworth's gates."

"Apologies, Milord," Rodor bowed his head. "I spoke hastily out of anger. Cynddylan's arrogance galls me. He behaves as a base-born mercenary. His demand was outrageous—surely you do not mean to let Powys rule as far east as Lichfield?"

Penda stretched his long legs out before him, and crossed them at the ankles. He fixed Rodor with a level gaze.

"I made a pact with Powys. In this instance, I thought it prudent to uphold our promises. We may need Cynddylan's assistance in the future."

Rodor frowned. It was unlike Penda to care about keeping oaths, or to bow to the demands of others.

"Mercia does not need the help of those Cymry dogs," Rodor replied, his lip curling.

Penda gave a humorless laugh. "You did not fight alongside them at Maes Cogwy, Rodor. They are formidable allies, and I am not done fighting. Northumbria might have been beaten to submission but I still have enemies to face. Annan of the East Angles has long been a thorn in my side. I will not rest till I gut that whoreson on my blade."

Rodor did not reply to that. He knew that the rancor between Penda and Annan ran deep. Mercia had beaten the East Angles at Barrow Fields, years earlier, and killed their king. The successor to the East Angle throne, Annan, was allowed to live only if he agreed to 'bend the knee' to Mercia. Penda had attempted to seal the agreement with an arranged marriage between his sister—Saewara—and Annan. Unfortunately, his plan had turned against him when Saewara fell in love with her new husband and betrayed her brother.

These days, it was forbidden to mention Saewara's name in Penda's presence. The king's hatred for his sister ran deep.

"Cynddylan of Powys will also become your bane," Rodor told Penda, his dislike for the prince overriding prudence. "Mark my words, he will be laughing at you right this moment—gloating over his good fortune."

Silence stretched between them then. When Penda replied, his voice was low, dangerous. "What would you counsel me to do?"

Rodor hesitated. He knew that tone well, and it warned him to proceed carefully. His king was on the verge of losing his temper. Rodor was close to bearing the brunt of the Mercian king's wintry rage.

"Send a war party after Cynddylan," Rodor told Penda firmly. "Kill him before he reaches Powys."

"What? And turn Powys against us? Have you not been listening to me—we need their alliance."

"Make his death look like the work of outlaws," Rodor continued. "No one has to know it was you."

The king did not reply for a moment. His gaze moved away from his thegn, to where Paeda was still clutching his ear and wailing curses at his smug younger brother.

"Finally," Penda drawled, "a suggestion that doesn't make you sound like a dolt. I was wondering if the trust I have placed in you all these years had been misguided."

Rodor stared back at Penda and felt his face flush hot at the insult. The king's response was offensive. Still he could see that Penda was starting to come round to his idea.

"It must be an assassination," Penda continued. "Swift and silent. The killers must move like shadows. Cynddylan's throat must be cut while he sleeps—and no one must *ever* suspect that I was behind it."

Rodor nodded, holding his breath.

Penda's gaze swiveled back to the warrior before him, and Rodor saw the calculating gleam in the king's gaze. "Who will carry out this task?" Penda asked.

Rodor smiled. They both knew the answer.

"I will, Milord."

"You, Rodor? Yet I see that you hate the Prince of Powys. Hate makes a man rash, foolish. I've lost many a good warrior to it."

"I'm one of your best. I do not succumb to the same mistakes as others," Rodor replied without a trace of arrogance. It was a simple fact. Penda knew it—that was why the king had left him behind to protect Queen Cyneswide while Penda marched his fyrd to war. He would only leave her in the hands of a warrior he knew to be his own rival.

Penda nodded. "You are—but this task requires more than skill with a blade. You will not be fighting Cynddylan on the battlefield. You must catch him unawares. Can you be as silent as a shadow?"

"I can," Rodor assured him. "I will gather a group of warriors—the best you have. We will track down the Cymry army and penetrate their camp at night. We shall make sure their prince never reaches home."

Penda sank back into his chair, his gaze hooded. "Very well," he finally acquiesced. "I give you leave to do so."

Victory surged through Rodor, sweet and heady as strong mead. With a nod he turned to leave.

"Rodor."

"Yes, Milord," Rodor swiveled back to face his king. Penda's pale gaze snared his, and held him fast.

"There can be no mistakes. None. If you fail, none of you must return here. You will die rather than reveal the truth—is that clear?"

Rodor nodded.

"Heed me well," Penda leaned forward in his seat, the intensity of his gaze making Rodor draw back slightly. "If you, or any of your men, return to me with tales of woe, I will show no mercy. Cynddylan must die quietly, and you must do it unseen."

Chapter Eleven

The Journey West

Grey mist clung to the trees like porridge. Merwenna struggled through the undergrowth. She cursed at the blackthorn that tore at her skirts and cloak, and at the rain that slashed across the woodland. She had no idea if she was even going in the right direction. Without the sun to guide her, she was traveling blind.

She was soaked through and chilled. It had been a long, miserable night, huddled under the trees while the tempest spent itself. The breaking dawn had not brought any solace. The storm moved on, but the rain remained. It was hard to believe that the kingdom had been enjoying the balmiest summer in years. All at once, autumn had arrived.

Merwenna's stomach growled as she walked; a constant reminder that she had eaten little since leaving Tamworth. She carried little money with her, for Seward had been looking after the pouch containing their precious gold. She had used her last thrymsa to buy bread and cheese before slipping out of the gates into the dusk, but that was nearly gone. What little she had left needed to be rationed. She had found some raspberries that morning and taken the edge off her hunger—yet it returned now, sharp and demanding.

Ignoring her empty belly, as best she could, Merwenna pressed on. More than her hunger, it was a growing sense of panic that bothered her. She had been so sure of her direction last night, before the storm broke. Now, she had the chilling sensation she was traveling off-course.

Still, she would find out soon enough—once the mist cleared—whether she was journeying toward home.

Eventually, the trees began to the thin, and the going grew easier. The ground squelched underfoot as the rain continued to fall in a thick, heavy mist now. Time lost any meaning.

Merwenna took a brief rest, under the sheltering boughs of a great oak, and chewed at a piece of bread. The rain had soaked it, making the staleness more palatable. She ate it slowly, forcing herself not to stuff the rest into her mouth.

She still had a long way to travel before reaching home.

Merwenna continued her journey west, eager to distance herself from Tamworth. The day drew out. Gradually the mist lifted, and the rain ceased. When the sun set in the west, Merwenna was relieved to see that she had not traveled as far off course as she had feared. Still, she altered her direction slightly—cutting right, across a shallow, wooded valley.

Warmed by the rays of the setting sun, Merwenna's spirits lifted for the first time all day. And when she discovered a patch of mushrooms growing in a shadowy dell at the bottom of the valley, she almost felt cheerful.

The mushrooms were small and earthy, and they took the edge off her hunger. Her clothes had started to dry out although the damp homespun itched against her clammy skin. She found a stream in the valley, but it was too shallow to bathe in. She did manage to slake her thirst from it and wash her face.

Night eventually settled over the softly wooded hills of Mercia, bringing with it a chorus of bird-calls. Merwenna would have liked to build a fire, but there was no dry wood about to make one with. Instead she sat under the canopy of twin beeches and leaned her back up against the rough bark, watching as darkness swallowed the world.

As a child she had been terrified of the dark, especially in the winter. She had been convinced a demon would creep out of the trees and carry her off. Her fears had been so real that she had kept both her parents awake for many a night.

Yet tonight it was not demons but thoughts of Beorn that kept her from sleeping.

It was easier to keep thoughts of her betrothed at bay during the day, when she was focused upon her destination. However, now that she had curled up amongst the trees, she could no longer outrun her worries.

Why did you have to go to war? Merwenna's chest constricted painfully. *You could have been happy farming the land in Weyham, building a life there with me. We could have had children. We could have grown old together.*

She brushed aside the tears that trickled down her cheeks and chided herself for railing against fate. It was futile to dwell on such things. Beorn was gone, and with him the focus that had given Merwenna her strength, her purpose.

What will become of me when I return to Weyham? I'll have to face Seward and my parents—who will be furious with me. But, after that?

The future was open, unwritten—empty. She did not like to dwell upon it. Instead, she drew her damp cloak close around her and shut her eyes against the encroaching darkness.

***

The scent of wood-smoke made her halt mid-stride.

Was she near a village? It was nearing dusk, on the second day of her journey west from Tamworth. Despite that she had stumbled upon the road west this morning, and followed it ever since, she had not yet set eyes upon a soul. She hoped it was a village nearby, for she felt light headed with hunger and her limbs ached with weariness.

Mingled with the wood-smoke was the aroma of roasting mutton. Her mouth filled with saliva, and she took another step forward. Then she hesitated.

It might not be a village. There could be a group of men camped ahead. They might be hunters, outlaws—or the king's men. The thought frightened her. She was wary of rushing forward to greet strangers without first knowing what lay ahead.

Out here in the woods, there was no one to protect her. If she ran into trouble, no one would hear her scream.

Merwenna took a slow, deep breath and stepped backward. On second thoughts, it was better to avoid company altogether. She was safer on her own.

"Wes hāl wench—so we meet again."

Her heart leaped in her breast, and she swiveled around. Her gaze shifted to the cloaked figure, carrying an armload of fire wood. He was a stocky man of middle age, balding, with a pugnacious face she would never forget.

Drefan of Chester—the cloth merchant.

Merwenna's heart started hammering against her ribs like a caged thing. Of all the individuals in the kingdom, this man was the last one she wanted to meet in the middle of the silent woods.

Drefan must have seen the terror on her face, for he smiled. It was not a pleasant smile, but one full of vindictive pleasure.

"We have a debt to settle," he said, throwing aside the twigs he had been carrying and dusting his hands off. "Do you remember?"

Merwenna swallowed, her mouth suddenly dry. "The queen paid you," she gasped. "Two thrymsas. I saw her man give them to you."

Drefan's smile faded and he shook his head, mockingly. "I'm not speaking of that debt, but of another. You insulted me, you dishonored me before the Queen of Mercia. You turned her against me. She will never buy cloth from me again—because of you."

Merwenna's eyes widened, her heart pounding so hard she thought it might explode from her chest. She backed away from him, every nerve stretched taut like a hemp bowstring.

"I owe you nothing," she whispered. "Leave me be."

"Slut," Drefan growled, looking around as he took a step toward her, his gaze narrowing in suspicion. "Where's your brother, eh? Aren't you going to shout for him?"

She backed further away, her gaze never leaving him.

The cloth merchant's smile returned, as realization dawned upon him.

"Wyrd shines upon me indeed," he grinned. "You're alone out here. Your brother has abandoned you. I don't believe my good fortune."

She shook her head, too terrified to speak.

"Come here, you little bitch."

He lunged at her, moving swiftly for a heavy-set man. Yet Merwenna moved just as quickly. A moment earlier, she had been frozen in terror, but his lunge caused her to spring away, toward the trees.

Unfortunately, her pursuer was fast, and Merwenna's limbs were clumsy with fear. After just a couple of strides, he barreled into Merwenna, pinning her to the damp ground under his weight. Winded, she gasped for breath as he climbed off her and pulled her to her feet by the hair. Agony burned across her scalp but she struggled nonetheless—earning a hard slap across the face from a calloused hand.

The pain did something then. Instead of subduing her, it chased away the paralyzing terror. It was like being woken from a deep, numbing sleep. Suddenly, she remembered the things her father had told her; methods of defending herself should a man ever try to force himself upon her.

Merwenna balled her hand into a fist and punched her attacker, hard, in the throat. She caught him, just under the chin.

Drefan's eyes bulged in shock. He had not expected her to retaliate. He choked and staggered back, grasping his injured windpipe. Seizing her chance, for she would not get another, Merwenna twisted away—and ran.

Chapter Twelve

Travelers in the Woods

Dylan was about to call his men to a halt and command them to make camp, when he saw a young woman burst from the trees up ahead.

They were riding on the edge of a shallow wooded valley, upon the road west as it followed the course of a gently meandering stream. His men had journeyed hard since leaving Tamworth, despite the bad weather. His instincts told him it was best to get as far away from Penda as possible—as quickly as possible.

Dylan had been brooding, mulling over the last words he had exchanged with the King of Mercia, and their significance, when he saw the girl.

She was wearing a thick brown cloak, made of coarse wool, and boots fashioned from rabbit skin and laced tightly around her feet and ankles. Her mane of brown hair flew behind her like a flag as she raced across his path, causing his stallion to start.

Cursing under his breath, Dylan sought to calm the beast, but a moment later, he was nearly thrown off the saddle when a heavy-set man of middling years crashed through the trees in pursuit of the girl.

He saw the black rage that twisted the man's features and knew that if someone did not intervene, it boded ill for her.

"That's the lass from Tamworth—the one who pestered Penda about her lover," Gwyn rode up to Dylan's side and pointed to where the female raced up the bank toward a copse of trees.

Dylan tore his attention from yanking up his stallion's head—the horse had just tried to throw him—and stared after the girl. "What is she doing out here alone?"

"About to get herself raped."

They could see the girl's pursuer was gaining on her. She may have been younger, but the man who chased her was surprisingly swift on his feet.

Dylan left his men and spurred his stallion up the bank, after the pair. Ahead, he saw the man catch the girl by the hood of her cloak and yank her backward.

Her strangled scream echoed down the valley.

"Bitch!" the man shoved his quarry to the ground, and kicked her viciously in the side. "I'll teach you to fight back!"

Dylan reached them and struck out with his fist, catching the man on the side of the head as he was about to kick the young woman once more. Dazed, the man staggered back, clutching his head.

Dylan swung down from the saddle and stepped in between the girl and her assailant. She gazed up at him, her blue eyes huge on her pale, frightened face. She had been in such a panic, she had not even noticed Dylan and his men. Likewise, her pursuer had been oblivious to the fact he had an audience.

"Who are you?" he bellowed, still clutching his head. "Clear off, this isn't your business!"

"I'm making it mine," Dylan replied. He helped the trembling young woman to her feet, but kept his gaze riveted on the man before him. "Leave her."

"I'll do as I please—she's my woman, and I'm teaching her some manners," the man spat at his feet.

"I know this woman, so don't bother with your lies," Dylan countered.

The man's gaze widened at that. Dylan could see that he did not believe him. However, faced with an armed man, and suddenly surrounded by leather-clad, glowering Cymry warriors, the girl's molester lost a little of his courage.

"Whoreson," he growled, glancing over at where Gwyn swung down from his horse and unsheathed his sword. "You'll pay for interfering."

"Men who hunt women like deer should be given the same treatment," Dylan growled.

"Oh, and you're a man of honor?"

"Compared to you, most men are. Speak your name?"

The man glared back at him sullenly, considering whether to answer. "Drefan of Chester. What's yours?"

"Cynddylan ap Cyndrwyn of Powys."

"The Prince of Powys himself," Drefan of Chester's mouth twisted although Dylan could see the fear in his eyes.

"That's right. Now that we've made our introductions, it's time you were on your way."

"I'm my own man; a jumped up Cymry princeling doesn't command me."

"Princeling?" Dylan raised an eyebrow. "Move on, Drefan of Chester, and I'll forget your face—otherwise things are about to go downhill for you."

"I won't be forgetting *your* face," Drefan of Chester glowered at Dylan before his gaze swiveled to where the young woman stood, silent and ashen, a few steps behind the prince. "Or yours, you little hōre."

Dylan drew his sword and took a step toward Drefan. "One more word, and you'll taste my blade."

Panic flashed across the man's face, momentarily replacing the defiance and anger. Something in Dylan's tone warned him that the Prince of Powys would make good on his threat. Reluctantly obeying, he turned, drawing his cloak about him. He staggered off back the way he had come, disappearing into the gathering dusk.

Dylan watched him go, waiting until Drefan of Chester had indeed gone, before he sheathed his sword and turned to the young woman. She had drawn his gaze in Tamworth, but it was a surprise to see her again.

"Remind me of your name?" he met her tear-filled gaze before his own gaze shifted to her full lips.

By the gods, she is a lovely creature.

"Merwenna of Weyham," the girl replied, her voice husky from the effort she was making to hold in her tears.

"And what are you doing out here?"

The young woman dropped her gaze to the ground. Dylan noted that she was still trembling.

"I was traveling home."

"Alone?"

"The queen was supposed to provide me with an escort," Merwenna replied, keeping her gaze downcast, "but when the time came, she didn't."

Dylan glanced across at Gwyn, who gave him a wry look and shook his head.

"Well, fortunately for you, we are traveling the same road. We'll camp here tonight. You will be our guest at the fireside."

Merwenna's head snapped up, alarm in her eyes. "I thank you for helping me," she said hurriedly, taking a step back from him, "but there's no need. I'll be on my way."

"And where do you think you're going?" Dylan asked, incredulous. "Drefan of Chester won't have gone far—he'll be waiting for you."

She stared back at him, clearly unconvinced.

"Fear not," Dylan drawled, gesturing for Gwyn to order the men to make camp. "You will be safe with us."

***

The fire hissed gently as the flames did their best to devour the damp wood. It was a cool, still night but dry enough to sit outdoors. A brace of conies roasted on a long spit at one end of the fire pit, where embers glowed bright. This was just one of many fires that ringed the heart of the Cymry camp—where around three hundred men, horsemen and spears, had constructed a makeshift township for the night.

The aroma of roasting meat drifted across to where Merwenna sat close to the fire's edge warming her fingers.

The smell made her stomach growl in protest. Despite it all, she was ravenous. After her ordeal she felt chilled to the bone. Her left side ached dully where Drefan had kicked her; she would have a livid bruise there in the morning.

Even now, her heart still raced when she recalled the terror that had coursed through her—the blind panic that had consumed her—as she ran. If Cynddylan and his men had not been riding through this valley and intercepted her flight, she shuddered to think of the state she would be in now.

She had looked into Drefan of Chester's eyes and had seen killing rage there. He would not have been content with rape, not after she had fought him and made him chase her down.

She shuddered at how close she had come to dying at that man's hands.

"Cold?"

Cynddylan's voice sounded in her ear before the man sat down with loose-limbed grace beside her.

"Not really, just tired and shaken."

"Here," he handed her a wooden cup. "Some mead ought to warm your belly."

Merwenna accepted the cup warily and took a cautious sip. The mead was hot and pungent, with the deep flavor of honey. As she swallowed the first two sips, she felt some of the chill leave her.

"The rabbits will be roasted soon," Cynddylan told her.

She nodded. "Thank you, Milord."

He stretched out his legs before him, and she could feel his gaze upon her.

"So, Merwenna of Weyham," he said finally, his tone bordering on offhand. "Tell me of that man who was chasing you."

She stiffened and glanced nervously at the prince. "What of him?"

"Drefan of Chester," he prompted. "There was more to him than appeared."

Merwenna glanced away, her gaze resting on the dancing flames before her.

"I met him when my brother and I arrived in Tamworth," she admitted finally. "He offered us passage, on the back of his wagon, into town. He's a cloth merchant and was traveling to sell his wares at Tamworth market. At the journey's end, we thanked him but he wanted payment for passage, and when we could not pay him in thrymsas, he demanded a different kind of payment.

My brother, Seward, intervened, and things were about to get out of hand when Queen Cyneswide came to our aid. She offered to shelter us in the Great Tower until I could discover the fate of my betrothed. The merchant was furious—especially when the queen told him she would not buy cloth from him."

"And your brother? You were alone at Tamworth—where is he?"

Merwenna dropped her gaze to her lap. She did not want to tell the rest of this tale.

"He went home."

"And left you unchaperoned in the King's Hall?"

Merwenna sighed.

She was tired of this conversation. Why could he not leave her be?

"He fell out of favor the first night we stayed in the Great Hall," she replied. She refused to meet the prince's eye as she continued. "He was found with one of the king's female slaves. He was whipped and banished from Tamworth the next morning."

Silence fell between them then, punctuated only by the crackling of the fire, and the rumble of voices of the men around them. Merwenna could feel her cheeks burning. Told so directly, the whole incident sounded even worse than she remembered.

When Merwenna looked at Cynddylan, she saw that he was watching her under hooded lids. Merwenna grew even hotter under the intensity of his stare.

"That's quite a tale of misfortune," he said with a wry smile. "Abandoned by both your lover and your brother."

"Beorn was not my lover, he was my betrothed," Merwenna replied stiffly. Her embarrassment was swiftly turning to anger; she did not like to be mocked. "He died serving his king and protecting our land."

"I expect that's cold comfort to you now," the Prince of Powys replied, rising to his feet and throwing the dregs from his cup into the fire. "He ran headlong into battle, desperate for glory. Only a fool offers up his life so cheaply."

Chapter Thirteen

An Honorable Man

A full moon was riding high in the night sky when the army finally bedded down for the night.

Merwenna watched them nervously. Many of the men stretched out around the smoldering fires, while others took their places around the perimeter of the camp, for the first watch. Cynddylan's men had erected a cluster of tents made out of goat-hide, for the prince and his highest ranking warriors.

Not knowing where she was supposed to sleep, Merwenna wrapped her cloak tightly around her and tried to get comfortable on the hard ground beside one of the fires.

"You're not sleeping there, wench," a gruff, heavily accented voice roused her.

Merwenna looked up into the face of Gwyn—the hulking warrior who appeared to be the prince's captain. "There's space for you in the prince's tent."

"Excuse me?" Merwenna sat up abruptly. "I can't sleep there."

"It's safer than out here."

"But, I can't share that man's tent."

"Go on," Gwyn hauled Merwenna to her feet and propelled her in the direction of the largest tent at the heart of the cluster. "You can trust him."

Merwenna threw Gwyn a resentful look, but reluctantly did as she was bid, making her way across to the prince's tent.

She stepped across the threshold, ducking through the narrow opening, and was relieved to see that the tent was empty. A small fire burned in a pit in the center of the space, smoke escaping from a slit in the conical roof. No beds had been made up; only a large pile of furs had been dumped in one corner.

Merwenna helped herself to two of the furs and arranged them on the far side of the tent. She had just seated herself upon them, and was unlacing her fur boots, when Cynddylan entered the tent. He was carrying a jug of water and two wooden cups.

"Comfortable?"

"Your captain insisted I sleep in here," she replied stiffly.

"It's for your own good." The prince untied a flap of leather from where it was rolled above the doorway and let it fall, sealing them inside the tent. "Drefan is likely to be nearby. He'll nurse a grudge for a long while—better if you stay out of sight."

"He wouldn't try and attack me here," she replied, stacking her boots at the foot of her furs. She then pulled her cloak tightly about her and snuggled down into her surprisingly comfortable bed. "Not in the middle of your camp."

"Never underestimate a man like that," Dylan replied tersely. "If you ever stumble across Drefan again, he'll slit your throat from ear to ear."

The prince placed the jug and cups near the hearth before crossing to his furs. There, he shrugged off his plush purple cloak and began to remove the heavy mail vest he wore beneath. He finally managed to shrug the heavy vest off his shoulders. It fell clinking to his feet, revealing a sleeveless linen tunic underneath.

Merwenna watched as the prince stripped off his tunic, revealing a lithe, finely muscled torso beneath. The firelight played across his broad shoulders and long back. Realizing that she was staring, she stifled a gasp and turned her back upon him.

"Very well," she said meekly, desperately wishing she had remained outdoors by the fire pit. "I will stay out of sight."

"Good. Tomorrow, we will escort you home."

"*Hwaet!*" Merwenna abruptly turned to face Cynddylan once more.

She instantly regretted the action, for he was now facing her. The sight of his naked chest, and the whorls of dark hair that dusted it, tapering down to the waist-band of his breeches, caused Merwenna's mouth to go dry and her heart to start racing. However, she ignored her body's traitorous reaction and focused on her anger instead.

"I don't need an escort!"

"Yes you do," he contradicted her smoothly. "And fortunately for you, Weyham is but a short detour on our way back to Powys."

"Thank you for the kind offer," she replied through clenched teeth, "but tomorrow I will go my own way."

"That wasn't an offer, Merwenna."

Rage rendered her momentarily speechless.

"You are insufferably conceited," she finally choked out. "How dare you make decisions on my behalf! You're not my father, my brother, or my husband. I'm not your property."

"No," Dylan cocked an eyebrow and started to undo the laces of his breeches, "but I will do my best to ensure you are delivered safely back to your family. A little gratitude wouldn't go amiss."

Merwenna stared at him, her anger simmering, before realizing that he had almost finished unlacing his breeches. In a moment, he would be standing naked before her.

"Stop," she gasped. "What are you doing?"

"Undressing. I always sleep naked. Don't you?"

"Not here," she replied, feeling herself shrink under his amused gaze.

"If my naked body offends you then I suggest you turn away," the prince continued. "Or, you can continue staring—I don't mind."

"Nithhogg take you!" she snarled, before turning her back to him once more. She was not in the mood to be tormented. After everything she had endured today, this was too much.

She had expected him to take offense. Cursing a man to the underworld, where his corpse would be feasted upon by the fire-breathing dragon that dwelt there, would usually rouse his anger. Instead, Cynddylan merely laughed.

"You'll have to do better than that if you want to enrage me, cariad."

She refused to answer him. Instead, she stared at the weather-stained goat hide wall of the tent. She listened to the rustle of Dylan undressing behind her, and squeezed her eyes shut in an attempt to erase the image of his lean, virile body, caressed by firelight.

He might have been mesmerizingly handsome, but the Prince of Powys only made her yearn for Beorn. Her betrothed had been a good, honorable man—and she would never forgive Cynddylan for insulting him this evening.

Mercifully, Cynddylan appeared to have tired of tormenting her. She heard him climb into his furs, and silence settled over the tent, broken only by the gentle pop of embers in the dying hearth.

Merwenna lay there, staring into the darkness, listening as the prince's breathing gradually deepened and slowed. A man who fell asleep that quickly had a clear conscience indeed.

In contrast, despite her exhaustion, Merwenna was wide awake. Her body was taut, her senses attuned to any movement behind her. She did not trust this man.

What if he tried to maul her during the night?

She rolled over, facing him across the fire pit. She intended to keep watch, and if she saw him make a move toward her, she would be up and out of the tent in a heart-beat.

***

Cynddylan's men broke camp at first light, packing up the tents, dousing campfires, and saddling their horses with practiced swiftness. A grey dawn stole across the world, bringing with it a chill mist that snaked between the trees like crone's tresses.

Merwenna wrapped her fingers around a mug of hot broth and watched their industry with awe. After a sleepless night, the delicious broth had a restorative effect on her. Even so, the sight of the Prince of Powys, striding toward her across the camp, from where he had been saddling his horse, made her stomach clench nervously.

"Ready to move on?" he greeted her.

Merwenna nodded, and took one last gulp of broth before pouring the dregs out onto the ground. "How long till we reach Weyham?"

"Three days if we ride fast."

"Ride—but I don't have a horse."

"Don't worry about that," the prince gave her one of his infuriating slow smiles. "You'll be riding with me."

Panic flared in Merwenna's breast. She glanced nervously at where the heavy-set, bay stallion pawed at the ground and jangled his bit, impatient to be off.

"Can't I just walk?"

"I'm afraid not."

Merwenna did not like the idea of spending three days in the saddle with this man. However, there seemed little point in refusing him. The Prince of Powys was used to getting his own way.

She refused to meet Cynddylan's eye as he sprang up onto the saddle and reached down to help her mount. She reluctantly took his hand, noting the warm strength of his fingers, and settled into place behind him. Her skin tingled from where she had touched him.

Layers of clothing separated them, and the Prince of Powys had donned his mail vest and cloak, but even so Merwenna could feel the heat of his body pressed up against hers.

Her throat constricted and tears filled her eyes.

Curse him, and curse her own traitorous reaction to him. She was grieving for Beorn, and she just wanted to be left alone.

A short while later, the small army of around three hundred men rode through the encircling mist. They followed the meandering course of the stream down the shallow valley. The thud of hooves on the soft ground, and the snorts of the horses, were the only sounds in the still morning.

Dylan looked down at the pale, slender hands loosely clasped around his waist, and silently admired their delicacy. The feel of the girl—for despite her luscious breasts, now pressed against his back, and sultry gaze, that was what she was—came as a pleasant distraction.

He knew he should not have taunted her last night, but he had not been able prevent himself. Still the sight of her pale face this morning, her eyes red-rimmed from crying, had given him a pang of guilt. He should not have insulted her betrothed.

What does it matter to me if she thinks that lad was the greatest warrior that ever lived?

Mist still shrouded them in a shadowy world, where trees emerged like the tattered spears and standards of a ghost army. It was a vaguely threatening scene, reminding Dylan of the recent battle against the Northumbrians. That memory brought him to the reluctant agreement Penda had made.

Fortunately, due to the pact that Penda had now honored, Powys was considerably closer. Lichfield, which now straddled the border between Powys and Mercia, was barely two days ride from Weyham.

Dylan had forced Penda's hand in the end, but victory was his.

He had been away from Powys for many months and delayed his crowning in order to go to war. It had been risky to do so, for had he not returned his brother would have been made king instead, but in the end it had worked in his favor. Now, he would return to Pengwern victorious, the first ever ruler of his land to unite Mercia and Powys against a common enemy.

Dylan gave a grim smile and urged his stallion into a brisk trot, making his way up to the head of the column. He was returning home with just over three hundred men—barely half of the number he had taken to Maes Cogwy. He thought about the years it had taken to reach this point. Powys and Mercia had been enemies for a long while; so long that the new alliance between them was as brittle as spring ice.

He only hoped it would last.

Chapter Fourteen

Temptation

Merwenna slid to the ground. She clenched her teeth as the impact jarred, sending pain up through her ankles. It had been a while since she had ridden.

On the morrow, I'll be suffering for it.

The day had been long and tiring. Relieved to be on the ground once more, Merwenna stretched her back and looked about the gentle slope where the men were making camp. They had left the wooded valley far behind, and were now traveling through grassy hills, interspersed with beech thickets. She stood at the midst of the army and watched the men with interest as they unsaddled and rubbed down horses, built fires, and raised tents.

Nearby, Cynddylan was rubbing down his horse, his back to her. Against her will, her gaze rested upon him, taking in the breadth of his shoulders, and the flex of his muscles as he worked. He had offended her yesterday, but that did not stop her from being a little in awe of him. It was not every day she rode with a prince.

Yet there was something about him that made her wary. He had looked at her with a hungry, almost predatory look in his eye last night. She felt flustered and nervous whenever he stood too close. Riding behind him, her breasts jiggling against his back with every stride of his horse, had been slow torture. The feel of his strong body pressed up against hers had distracted her for most of the day.

Merwenna turned her back on Cynddylan, cursing herself for being so easily seduced. Vowing to keep her distance from him from now on, she moved across to the largest of the fires that had just been lit. A young man had just sat down to skin a pile of conies they had trapped the night before.

"Can I help?" Merwenna asked shyly, aware that she was the only one in the camp that appeared to be idle.

The warrior, only a couple of years older than her, glanced up and smiled. He was slightly built, compared to the men she had grown up with. Lean and sharp featured, he had a mop of dark hair that kept falling in his eyes.

"Sit down," he gestured to the rock beside him. "I could use a hand."

He spoke Englisc haltingly, with a very thick accent. Since Merwenna knew no more than a handful of words of Cymraeg, she was grateful.

She perched on the rock and took the bone-handled knife the warrior handed her. Then she plucked a dead rabbit from the top of the pile and began to skin it with practiced ease. Over the years, Merwenna had lost count of the evenings she had spent beside the hearth, skinning rabbits with her mother and sister at her side.

The act brought back memories that made her smile and caused a wistful pang of homesickness for Weyham, and for her kin. Fear of what awaited her there caused her nostalgia to fade.

"My name's Merwenna," she said eventually, after skinning and gutting her fifth rabbit. "What's yours?"

"Owain," he replied.

"You must be looking forward to returning home."

The man nodded.

"How long have you been away?"

"Since last winter," Owain replied. "Many months."

Merwenna nodded, trying to imagine the life he would have left behind.

"Do you have a wife and children waiting for you?"

He nodded. "My wife and son. Ifan will be walking now; he was just a babe when I left."

Merwenna smiled. The love and pride on Owain's face were evident.

"Do they know you survived the battle?"

Owain shook his head, his expression growing grim. "There's been no time to send word. My wife, Eira, will be worrying."

Merwenna's smile faded. She remembered the gnawing worry that had gripped her upon waking, every morning after Beorn's departure. In the end, it had become unbearable.

"It's the waiting that's the worst," she replied softly, "and yet it is a woman's lot."

***

Merwenna picked the last scraps of meat off her rabbit carcass and threw the bones on the fire. The flames hissed and popped as they devoured them. Licking grease off her fingers, she sat back from the fire and stretched out her legs in front of her.

It was a mild evening without a hint of a breeze. Autumn was not far off although the air still held summer's warmth tonight. Night had fallen, and the sky was a curtain of black. The stars twinkled in sharp relief overhead.

Merwenna sat back on her hands and craned her neck back so that she could study the stars more closely. Their majesty made her feel so small.

Suddenly, she was aware of a man's gaze upon her.

She inclined her head, her own gaze traveling across the faces of the men who sat nearby. It came to rest upon

Cynddylan. The Prince of Powys was staring at her, the firelight playing across the chiseled contours of his face.

He was used to having his way with women. She had never lain with a man but knew the gaze of one who stripped her naked with his eyes. The heat of his gaze caused her breathing to quicken. She struggled to keep her face expressionless although inside she was churning with a wild, dangerous excitement. He looked at her in a way that made her skin ache to be touched, her mouth burn to be kissed.

Merwenna gasped at her body's betrayal and tore her gaze away from the prince's. He cared not that she grieved for her betrothed. Instead, he wielded his devastating charm like a weapon, drawing her in against her will.

How many women had melted under that stare?

Merwenna took a slow, shuddering breath and glanced back up at the heavens. Was Beorn looking down on her right now? Did he despise her for her weakness?

I'll not betray you, my love, she vowed silently. *You were everything to me.*

Those words were true. She had loved Beorn. Why else had she run away to Tamworth? She had risked much in doing so—for her family would not be quick to forgive her behavior. He was the man she had planned to spend the rest of her life with. The only man for her.

Yet, if that was the case, why did her body burn under the gaze of another?

Chapter Fifteen

Drefan of Chester

Sunlight on his face woke Drefan of Chester from a deep slumber. He slowly opened his eyes, struggling to gain his bearings for a moment or two, till the fog of sleep lifted.

Cursing foully, he struggled to his feet.

Dawn had broken some time ago. He should have already been on his way, not snoring by the fire as if he had all the time in the world. He would never keep up with Cynddylan and his rabble at this rate.

Drefan's head felt twice its size this morning, and his mouth tasted like rank, old leather. He had downed two large skins of mead last night and was now paying the price. Ever since Cynddylan had ripped his prize from him, and humiliated him in the bargain, Drefan had been in an evil mood. Before running into Merwenna in the woods, he had been planning to travel south, to trade his wares in the Saxon settlements.

Now, he had changed his direction to the west.

That bitch had made a fool of him twice now, and she would have to pay. Thanks to her, the Queen of Mercia would no longer buy his cloth; something that could potentially ruin him. Tamworth had always been his most lucrative stop on the way north.

Merwenna of Weyham had made him a leper in Tamworth.

Drefan was not a man who easily forgave—and he never forgot. He would follow Cynddylan's army, and when the chance presented itself—for one day it would—he would take Merwenna from her new protector and make her rue the day her mother birthed her.

Drefan unloosed the ties on his breeches and relieved himself on the smoldering embers of last night's fire. His urine, dark and stinking of mead, hissed on the hot coals. As he pissed, Drefan closed his eyes, imagining what he would do to Merwenna, once he caught her. He was just retying his breeches, when a sound behind him made him start.

The tread of a heavy foot on the leaf-strewn ground.

Drefan whirled to find a group of men gathered at the edge of the small clearing, watching him.

His gaze traveled across their faces. They were big men, dressed in leather armor and fur cloaks. They were also well-armed. Swords hung at their sides, shields from their backs, and most of them carried quivers of arrows and longbows. He would have thought them a hunting party, but his well-honed instincts told him that was not the case.

Drefan's gaze rested on the face of the biggest warrior among them—a good-looking man with shaggy brown hair and a wintry gaze—and his breath stilled. He recognized that face; the sight of it bringing him back to his humiliation in Tamworth's market square. This man had been one of Queen Cyneswide's guards. The one she had called Rodor. It was he who had placed the coins in Drefan's outstretched palm.

The recognition was mutual, for Rodor smiled under Drefan's scrutiny. Then he stepped forward, unsheathing his sword in one smooth movement. The sound of iron scraping against leather echoed across the still clearing, and Drefan's bowels loosened.

"Taking your cloth elsewhere?" Rodor motioned to the small cart sitting a few yards away, and the stocky ponies hobbled next to it.

"Well, I won't be selling it in Tamworth, will I?" Drefan replied with a sneer.

"No," Rodor stepped forward, his sword blade glinting in the pale morning light. "I'm afraid you won't be peddling it anywhere."

Panic flared, and Drefan backed away from the warrior.

"What do you want from me?"

"Nothing."

"Then why are you about to kill me?"

"Because you recognize me—and I can't have that."

"I won't tell anyone you were here." Drefan's gaze locked on the blade that was slowly advancing toward him. "There's no one to tell."

"Have you not seen anyone on your travels then, merchant?"

"My name's Drefan—and yes, I've seen plenty of folk of late. That little whore you paid me for in Tamworth for one."

Rodor went still at that. "Really?"

"I ran into her just over a day ago," Drefan rushed the words out, taking advantage of Rodor's pause. Drefan was unarmed, save for the boning knife at his belt. He was a worthy opponent, and knew how to fight with low cunning. However, faced by this warrior with eyes the color of ice, wielding his sword as if he had been born with it, he did not rate his chances.

If Drefan did not talk his way out of this, he was dead.

"And where's Merwenna now?"

"She ran off."

"Did she?" Rodor cocked an eyebrow and continued his path across the glade toward Drefan. "Why don't I believe you?"

"Actually, there is more to it than that," Drefan swallowed, feeling sweat slide down his back. "She did run off, and I followed. However, she ran straight into the path of the Cymry army, and their prince rescued her."

"You saw Cynddylan of Powys?" Rodor stopped once more, his expression hardening. "How far ahead are they?"

"No more than a day. I overslept this morning or I would already have been on their trail."

"You're following them?"

Drefan licked his lips, considering whether to tell this man the truth. Rodor was watching him closely, and he could see he was no idiot. It was perilous to lie to clever men.

"Yes—that wench made a fool of me once again, and I'm not having it. I'd wager they are escorting her home, on their way back to Powys. I intend to follow them there."

"She is from Weyham, is she not?"

Drefan nodded, his gaze flicking from Rodor's sword to his face. "You're tracking Cynddylan's army, aren't you?"

Drefan saw Rodor's gaze narrow at that, and so he rushed on, aware that he only had moments to convince this man he was not worth killing.

"Let me come with you. I know these lands well—and I know a short cut to Weyham. If you're wanting to catch up with Cynddylan and his men, I can help you."

Rodor gave a chilling smile. "Is that right?"

"Look," Drefan raised his hands pleadingly. "I don't know why you're after him, and I don't care. I only hope it's to slit his throat. You can trust me, I have no love for the Cymry—least of all that whoreson."

"That may be the case," Rodor replied, "but I trust no man unless he proves himself worthy of it."

"I can prove myself. If you want to kill Cynddylan of Powys, I'll help you. Just let me have Merwenna."

Rodor glanced back at his men. They were all silent, observing the scene with obvious amusement. Some were openly sniggering, while others stood there smirking.

"What do you think boys? Shall we let him live?"

"Don't think so," one of them—a tall, lean warrior with lank blond hair and a stubbly beard—replied with a grin. "I'd say he's lying to save his hide."

Rodor smiled back. "Well said, Caedmon. Of course he is."

Drefan watched, cold dread washing over him, as Rodor closed the gap between them in two long strides.

"Wait!" he choked out, stumbling back. "I can help you."

Yet Rodor had finished talking.

Drefan of Chester saw the glint of Rodor's blade—as it swung toward him—and knew his end had come.

Chapter Sixteen

The Kiss

Merwenna added another stick to her armload of kindling. The wood was damper than she would have liked. She had been forced to venture into the trees, away from the fringes of the woods, to find anything worth burning.

It had been drizzling for most of the day, and around her the daylight was slowly fading into a murky twilight. She would not linger out here for much longer, for it was becoming difficult to see. She picked up one final piece of kindling and was about to retrace her steps back to camp, when she heard footsteps behind her.

She whirled around, and in her fright, dropped the wood she had been carrying.

Cynddylan was standing a few feet behind her.

Merwenna stared at him, her heart hammering. "What are you doing here, Milord? You scared me."

"Sorry," he gave an apologetic smile. "You were gone awhile, so I thought I'd better come find you."

"Well, as you can see I'm unharmed," Merwenna's face flamed as she bent to retrieve the sticks. "I thank you for your concern."

"It was well meant, Merwenna," he replied. "I've seen the way my men look at you. Many of them are hungry for a woman. Seeing you wander off alone into the woods is too much temptation."

I've seen the way you look at me, Merwenna tried to ignore her palpitating heart. *It's you I need to be wary of.*

The only man she feared in the Cymry encampment was the one standing before her.

"I don't need your protection," she insisted, lifting her chin stubbornly. "Please leave me be."

"We both know that's not true," he raised an eyebrow. "Drefan of Chester may have followed us. Such a man does not abandon his quarry without a fight."

The mention of the cloth merchant's name caused a shiver of dread to run down Merwenna's spine. She cast a nervous glance around her, as if she expected Drefan to leap at her from the shadows.

"Well then," she clutched the wood to her breast, feigning courage. "Escort me back to the camp, if it pleases you."

The Prince of Powys nodded, but instead of turning and leading the way back through the trees—he slowly walked toward her. He stopped, so close that they were barely touching.

"It pleases me to look upon you," he murmured.

Merwenna swallowed, her mouth was suddenly dry, and her heart was racing as if she had finished a sprint.

Gods, no.

"Please don't," she finally managed, gripping the twigs as if they were keeping her afloat.

"Don't what?" he asked, his gaze roaming over her face.

"Stare at me."

"But I can't help myself. You are lovely, Merwenna."

"Well, you should stop," Merwenna's voice was barely above a whisper. "It's wrong. I am grieving for Beorn. I just want to go home."

Even to her own ears, the words sounded hollow.

He stepped closer still, his hand reaching out to lightly caress her cheek. Merwenna trembled under his touch and hated herself for it.

"I can't stop," he said simply. "You are too lovely. I am but a moth to your flame."

"But I . . ."

The prince's mouth came down over hers, cutting off her protest. The shock of his lips against her own caused her to gasp. The twigs slid from her arms and fell to her feet.

With a groan low in his throat, Cynddylan pulled her hard against him. In moments, his kiss changed from a gentle caress, to hungry, hot, and demanding.

Merwenna struggled against him at first—but a moment later, she was lost. The feel of his lips on hers caused all rational thought to cease. Her body and senses betrayed her completely. She melted into his arms, her mouth opening under his.

He kissed her hungrily, pulling her body against the length of his. The hardness of him, the musky scent of his skin, the roughness of his new growth of beard, the taste of him—together unleashed something within Merwenna.

With a groan of surrender, she gave herself up to the kiss.

Cynddylan's hands slid up the length of her back, up her neck, and tangled in her hair. He then deepened the kiss further, exploring her mouth with his tongue. Merwenna's knees gave, and had he not been holding up upright, she would have crumpled to the ground.

The kiss drew out. Yet—eventually—it was the prince who broke it.

Merwenna's pulse was throbbing in her throat, and her head was spinning. Cynddylan was breathing heavily. His cheeks were flushed and his eyes had gone dark. His gaze still locked with hers, the prince released Merwenna and stepped back from her.

Around them, the rain fell in a gentle, silent mist.

Mortification slowly crept across Merwenna's body. The desire that had momentarily overtaken her was seeping away, replaced with burning shame.

What had she done? Beorn's ashes were barely cold, and here she was kissing another. Not only that, but she had enjoyed it.

A sob rose in Merwenna's chest. She had not deserved Beorn, and it was for that Tiu—God of war and the sky—had taken him from her. This was her punishment.

"Leave me be," she gasped, hating herself as much as him in that moment.

The firewood forgotten, she pushed past Cynddylan and without another word, fled back to the camp.

Chapter Seventeen

Homecoming

"I'm walking today," Merwenna informed the prince coldly.

They had not spoken since their kiss the night before. Dawn had just broken, and the army was packing up. Cynddylan had been in the midst of saddling his horse when she strode up to him.

"Excuse me?" he turned and regarded her, clearly amused.

Merwenna wished she had the courage to strike him. "You heard. I'm not riding with you. I will travel on foot."

Merwenna clenched her fists by her sides as she finished speaking and braced herself for his refusal. However, she would not be swayed. She had spent most of the night in tears but had woken ready for a fight. The only way he would get her to ride with him today would be to tie her up.

Cynddylan observed her silently for a moment before, unexpectedly, shrugging. "As you wish, cariad."

Merwenna ground her teeth. She hated when he called her 'sweetheart' in Cymraeg. After what had happened last night, it was like a slap in the face. Without another word she turned and stalked off to retrieve her things.

She was still seething when the army moved off, traveling northwest down the shallow Weyham valley. She walked amongst the sea of men, anger a painful knot in her belly. The Prince of Powys had been playing with her. He had known she was grieving for her betrothed but had wanted to prove he could have her nonetheless. No doubt he had congratulated himself on how easily she had succumbed to him.

Is that what power did to a man? She only hoped that now he had made his point, Cynddylan would leave her alone.

Merwenna walked behind the horsemen, where the first of the spearmen marched. They carried long ash spears and walked with shields slung across their backs. Some of them also carried throwing axes notched in their belt and scramasax—fighting daggers—at their sides. It was a mild morning. There had been a little mist at daybreak, but as the sun rose into the sky, it quickly burned off and the day began to warm.

They were close to her home now. She knew the brook that babbled its way over the smooth stones here—the Larkflow. In the upper reaches of the valley, the Larkflow was a gentle stream, however, it widened and deepened by the time it reached Weyham. Merwenna had many memories of bathing in its cool water, of sitting with her little sister on in its banks watching her brother skim stones across its gently rippling surface.

The sight of the river distracted Merwenna from her rage and made her focus on what lay ahead.

***

They reached Weyham in the late afternoon, as the shadows were beginning to lengthen, and the sun drenched the world in a veil of gold. It was the perfect afternoon for a homecoming. Yet Merwenna's stomach was knotted in dread when Cynddylan's army drew up in the meadows.

To the west was a belt of woodland. Beyond those trees lay Weyham.

Merwenna made her way up to the front of the column, where she knew she would find the prince. He was waiting for her, still mounted upon his stallion. Around him was a small company of riders, who also waited while the rest of the army made camp for the day.

"Are you ready?" Cynddylan asked, his face impassive.

Merwenna nodded.

"Ride with me."

She shook her head. "No thank you, Milord, I'll walk."

"I'm not asking you. I'm telling you. Climb up or Gwyn will throw you across the saddle. Your choice."

Merwenna glanced across at where Gwyn stood, frowning at her. His thick arms were crossed before him, and he looked in an ill temper.

Conceding with a glower, she took Cynddylan's proffered hand and vaulted lightly up onto the stallion's back. She had hardly settled into place, when Dylan wheeled the horse around and spurred it toward the trees.

"Let's get you home."

The company of riders cantered to the tree line, before slowing to a trot. They entered the woods single-file along a narrow track through dappled sunlight, under a canopy of oak and beech. They rode in silence; the only sound the clump of the horses' heavy hooves on the damp earth.

Merwenna was thrown against Dylan with every stride although she was thankful he did not speak. He had not shared the tent with her last night, leaving her alone with her tears and self-recrimination. For that she had been grateful.

They passed through the woods quickly, past the very spot where Merwenna and Beorn had stood on that early spring day, when he had proposed to her. It was only four months ago, but it seemed as if years had passed since that moment.

Merwenna did not feel like the same person. She had changed—and not for the better. She had been happier before, cloaked in the security that ignorance brings. Only, once that cloak fell away, there was no going back to the way things were. The thought of returning home suddenly filled her with dread.

The horses emerged from the trees and rode down a dirt track in-between fields of barley. Folk were out harvesting, sweating in the humidity of the late afternoon. Up ahead, Merwenna spied the thatched roofs of Weyham, with the ealdorman's hall rising above the others.

"Where do we find your parents?" Cynddylan asked.

"On the far side of the village," Merwenna replied, averting her gaze from the curious faces of the villagers they passed.

It was difficult to maintain her composure. Here she was, escorted by Cymry warriors on Mercian land. All those who gazed upon her would recognize her face. Weyham was small enough that she knew everyone by name. Some folk even called out to her and waved. Merwenna pretended that she had not heard, keeping her head downcast. She wished she had donned her cloak before riding here; at least then she could have pulled up her hood to protect her identity.

Weyham was little more than a scattering of dwellings around a central grassy area. On the way in they passed the village's mead hall; a low-slung, wedge-shaped, windowless building. It was empty at this hour although as soon as dusk settled it would be full of thirsty men. Further in, they rode before the ealdorman's hall.

"I should stop and give my regards to the ealdorman, lest he takes offence," the Prince of Powys commented as they rode by the impressive timbered hall. "However, I know how keen you are to be free of me—so I'll take you home first."

Merwenna did not reply. They both knew the truth of it.

The house belonging to Wilfrid was made of oak with a thick thatch. It was far humbler than the ealdorman's hall but, at the same time, much grander than most of the wattle and daub dwellings in Weyham. It sat apart from the other houses, on the edge of tended fields, and had two out-buildings: a food store and a chicken coop.

Cynddylan drew his horse up outside the dwelling and looked about.

"This is a fine home," he observed.

Merwenna ignored him and slid off the stallion's back.

"Where are your parents?" Cynddylan turned in the saddle, regarding her.

"They'll be out in the fields at this hour," Merwenna replied. "Harvesting."

"Well then," Cynddylan dismounted and tossed his reins to one of his men. "I'd better deliver you to them."

"That's not necessary, Milord," Merwenna replied coldly. "I can deal with them myself, thank you."

"Oh, but I insist," Cynddylan smiled. "I've brought you all this way. I intend to make sure you're safe before I take my leave."

"I'm not a child," Merwenna answered through gritted teeth.

"I'm well aware of that," the prince gave her a lingering glance before he turned to his men. "Llywelyn, Ifan—come with us."

Merwenna and Cynddylan skirted the edge of the timbered dwelling and walked out into the fields with two warriors trailing them. Merwenna spotted her family immediately. She could see four figures, hard at work in the distance. The fields grew enough food to feed them, and enough to trade with neighbors. Her father, who had spent his younger years as a warrior, had shown a flair for farming in middle-age; one that had kept his family well-fed through poor harvests and bitter winters.

The newcomers walked across the tended fields in between rows of cabbages, carrots, and onions—still much of it to be harvested. Merwenna grew steadily more nervous as they approached her family. The rock that had settled in the pit of her belly was growing heavier by the moment. Her step faltered, but the prince took her by the arm and gently propelled her forward.

"Go on—they are waiting for you."

Merwenna threw him a venomous look, wrenched her arm free, and stalked off ahead. As she neared the group, she could make them all out individually. She could see her father and Seward scything barley. Aeaba and her mother trailed behind, gathering up the fallen stalks and bundling them into sheaves.

"Merwenna!" Aeaba was the first to spot her sister's approach. The little girl threw down the sheaf she had just finished tying and sprinted across the stubble toward her. Merwenna had to physically brace herself for the onslaught; Aeaba was more powerful than she looked. The force of her sister's hug nearly knocked Merwenna off her feet.

Merwenna hugged her sister fiercely, her eyes stinging with tears. Finally extracting herself from Aeaba's bone-crushing embrace, Merwenna looked up to see that the rest of her family approached.

The moment she had been dreading had finally come.

Chapter Eighteen

Keeping Secrets

Her parents did not rush to her, as her sister had, and Merwenna's heart sank.

It was as she had feared.

Their faces were pale and taut. Her mother's blue eyes brimmed with tears, and her father's expression was stony. His hazel eyes—so like her brother's—were harder than she had ever seen them. A few feet behind him, Seward looked on, his face a cold mask.

If the Prince of Powys had not been standing behind her, Merwenna would have turned and fled.

"Hello mōder," she smiled wanly at her mother. Cynewyn stared back, her expression suddenly torn. Merwenna could tell she wished to embrace her, but anger held her back.

"Merwenna," Cynewyn finally managed. "I was beginning to think you would never return."

Merwenna gave a tearful smile, her gaze shifting to her father. "Fæder?"

Her father, Wilfrid, did not speak. Instead, his gaze was riveted upon the men who stood a few paces behind her.

One in particular drew his eye—Cynddylan.

Wilfrid stepped forward, still gripping his scythe. "Who are these men?"

Merwenna stepped back from her mother and hastily wiped away the tears that had wet her cheeks. Now was not the time for weeping. She had done something selfish and foolish, and she would have to deal with the consequences. "They are my escorts from Tamworth. This is Cynddylan ap Cyndrwyn of Powys."

"Wes hāl," the prince greeted Wil.

"Prynhawn da," Wil replied, bidding the newcomer good-afternoon in Cymraeg. "Thank you for bringing our daughter home safe."

Cynddylan nodded in response. "It was no bother. We were traveling the same road. My men are camped just outside the village."

The prince then inclined his head toward Merwenna and gave her an enigmatic smile. "Hwyl fawr, cariad. I wish you well."

With that, the Prince of Powys turned, his purple cloak billowing behind him, and strode away. His men, Llywelyn and Ifan, fell in behind him without a word.

Merwenna watched him go, suddenly overwhelmed by a strange, and unwelcome, sense of loss. The man had caused her no end of stress on the journey home, yet he had also been her anchor. Now that he was leaving, she would have to navigate treacherous waters alone. Forcing herself to look away from him, she turned back to her waiting family.

"You have made powerful friends on your journey home I see," Wil observed, his expression even grimmer than before. "Have you forgotten Beorn already?"

Merwenna flushed at the scorn in her father's voice. Never, had he spoken to her thus.

"Of course not," she gasped as if he had slapped her. "Fæder, Beorn is dead."

"And you wasted no time finding another," Seward spoke up for the first time. "Such is the allure of power."

"No!"

Silence fell then, punctuated only by the chirping of crickets, and the whisper of the wind through the barley. It was Wilfrid who broke it.

"We know about Beorn," he said, his tone softening. "Word arrived two days ago."

Merwenna did not reply. It was all she could do not to dissolve into tears.

"Merwenna." Wil stepped forward so that he and his daughter were only two feet apart. He then reached out and took hold of her chin gently, forcing her to meet his eye. "Why?"

Merwenna's gaze flicked over to Seward—obviously he had not provided much of an excuse. In fact, after what had happened in Tamworth, he would have laid the blame entirely at her feet.

She expected nothing less, for it was the truth.

"I'm so sorry fæder," she began, choking back a sob. "I thought that if I traveled to Tamworth in search of Beorn, it would bring him safely home. I knew it was wrong to leave in the midst of harvest, but I could not think of anything except finding him. I realize my mistake now."

"It's too late for that. The pair of you have gravely disappointed me."

"Please don't blame Seward," Merwenna pleaded. "He only went because I asked him."

"He holds as much blame as you," Wil countered, his voice as harsh. His baleful gaze shifted to Seward. "He should never have left Tamworth without you."

"Merwenna's stubborn," Seward protested, his face growing pink under his father's glare. "I couldn't force her."

"That's no excuse," Wil snarled. "Leaving your sister to fend for herself in the King's Hall is unforgivable."

Merwenna watched the exchange between her brother and father, before her gaze flicked to her mother's face. Suddenly, the truth dawned on her. She had been a fool for not realizing sooner.

Seward had not told them of his disgrace.

***

Merwenna took a bite of leek and rabbit pie and chewed slowly. She had sorely missed her mother's cooking. Still, the atmosphere at the table meant that the evening meal was a tense affair. Even Aeaba, who usually chirped like a bird during mealtimes, kept silent this evening.

Seward sat opposite Merwenna, digging into his pie without a glance in her direction.

He would be wondering when—not if—Merwenna would betray him to their parents.

Taking another bite of pie, Merwenna glanced to where her father sat at the head of the table. Wilfrid's mood had not improved since her arrival. He was usually such an even-tempered man, it upset her to see him so angered. Trust was everything to her father. Perhaps things would never go back to the way they had been.

They concluded the meal in silence, fraught with the tension of unsaid things. Merwenna helped her mother and sister clear the table and wipe it down. Meanwhile, her father went outside to chop wood, and her brother sloped off to the mead hall.

"Merwenna," Cynewyn spoke finally, once they were alone. She had sent Aeaba out to shut the chicken coop for the night, and Merwenna knew that her mother had been waiting for a chance to speak to her on her own. "The news of Beorn's death saddens us all—but how are you coping?"

"I'm fine," Merwenna lied, refusing to meet her mother's eye as she scrubbed down the table with more force than was necessary. "It was a shock, but I will have to learn to live with it."

"Stop that and come here," her mother replied gently. "I can see you're suffering. There's no need to hide it from me."

Merwenna hurriedly brushed at the tears that now trickled down her cheeks.

"Crying won't change anything," Merwenna whispered. "He's gone."

She dropped the cloth and covered her face with her hands in an attempt to stifle the sobs that were building inside her. Yet her mother's gentle concern, her understanding, unleashed the tears Merwenna had been holding back since her arrival. She was vaguely aware of her mother wrapping her arms around her and whispering soothing words into her ear, before the dam burst.

Then, she wept as if her heart would break.

***

A waxing gibbous moon rose high into the sky, a silver crescent against an inky curtain. It was a warm night, slightly sticky, and the air smelt of grass and sun-warmed earth. Merwenna sat on a tree stump outside her home, listening to the croak of frogs. Inside, her mother and father had already retired for the night behind the goat-skin partition at the back of the dwelling.

Merwenna had left her sister sleeping soundly, curled up on a pile of furs near the fire pit, and ventured out into the crisp night air. After her tears earlier, she felt wrung out, tired. She would not sleep tonight until she had spoken honestly with Seward.

He was still at the mead hall, and Merwenna would not seek him out there. The mead hall was the domain of men, not women. If it took all night, she would wait. He would come home eventually.

It was a restful eve, apart from the distant rise and fall of drunken voices at the mead hall on the other side of Weyham. Merwenna felt safe and relieved at being home again. She knew this village so well. The surroundings were all so familiar to her, like the faces of her kin. Despite her relief, she felt melancholy settle upon her in a heavy mantle this evening. Her tears had not washed away her sadness.

Weyham had been where she and Beorn were going to make their future. She had wanted a little home, timbered rather than wattle and daub, with a thatched roof. She had planned to grow a garden and raise animals. She had wanted to bear his children.

Weyham was a reminder of her dreams, which now lay in ashes at her feet.

Now, it felt strangely empty. With Beorn gone, and her father angry, what did her future hold?

The sight of a figure approaching drew Merwenna from her contemplation. Immediately, she knew it was Seward. She recognized the set of his shoulders, his long-limbed stride. He had his head down, and was deep in thought—and so he did not see his sister till he was nearly on top of her.

"Good eve, Seward."

Seward came to an abrupt halt, his head snapping up. In the silvery moonlight, his expression was hostile.

"What are you doing out here?"

"Waiting for you," Merwenna smiled timidly, nerves getting the better of her. "Only I didn't expect you back so soon."

"The hall was full of your Cymry friends—drinking and making merry like it belongs to them. Let's say, I suddenly lost my taste for mead."

Merwenna noted the sarcasm in his voice, but ignored it. Instead, she swallowed her nervousness and focused on the reason she had waited for him.

"Seward, I need to talk to you."

"I have nothing to say." Seward moved to step around her, but Merwenna jumped to her feet and blocked his path.

"Please, Seward."

"Get out of my way, Merwenna."

"No," Merwenna stared him down, her heart hammering against her ribs. She had rarely seen Seward this angry. "You're my brother, and there are things that need to be said. Mōder and fæder don't know what really happened in Tamworth, do they?"

Seward grew still. "Are you planning to tell them?"

Merwenna flinched at the harshness of his tone. "No, not unless you want me to."

Silence stretched between brother and sister. Merwenna stared up into Seward's face, trying to gauge his expression in the moonlight.

"You think fæder was angry today," he said finally, "but you didn't see him when I arrived back a couple of days ago. He was livid. He nearly cast me out; if it had not been for mōder, he would have. He said that once the harvest was over, we were traveling back to Tamworth to find you. He told me that if any harm had befallen you, I would no longer be his son."

Harsh words, and yet they would have not been spoken lightly.

"I'm sorry, Seward," Merwenna breathed. "This was all my doing."

Seward gave a deep sigh, and Merwenna sensed his turmoil. "No," he replied quietly. "It was not."

"How is your back?" she asked.

"Healing," he replied. "Although I haven't been able to take my shirt off since I returned."

"Will it scar?"

"I expect so."

Merwenna lapsed into awkward silence. There was so much she wanted to say, but she did not know where to begin.

"Don't worry," she told her brother, "I will say nothing about what happened. I only have one question."

"What?" he asked warily.

"Why did you do it?"

Seward's eyes gleamed in the darkness. Then, he shook his head and gave a humorless laugh.

"I wanted her," he said finally, "and I took her. I can honestly say that I gave no thought to the consequences."

Merwenna stared back at him, unsettled by the baldness of his answer. A few days earlier, she may not have understood his meaning but now she did. She had recently learned just how powerful lust could be; had Cynddylan not ended the kiss, she would have been his. The realization that she could be grieving for one man and display passion for another disturbed and upset her.

"But, it's so dangerous," she murmured. "To give in to something that takes you over so completely."

"It is," Seward replied with another wry laugh, "and I have the scars to prove it."

Chapter Nineteen

Alone in the Woods

"This is a good brew."

Gwyn raised his cup, filled to the brim with frothy honeyed mead. He then toasted the Prince of Powys, for the tenth time since they had taken a seat at one of the long tables inside the mead hall, and took a deep draught.

Dylan suppressed a grin before sipping from his own cup. Gwyn was, indeed, in high spirits this eve. His captain was always his happiest in a mead hall.

They had visited the ealdorman at dusk and had shared some of his supper, only to find themselves invited to Weyham's mead hall afterwards. After a long day in the saddle, Dylan had wanted to return to camp and stretch out in his tent. He felt weary this evening. Still, it would have been rude not to accept the ealdorman's invitation.

The ealdorman's name was Godwine. Seated opposite Dylan at the table, Godwine of Weyham was starting on what must have been his eighth cup of mead. He was a huge man, with shaggy, grey-streaked blond hair and beard. Dylan had recognized him from Penda's campaign against the Northumbrians; the ealdorman had fought alongside Dylan, and had been formidable on the battlefield. Off it, he was amiable and hospitable.

Unlike many of the other men seated around the room, who watched the Prince of Powys and his companions with veiled hostility, there was no such undercurrent in Godwine.

"You and your men fought well at Maes Cogwy," Godwine bellowed across the table.

"I thank you, Godwine," Dylan raised his cup to the ealdorman. "It's good to be appreciated."

"All of us do, it's just that no Mercian likes to admit he can't take on all of Britannia's armies without a little help."

Dylan laughed, his fatigue lifting slightly. Still, the mead tasted cloying in his mouth, and he had been nursing one cup—in contrast to Gwyn's four—since their arrival.

'Drink up, Lord Cynddylan," Godwine motioned to a lad, who was circling the table with a jug of mead, to refill Dylan's cup. "You're sipping that like a wench!"

This comment drew a roar of laughter from the table, Gwyn included.

Dylan gave a lazy smile and waved the lad away. "We've got an early start tomorrow," he replied. "And if Gwyn keeps trying to keep up with you, he'll be hanging over his horse in the morning, not riding it."

Gwyn swore at him in Cymraeg. The tone of his voice needed no translation, and another boom of laughter rippled down the table. Dylan felt the tension inside the mead hall lessen somewhat.

"Come, Gwyn," Dylan stretched, rose from the table and nodded to the ealdorman. "I thank you for your fine hospitality Godwine, but my men and I had best retire for the night."

"What?" Gwyn glowered at him, flushed in the face. "But I'm not finished."

"Drink up," Dylan slapped his captain on the shoulder before turning his attention back to the ealdorman. "May we meet again, Godwine of Weyham."

"Aye," the ealdorman raised his cup to Dylan. "And may it be, once again, shoulder to shoulder, not on the opposite sides of a shield wall."

"I'll drink to that," Dylan replied, before raising his cup and draining the last of his mead.

***

Merwenna walked slowly through the woods, along the moonlit path, deep in thought.

She knew she should retire for the night, for her eyes burned with fatigue and her limbs felt leaden. Yet, after her conversation with Seward, she had needed to walk a while.

Her mind was churning, and she knew that sleep would not come easily this night.

Without even realizing it, she found herself walking into the woods behind Weyham and toward the clearing where Beorn had proposed to her.

Moonlight filtered through the tall trees, caressing Merwenna's face as she walked. It was quiet in the woods and the peace soothed Merwenna's anxiety. She arrived in the clearing and sat down in the center of it, upon the stump of an old oak.

The woods had always been her refuge, a magical place where she could be alone with her thoughts. She had often walked here with Beorn; the clearing brought back memories of stolen moments together.

Seated upon the stump, Merwenna thought back to the morning of the proposal, of the joy she had felt when he had asked her to be his wife, and of the anguish that swiftly followed when he announced he would be marching off to war.

I tried to tell him, she thought sadly. *If a woman knows that battle is not like the songs, why doesn't a man?*

She had no idea what had become of his corpse; she imagined it had been burned upon a pyre, with the rest of the Mercian dead. This clearing was the only remnant of Beorn she had left. She had expected to feel his presence here, but she was only aware of the empty quiet. Beorn's spirit had left this world and closed the door behind him.

Merwenna was so immersed in her own thoughts, lost in the fog of past words and deeds that could never been changed, that the glow of torchlight up ahead did not intrude at first. Then the sound of men's voices reached her.

Merwenna froze upon the tree stump, momentarily stunned by the light.

She was not alone in the woods.

It was late—she had not thought anyone would be about at this hour. By the time she had gathered her wits enough to think about diving for cover, the men were just a few yards from her.

"Helo!" one of them called out in Cymraeg.

Merwenna went cold. It was Cynddylan and his men. She cursed her stupidity, suddenly remembering that Seward had mentioned that they had gone to Weyham's mead hall. It was too late to run, and moments later she was surrounded.

"Merwenna?" the Prince of Powys stepped forward beside Gwyn, who held a torch aloft. "What are you doing out here?"

Cynddylan was plainly surprised to see her.

Merwenna rose to her feet, gathering her cloak tightly about her. "I was taking a walk," she said hurriedly. "I must have lost track of the time."

"A walk?" the incredulity in the prince's voice was mirrored in the faces of his men. "At this hour?"

"Yes," Merwenna took a step back from them, her pulse starting to quicken. Cynddylan and his men had kept her safe on the journey back to Weyham, but suddenly they appeared threatening, their gazes wolfish in the torchlight.

"I think she was waiting for you, Cynddylan," Gwyn grinned. "Hoping to catch one last glimpse of the great battle lord."

His comment drew laughter from some of the men. The prince, however, did not join them.

"No, I wasn't!" Merwenna choked, anger at Gwyn's lewd expression curling like a serpent in her belly. "These woods are my home. I have more right than you to be here."

That wiped the smirk of Gwyn's face. He glowered at her but did not reply. She watched the prince exchange a glance with his captain.

"Go on ahead," Cynddylan commanded him. "I want to speak to Merwenna alone."

Gwyn grunted, and with a speculative glance in Merwenna's direction moved off. The others followed him along the woodland path, bringing their torches with them.

Merwenna and Cynddylan were left, facing each other, illuminated only by the moonlight that filtered through the trees.

"You should go with them," Merwenna told him, her voice flat with simmering anger. "Gwyn is wrong. I have no wish to see you."

"I will go soon enough," he replied with a half-smile. "After we have spoken."

"I have nothing to say to you."

The prince gave a soft laugh, and Merwenna was aware of how close he stood to her. She could feel the heat of his body. His nearness was making her light-headed, and she struggled to focus.

“So you make a habit of waiting on woodland paths at night, do you?”

“No,” Merwenna glared at him, “but tonight is different. I’ve just returned home—and I’ve realized what awaits me.”

“And what’s that?”

Emptiness. Loneliness. Sadness.

“A life without Beorn.”

The humor faded from Cynddylan’s face at the mention of her betrothed. His eyes gleamed as he gazed down at her.

“Ah, him again,” there was a hardness to his voice that had not been there earlier. If she had not known better, she would have thought him jealous.

“Yes, him,” Merwenna straightened her spine and returned his stare. “I loved him.”

“I’m sure you did,” the prince drawled, “but pining here, alone in the woods won’t bring him back. Contrary to what you believe, love doesn’t rule the world. The lust for power and dominance over others is what drives men—always has, always will.”

“Are all high born men so callous and cruel?” Merwenna countered, anger making her reckless. “You’re no better than Penda, incapable of caring for anything beyond your boundaries. You love nothing but your throne.”

With that, Merwenna stepped back from him and turned on her heel. Enough. Her nerves were frayed raw; she had no wish to tarry here a moment longer.

Cynddylan’s hand on her arm stopped her, and he pulled her round, none to gently, to face him.

“I didn’t give you leave to go,” he ground out. Merwenna saw that she had succeeded in angering him. The air suddenly crackled with danger, but her own rage made her disregard it.

"I'm not your subject," Merwenna snarled back, struggling to free her arm. However, his grip was like iron. "You don't command me!"

Cynddylan gave a muffled curse and pulled her into his arms, his mouth slanting over hers. His kiss was rough, possessive.

Merwenna pushed against his chest to no avail; he was as immovable as one of the oaks surrounding them. She opened her mouth to protest, which was a mistake, for his tongue plunged between her lips and tangled with hers.

Despite her anger, Merwenna's body betrayed her, as it had the evening she had been collecting firewood. Suddenly, her skin felt bathed in fire. The feel of his hard body, and of his mouth devouring hers, turned her body molten.

"No," she gasped, as his mouth left her lips and grazed the column of her neck. He ignored her protest and continued his sensual torture. The sensation of his tongue on her skin turned Merwenna's limbs boneless. A deep ache pulsed between her thighs, melting her lower belly.

The prince's mouth claimed hers once more, and this time his kiss was deeper and more yielding. He tangled his hands in her hair, his fingers gently massaging her scalp. The roaring in her ears made Merwenna feel as if she were standing beneath a waterfall.

The hunger he unlocked inside her made Merwenna shudder with need. When Cynddylan kissed her, she no longer knew her own name.

Yet now that she had told him 'no', the spell had been broken. Like a swimmer kicking toward the surface of a deep pool, she tore her mouth from his and took a deep breath.

"Stop," she sobbed, pushing at Cynddylan's chest with all her might. Anguish bubbled up inside her, and she began to cry. "Please, just stop!"

Chapter Twenty

Unsaid

Dylan looked down at Merwenna's tear-streaked face and realized he had taken things too far.

He had not meant to kiss her. It was not his fault she was out here alone in the woods. He had never thought to set eyes on her again, and here she was sitting on a tree stump looking like a fairy maid sent to trap mortal men with her beauty.

Indeed she had—for he had been ready to strip her of her clothes and take her on the acorn-strewn ground. Had she not started to weep, he would have.

Merwenna may have been a sheltered young virgin from a Mercian backwater, but she had the capability to make him forget who he was.

Dylan took a deep, shuddering breath and released her. She stumbled back from him, and her legs gave way. She would have fallen, if he had not caught her.

"Leave me be!" she cried out, cringing away from him as if he were a leper.

Dylan's lust drained from him. He had never seen a woman shrink from his touch; it shocked him as if she had struck him.

"Merwenna," he rasped, guiding her to the tree stump. "Calm yourself—I won't hurt you."

"You were about to rape me!" she replied, the words coming out in gasping sobs. "I told you to stop, but you wouldn't."

"I've stopped now," he hunkered down before her, so their gazes were level, and placed his hands on her trembling shoulders. "Listen to me, Merwenna. I'm sorry I lost control, but believe me, I would never take you against your will."

She stared at him, her eyes huge on her pale, wet face. Seeing the depth of her anguish, Dylan silently cursed himself.

He was the Prince of Powys, a leader of men. What was he doing terrifying young virgins? Back in Pengwern there were plenty of women willing to share his bed. He had no need to force himself on girls who wanted to be left alone.

"I know you're grieving," he finally ground out.

"Then why did you do it?" she wiped at her wet cheeks with the back of her hand.

"Because, like a lot of men, I want what I can't have," Dylan replied with a frankness that caught him by surprise. He had not realized he felt that way until he uttered the words. "Your Beorn was a fortunate man indeed."

Merwenna gazed at him, clearly confused by his admission. He could see that she was struggling to believe him.

Dylan gave a lopsided smile and, reaching out, brushed away the last of Merwenna's tears. Something twisted inside him as he did so, and he suddenly wished he was a better man than he was.

"I never thought to see you again," he murmured. "You are sweet and tender, an entrancing beauty. Without realizing it, you left your mark upon me, Merwenna of Weyham. It took me till now to realize it."

"But you could have anyone," she replied, a crease forming between her eyebrows. "Don't you have a betrothed back in Powys?"

He smiled at that, relieved that she was no longer hysterical. "No, although my father pressured me to take a wife for years."

"So why didn't you?"

"I had an army to manage, wars to fight. A wife was not my priority. Now that my father is dead, I will be crowned upon my return to Pengwern. Only then, will I think about finding myself a wife."

"You make it sound as if you were selecting a cow at market," she replied, lifting her chin, some of her fire returning.

"That's what high born marriage is," he replied with a shrug. "You marry to strengthen your bloodline, to build alliances, make pacts. You marry a woman who will breed strong sons—for no other reason."

"Makes me glad I am not high born," she replied, and their gazes met once more.

"Life isn't easy, whichever rank you're born to," he replied before taking a seat on the ground next to her. "Our women are pawns in a man's world; but low born women face cold, hunger and back breaking work that ages them before their time."

He looked away then, thinking of his mother, who had died giving birth to his sister, Heledd. She had been much like Penda's wife, Cyneswide. A beautiful but submissive woman living in the shadow of a hard, uncompromising man.

When he looked up, he saw that Merwenna was studying him, her face serious.

"You are far more complex than you seem, Milord."

The prince gave a soft laugh. "You give me too much credit, cariad. And, please, call me Dylan."

"Very well," she gave a sweet smile that made him ache to reach for her. "*Dylan.*"

She really had no idea how lovely she was, he realized. Perhaps that was part of her allure.

They lapsed into silence then, and when the quiet started to become uncomfortable, Dylan climbed to his feet and dusted the leaves off his cloak.

"I will go now," he told Merwenna, gazing down at her face, "and you should do the same."

She nodded, remaining silent as she too rose to her feet and faced him.

"Goodbye, Merwenna," he said softly, resisting the urge to lean down and kiss her. They both knew where that led. "I wish you all the happiness in the world. You deserve it."

"Farewell, Dylan," she replied, her voice suddenly throaty, as if she were on the verge of weeping again. "For what it's worth, I think you will make a good king."

They stood for a few moments, their gazes fused one last time. Dylan then smiled, and let what he really wanted to say at that moment go unsaid. He did not deserve her kindness, but to say so would only upset her.

Then, without another word, the Prince of Powys turned and walked away through the trees.

Merwenna watched Cynddylan go, keeping her gaze upon his back until he disappeared from sight. Then she let out the breath she was holding.

Frankly, the prince had surprised her. Not only that, but he had confused and touched her. She had not expected him to react the way he had when she had refused him. Even now, she trembled at how close she had come to surrendering.

Merwenna shivered and pulled her cloak tightly about her. Dylan was right, she should not linger here. She took the woodland path toward Weyham. Walking briskly, she made her way through the slumbering village, prudently skirting the mead hall where she could hear the strains of raucous singing. She arrived home to find her family all asleep.

Aeaba was curled up like a puppy on her furs next to the glowing fire pit, and Seward was stretched out nearby. The soft, rhythmic sound of his snoring filled the room.

Merwenna tip-toed across the rush-matting floor and lay down on her own furs, which Aeaba had laid out for her before going to bed. The furs were soft and Merwenna's body ached with tiredness. Sleep would not come.

She tried not to think of Dylan. She tried not to run their last conversation over and over again in her mind but thoughts of him kept creeping back. At the memory of his tongue tangling with hers, his hands massaging her scalp as he kissed her, heat began to pulse between her thighs once more.

Damn him.

Merwenna rolled over on to her side, away from the fire pit and clenched her eyes shut.

She had come home, and yet she had never felt so lost.

***

A golden sunrise blazed in the east as Dylan and his army rode away from Weyham. It was a mild morning although the scent of autumn was in the air, along with the smell of wood smoke.

Dylan rode near the front of his men, alongside Gwyn. His eyes stung with fatigue; after a sleepless night, the last thing he needed was a long day in the saddle. Powys still lay at least two days' ride from Weyham, and Dylan was eager to move on.

They had delayed in Mercia long enough.

"Where did you get to last night?" Gwyn asked as they rode up the sloping hillside, his dark gaze gleaming with mischief. “I was about to send out a search party for you.”

Dylan gave him a sidelong glance.

His captain grinned. “Judging from the cycles under your eyes, I’d say the lass wore you out.”

Dylan gave a wry smile. “Would you believe me if I told you we just talked?”

Gwyn roared with laughter. “I’d say you were lying through your teeth.”

“Well then, you’ll just have to call me a liar.”

His captain’s laughter died away, and his gaze narrowed in disbelief. “You’re telling me the truth—you didn’t take her?

“I am,” Dylan admitted, “although I can’t say I’m crowing about it.”

Gwyn snorted rudely. “What’s happened to you? Time was, you saw a girl you wanted and you took her.”

The prince shrugged. He cast his thoughts back to the night before, and how Merwenna had shrunk away from his touch.

For some things, the price was too high.

With that, he urged his stallion into a canter and rode up to the head of the column, leaving Gwyn ruefully shaking his head behind him.

Chapter Twenty-one

Consequences

Merwenna's first day back in Weyham fell into a timeless rhythm that made her feel as if she had never left. It was easier than she had thought to slip back into old routines.

She spent the morning threshing barley with her sister and mother. They laid out sheaves across a large rectangle of sacking and set to, taking turns at flailing the barley in order to separate the grain from the chaff. It was hot, laborious work but the women fell into a rhythm, chatting amongst themselves as they worked.

Merwenna was grateful to be kept busy. It helped keep her mind from thoughts she would rather not dwell upon. She had hoped that she would awake with a fresh perspective, ready to begin a new life in Weyham. However, she had just woken feeling depressed.

What future awaited her here?

Weyham was an isolated village. Like Beorn, most of the young men her age had ridden off to war against the Northumbrians. Few had returned. By now, the whole village knew what she and Seward had done. Then, they had seen her return with the Prince of Powys, and Merwenna shuddered to think about the conclusions they had drawn.

Whether she wanted to admit it, or not, life would not go back to the way it was.

After an industrious morning, the family stopped for the noon meal. Wilfrid and Seward came in from the fields, and they shared fresh griddle bread, cheese, and small, sweet onions. It was a warm day, so they sat outside under the shade of their home, enjoying the light breeze that whispered down the valley.

Even so, the meal was consumed in silence. Merwenna stole a glance at her brother as she ate. After last night's conversation, his attitude had thawed toward her somewhat; however, he barely spoke to anyone, withdrawn in his own thoughts.

Merwenna picked at her lunch, her stomach closed.

Things were still not right with her parents, either. At dawn, the family had broken their fast together, as always, but a tense silence remained. Cynewyn had appeared the readiest to forgive both her children for their transgressions, but Wilfrid had lapsed into stubborn silence, his anger a brooding presence.

Now, he sat silently chewing his meal, saying little and avoiding her gaze.

Merwenna could see that she had deeply hurt him, and she felt a lingering guilt over it. Wilfrid had only ever treated his daughter like his princess, and in return, she had shamed him before the whole village.

"How much more of the harvest is there?" Merwenna asked eventually, breaking the weighty silence.

"Still quite a bit," her mother replied, handing her a cup of water. "We will need to hurry before the weather turns."

"The carrots and onions in the lower field are getting past their best," Wil spoke up for the first time since sitting down to eat. "They need picking today."

"Yes fæder," Merwenna replied hurriedly, anxious to please him. "I will do it this afternoon."

Wil regarded her, his gaze narrowing. She realized, with a sinking feeling in her belly, that he was not so easily appeased.

"You let your family down," he accused. "Do you think survival is easy out here on the fringes of the kingdom? Don't you care that because of your selfishness, your sister might not have enough to eat this winter?"

"Wil," Cynewyn interrupted gently, "Merwenna knows what she's done." She placed a hand on her husband's thigh to calm him, but he brushed it aside.

"Does she?" Wil got to his feet and brushed crumbs off his breeches. "I've only ever wanted what's best for my family. I stepped away from a warrior's life to ensure you all had a roof over your heads and food in your bellies. In return, my son and daughter run off at harvest, without a thought to the consequences."

"I'm sorry," Merwenna pleaded, "I will do my best to make amends for what I've done."

"Good," Wil grunted, not remotely placated by his daughters apology. "Make sure that you do."

With that, he turned on his heel and stormed back to the fields.

***

"Merwenna, I can see something is troubling you." Cynewyn gave her daughter a sidelong glance. It was mid-afternoon, and the two of them were alone in the fields, harvesting carrots. "Are you going to tell me what it is?"

Merwenna grimaced and pulled up a bunch of carrots up, before brushing soil off them.

"I wouldn't know where to begin."

"Sometimes it helps to speak of such things," her mother took the carrots and placed them in the enormous wicker basket she carried. "Don't worry about your father. He is hurt, but he will recover in time."

Merwenna looked down at her dirt-encrusted hands and frowned. "I'm not sure I deserve his forgiveness, or yours. I'm sorry, mōder, I have behaved selfishly."

Cynewyn nodded. She obviously agreed with her daughter on that. "I'm not going to ask you why you did it. I was young once—and I know youth is rash and extreme."

"Part of me knew Beorn wasn't coming back." Merwenna uprooted another bunch of carrots with more force than was necessary. "Perhaps, I went looking for him because I didn't want to admit it to myself."

"It's easier to take action rather than be made to wait," Cynewyn replied. "Whatever the reason—it is done with now."

"Beorn was my future," Merwenna sat back on her heels and met her mother's gaze. "Now that he's gone I feel as if I'm just drifting."

"You will find your path soon enough," Cynewyn smiled. "You may not realize it, but you have already started."

Merwenna frowned, not understanding her mother's meaning. "How so?"

"I saw how the Prince of Powys looked at you, Merwenna. And the way you looked at him."

"Mōder!" Merwenna gasped, turning on her mother. "What are you saying?"

"You stayed out late last night," Cynewyn pressed on. "Were you with him?"

"No!"

"Listen to me," Cynewyn put the basket of carrots to one side and took hold of her daughter's hands. "There's no shame in it. Sometimes we believe we're in love, but it's really something else. You're not betraying Beorn by wanting Cynddylan."

"Are you saying I didn't love Beorn?" Merwenna was angry now and near to tears.

"No—I'm just saying that love isn't as clear-sighted as you think it to be. You wouldn't be the first young woman to make that mistake. I did."

"What do you mean?" Merwenna extracted her hands from her mother's grip. She did not like what she was hearing. Of course she loved Beorn, and she was furious that her mother would suggest otherwise.

"You know I was married to another man before your father?"

Merwenna nodded. She knew her mother's first husband had been an ealdorman killed during a Saxon raid. She had heard the story of how her parents came together many times. Her parents were from the village of Went in the Kingdom of the East Angles; her father had once served King Raedwald of the East Angles—the greatest of all the Wuffinga kings. Cynewyn and Wil had been reunited a decade after she had rejected him, and the lovers had ended up running away from their old lives together, to begin again in Mercia.

"Aldwulf was every young maid's dream—confident, blond, and charming," Cynewyn continued with a wistful smile. "He was everything Wil wasn't. It took me a decade, and a lot of heart-ache to realize that a young woman often loves for what she wants to see—not for what's truly there."

"I don't see what this has to do with me," Merwenna replied stonily.

Cynewyn continued to watch her daughter's face, the sad smile lingering.

"What I'm trying to explain is that none of us know what lies ahead. A blessing can end up a curse, and tragedy can open doors you never knew existed."

Cynewyn rose to her feet and picked up the basket, which was now overflowing with carrots.

"I won't go on. Just remember that your life didn't end because Beorn died. Don't torture yourself over what you cannot change."

Chapter Twenty-two

Newcomers to Weyham

Light seeped out from the mead hall and pooled like molten iron on the path ahead.

Seward and his father approached the long, low-slung, thatched building weary after a hard day in the fields. They did not converse. After the initial confrontation upon Seward's return, father and son had spoken little. Yet Seward knew the matter was not closed. He could tell his father's anger still simmered. They would face off again sooner or later.

Seward paused at the entrance to the mead hall, allowing his father through the low doorway first. Immediately the sweet scent of mead hit Seward, mingled with the less pleasant smell of sweating male bodies.

Ducking through the entrance, Seward saw that the hall was packed this evening. It was far busier than he had seen it in a while. The Cymry army had departed; these newcomers were Mercian.

Seward waited, as his father joined the line for a cup of mead, and cast a glance to the far end of the hall, where a loud burst of drunken laughter had erupted.

Seward's gaze focused on the man in the center of the group. Suddenly, he felt as if he had just plunged head first into a trough of icy water.

The man was ruggedly handsome, with shaggy brown hair and cold eyes. His mouth was twisted in a smirk as he listened to the man beside him.

Rodor of Tamworth.

A group of warriors surrounded Rodor. They were rough, dangerous-looking men who were drinking fast—too fast.

Seward swallowed hard, his bowels cramping. Rodor was the last individual he wished to see in this world, or beyond. The warrior had not yet looked his way, but Seward knew the moment he did, he was likely to recognize, and then humiliate, him.

His parents knew nothing about what had really happened in Tamworth, and he was in no hurry to tell them. They would not look kindly on their son rutting with one of the king's slaves, but what would anger them even more was that he had been foolish enough to get caught.

"Seward?" his father must have noticed his son's sudden pallor, for he was frowning at him. "What is the matter?"

"Nothing," Seward muttered, turning away. "I need to piss—back soon."

Not waiting for Wil's reply, but feeling his father's gaze burning him between his shoulder blades, Seward ducked out of the mead hall and into the gathering dusk.

Outside, he strode away, forcing himself not to run.

***

His family were seated companionably around the gently crackling fire pit—his wife and daughters sewing, his son whittling a piece of wood—when Wil returned home from the mead hall.

Wil halted in the doorway, his gaze immediately going to Seward.

"Where did you get to?"

Seward shrugged, keeping his gaze focused upon the piece of wood he was whittling. "Wasn't in the mood for mead."

"A pity," Wil stepped inside and pulled the door closed behind him, "for there was intriguing talk inside the mead hall. There are visitors to Weyham this night, a group of the king's men."

"Really," Cynewyn put down her sewing. "Why would they be here?"

"They didn't say initially—although drink loosens men's lips, and I gained the ear of one of the men. He was well into his cups by the time I spoke to him. What he told me was very interesting indeed."

Seward looked up at that, his young face milk-white in the fire light.

"You're as pale as a shade, Seward," Wil said, his tone sharpening. "Why do those men frighten you?"

"Who's says I'm scared?" Seward replied belligerently.

"I do."

"Those men," Cynewyn interrupted, "did you learn why they're here?"

"They're led by a man named Rodor," Wil replied, his gaze still upon his son. "One of the king's finest warriors. He and his men are tracking the Prince of Powys. They plan to kill him before he reaches the border."

"Kill him?" Merwenna spoke up, her face taut in the firelight. "But Mercia and Powys are allies."

"They are—but it appears that Cynddylan insulted Penda at Tamworth. He now seeks reckoning against him."

"Cynddylan and his men rode to Mercia's aid, and this is how Penda repays him?" Merwenna countered angrily.

Wil's gaze shifted from his son to his eldest daughter, his gaze narrowing.

"You forget—our village lost good men for Penda too."

"But Cynddylan lost half his army! This is a reckoning without honor."

Wil's frown deepened. "You are right, they are without honor. They intend to sneak into Cynddylan's encampment and slay him while he sleeps. Yet, whatever their motives, it has nothing to do with us—or you. We must look after ourselves, if we want to survive."

Merwenna's gaze left his, settling upon the tunic she was mending. Her cheeks were flushed and he could see she was upset. "Yes, fæder."

Satisfied that his daughter had minded him, Wil turned his attention back to his son.

"You still haven't answered my question, Seward."

"What's that?" Seward replied, his expression sullen.

"You took one look at Rodor and nearly collapsed. Why?"

Seward stared back at him, his face set in hard lines of defiance.

"We're not finishing this conversation till I get the truth out of you," Wil folded his arms across his chest. "It's not enough that you abandon your family in the middle of harvest, but you are now covering up something. Tell me what it is."

Merwenna sat, clutching the tunic with numb fingers, her heart hammering against her ribs, and waited for Seward to respond.

Although she feared her father's reaction when he heard the truth about Tamworth, she was still reeling from the news that Penda planned to murder Cynddylan. All she could think about was that the prince had no idea of the danger stalking him.

"We . . . I had a problem in Tamworth," Seward reluctantly admitted. He hesitated then, the only sound in the dwelling the crackle and pop of the hearth. When he continued, his shoulders had slumped in defeat, his manner far less defensive.

Merwenna listened intently as Seward recounted the tale of what had occurred upon their first night in the Great Tower of Tamworth. When her brother finished speaking, Wilfrid's face was thunderous.

A tense silence followed, and Merwenna found herself holding her breath.

"Take off your shirt, Seward," Cynewyn broke the silence. "Let me see your back."

The young man rose to his feet and did as she bid. He winced as he pulled his sleeveless tunic over his head.

Merwenna let out her breath in an explosive gasp. Her brother's back was crisscrossed with livid, scabbed marks. He would carry those scars with him for the rest of his life.

"I did not bring you up to abuse the hospitality of others," Wil finally spoke, his voice hoarse with anger. "The Queen of Mercia invited you into her hall, and this how you repay her?"

"I didn't mean to hurt anyone," Seward replied, his defensiveness returning. "I'd had too much mead, and the slave was willing. The next thing I knew . . ."

"Enough!" Wil roared, his temper finally snapping. "You have shamed our family!"

"I haven't shamed anyone!" Seward shouted back, his face turning red. "It was a mistake, and I've paid for it."

"You haven't finished paying for anything! You're a fool! A selfish clod!"

Merwenna rose to her feet, backing away from where her father and brother stood, nose to nose, roaring at each other. Little Aeaba was weeping, clinging to her mother's skirts. Cynewyn tried to intercede but Wil and Seward's shouting drowned out her protests.

Unnoticed, Merwenna slipped outside. Her brother and father's angry shouts following her.

"You always think the worst of me!"

"And with good reason—you're a dolt!"

The darkness enveloped Merwenna like a soft cloak; the cool air a balm after the smoky interior of her home. The moon was rising above the trees, and all was quiet save for the muffled argument inside.

Merwenna was in turmoil. The news that Rodor and his men were on their way to kill Dylan had been like a punch to the stomach. Yet it was her own reaction to these tidings that shocked her, as much as the news itself. It had been instinctive—there was no question in her mind about what she must do.

She had to warn him.

She had little time. The argument, as explosive as it was, would burn itself out soon enough. They would soon notice her absence.

It was time to go.

Merwenna crossed to the store house and unbarred the door. Inside, she worked by feel, knowing what she would find. The ripe smell of cheese assailed her nostrils as her fingers curled around the bone handle of a knife that hung from the wall. She cut herself a wedge from one of the wheels of cheese her mother had left to cure. She then stuffed the cheese and an apple into the deep pocket of her skirt. It was not much, but it would have to do.

Moving like a shadow, quiet and fleet, she left the store house and skirted the edge of the yard before her home and made her way toward the fields.

To one side, sheltered by oaks, was a fenced area where her father kept his two horses. They were cantankerous beasts, both shaggy and jet-black. Her father had named them Huginn and Muninn—the names of Woden's ravens. Huginn represented 'thought', and Muninn 'memory'. The birds perched on the King of the God's shoulder and whispered to him about the goings-on of the world below.

Merwenna crept down to the enclosure and caught Huginn. He was slower but far more biddable than his brother; a safer choice if she did not want to be thrown off mid-journey. There was no time to saddle her mount, she would have to ride bare-back. She slipped on Huginn's bridle, led him out of the enclosure and vaulted up onto his broad back.

Then she dug her heels into his flanks, and they were off.

They skirted the edge of the fields, avoiding the village itself. Instead, they made for the woods. Merwenna guided Huginn in and out of the trees and, a short while later, they emerged from the woods onto the meadows where the Cymry army had camped. Cynddylan would be some distance ahead by now. She would have to ride all night and most of the day to catch him up.

Merwenna clenched her jaw in determination. She had time. Rodor and his friends were likely to leave at first light. If she rode fast, she would keep ahead of them.

"Are you ready?" she whispered to Huginn, reaching forward and stroking his furry neck. "We have a long ride before us."

BOOK TWO

Powys

Chapter Twenty-three

The Long Ride West

They followed the road west, traveling under the incandescent light of the moon.

Huginn's unshod hooves beat a steady rhythm on the dirt road. It was rough going, for the way was little more than a rutted track in places. Merwenna crouched low over the horse's bristling mane, her eyes watering as the cold night air whipped past.

She focused on nothing but what lay ahead. In truth, had she stopped to consider her actions, she may never have done it. Instead, she clamped down on any wayward thoughts and told herself it was too late to turn back, too late for second thoughts. They were now far from Weyham and gaining upon Cynddylan's army with every stride.

I have to reach him before Rodor does.

The first rays of sun were peeking through the trees to the east when she stopped briefly, next to a babbling brook. Here, she let Huginn rest and take a light drink of water. She too drank from the brook. There had been no time to bring a water bladder with her, something she now regretted. She only hoped they would find water along the way.

Although she was exhausted, and her body cried out for sleep, Merwenna did not linger by the brook long. Rodor and his men would have left Weyham by now. Soon, they would be breathing down her neck.

A chill wind blew in from the north as they continued west. Merwenna was grateful for it, for the sting of the wind on her cheeks kept her alert. Huginn revealed his tough breeding and stubborn will, ploughing on through the morning without showing signs of tiring. Merwenna, having been taught well by her father, took care to rest him every so often. She left the reins loose, allowing the horse to pick his way over the rough ground.

Gradually, moving ever further west, the land grew more hilly and the woods thicker. The way grew harder to follow, narrowing to something resembling a goat path in places. Yet Merwenna knew this was the road the band had taken. She saw signs of horses and men—trampled undergrowth, as well as dung and grooves in the dirt. The army had recently passed this way.

The morning gradually turned into afternoon, and still horse and rider pressed on. This day was the longest one that Merwenna had ever known. Exhaustion dragged at her, obliterating all thoughts except for one.

I have to warn him.

It was growing late in the day, and the light was beginning to fade, when Merwenna and Huginn caught up with Cynddylan's army at last.

She was so thirsty that it was painful to swallow. They had not passed a water way since noon, and both horse and rider were beginning to suffer the effects of dehydration. Huginn's head hung low, his flanks slick with sweat. Merwenna slumped on his back, her eyes stinging, and her body aching.

The Cymry had camped on the brow of a low hill on a south-facing slope. The road skirted the base of the hill at this point. Looking up the hill, Merwenna could see the outline of tents and standards, flapping in the wind, outlined against the darkening sky.

Relief rushed through her, and she drew Huginn to a halt. Any further, and a sentry would spot her. It was time to dismount and travel the last stretch on foot. Sliding to the ground, Merwenna gave a loud groan of pain.

It had not been a clever idea to dismount. She could barely walk. However, Huginn gave a great sigh of relief and to her surprise, nuzzled her side. Huginn had lost his ill-temper half-way into the journey and had been a pleasant companion for the rest of the day. His endurance had humbled her.

"You did well, boy," she stroked his velvety nose, reaching up to tussle his fluffy forelock. "We're almost there. Just a few steps more."

Moving stiffly, Merwenna led the horse off the road and up the hillside toward the camp. A few moments later, she encountered two warriors who were keeping watch.

One of them shouted something in Cymraeg and raised his spear threateningly. Merwenna stopped, fear involuntarily rising in her breast.

"I'm here to see Cynddylan ap Cyndrwyn of Powys," she called to them.

The two warriors exchanged looks. Then the one who had shouted out approached her cautiously, spear still raised.

"You're the girl we escorted to Weyham," he observed in halting Englisc.

"My name is Merwenna. Please, I must see the Prince."

The warrior's companion joined them, and the two men grinned at each other. Merwenna recognized neither man and dearly wished it had been Owain out here, guarding the perimeter—a man she liked and trusted. She hoped these two men were more honorable than they appeared.

"You're a foolish girl," the warrior lowered his spear, still grinning. "Running after a man so desperately. Are you looking for trouble?"

Merwenna's stomach churned. Her fears were becoming real. At this rate, she would not even be able to speak with Dylan. To travel all this way and fail now would be a cruel twist of fate. Worse than that, she knew she was in danger of being raped.

"No, I'm not looking for trouble," she replied, forcing herself to meet the warrior's gaze. Her skin crawled at the heat of his stare.

"No? Well, I'd say you've found it all the same."

"Look here," Merwenna snapped. Anger flooded through her, drowning her fear. "I haven't ridden like night and day to be treated like a half-witted slut. Your leader is in grave danger—and I'm here to warn him." She glared at the men, enjoying the look of surprise on their faces. "Take me to him!"

***

"How long has he been like this?"

Dylan looked down at the man who lay on the ground before him. The warrior was feverish, his eyes unfocused. He was tall and dark-haired; the flesh now hung off what had once been a muscular frame.

"He took a wound at Maes Cogwy although he only started to noticeably weaken in the last few days." Owain replied from where he crouched at the injured man's side.

Then Owain peeled up the wool tunic, revealing the warrior's torso—and the puncture wound on his side. The injury was not large, but it was swollen, red, and angry, with livid marks running out from it. The sickly sweet odor it emitted made Dylan's bile rise.

He had seen enough war wounds to know that this one had turned septic and had poisoned the man on the inside. He let out a frustrated hiss between clenched teeth.

"Did he not see a healer in Tamworth?"

"He did—but it was obviously too late. The wound had already started to fester."

"What's his name?"

"Madog."

"Can he hear us?"

Owain shook his head.

Dylan sighed and knelt down at Owain's side, staring down at the contorted face of the young man who had loyally followed him into battle. He stared at Madog's face for a few moments more before he turned to Owain.

"He has little time left. Make him comfortable."

Owain nodded, resigned. Like his leader, the warrior knew the signs. Madog would be dead by morning.

A chill wind buffeted against Dylan as he rose to his feet. It was more exposed here than he would have liked, but it was the only spot flat enough for the army to comfortably make camp. Around him, a sea of tents was being erected, and to the west, the shadowy outlines of the mountains of his homeland were now visible.

Just one more day till the border.

After months away from Powys, Dylan was looking forward to setting foot on friendly soil once more. He also looked forward to being welcomed back to Pengwern, a hero to his people, and to receiving the crown he had rightly earned. He had never been prouder of the men who had followed him than at the end of the battle at Maes Cogwy. Songs would be composed about their valor, and sung for generations to come.

Still, his mood was flat this evening, as it had been since riding from Weyham. Victory was sweet, but it could not fill the sudden emptiness that visited him at unexpected times—like now.

Dylan strode back toward his tent and the large fire pit that burned before it. The prince reached the fire and saw his men were already roasting a brace of conies. The aroma of roasting meat wafted across the camp. He stood near the fire for a while, staring at the glowing embers, lost in thought.

"Milord!"

A voice behind him roused Dylan from his brooding. He swiveled round to see two of his men making their way toward him. One of them hauled a slight figure wearing a home spun wealca behind him.

Dylan's breathing stilled for a moment. He would know her walk, her creamy skin, her mane of light brown hair, and those piercing blue eyes, anywhere. The sight of her came as a shock. He had put this woman out of his thoughts. He had left her in the past, where she belonged. Yet here she was, returning to torment him.

"Merwenna!"

The young woman's gaze met his and held. He could see the lines of fatigue, the dark smudges under her eyes. Irritation swiftly followed surprise. He could not believe she had been foolish enough to follow him. He had credited her with more intelligence.

He stepped forward to meet her, his expression hardening. "What in the gods are you doing here?"

Chapter Twenty-four

By the Fireside

Dylan and his men listened to Merwenna in grim silence.

She finished her tale and felt anger stir around her. News that King Penda had betrayed them, and was planning to murder his ally, rippled around the camp.

"There will be reckoning for this treachery," Gwyn muttered, his craggy face dark with rage.

"There will," Dylan replied with surprising calm. Merwenna watched his face, and searched for some clue as to his thoughts, but found she was looking into a handsome mask that gave nothing away. "Make sure the camp is secure and tell the men to keep their heads. Then return here—we have much to discuss."

Gwyn nodded, before striding off to do his lord's bidding. Dylan turned, meeting Merwenna's eye once more. His gaze was suddenly hard, and she felt a pang of misgiving. Till now, her focus had been entirely on reaching her destination and delivering her warning. She had deliberately avoided thinking about how Dylan would react to her arrival—now, she realized why.

"Come with me," he instructed her.

Merwenna followed him to his tent, her stomach fluttering nervously. The moment they were inside, out of sight of his men, the prince rounded on her.

"You should not have come."

"But I had to warn you," she replied, flustered by his anger.

"Then send someone else. You did a foolish thing, coming here on your own. Have you forgotten Drefan of Chester? At the very least, your father or brother should have escorted you."

Merwenna lifted her chin, her own anger rising. "I don't need an escort. I can ride as well as any man. You needed to be told—there was no time to ask anyone for help."

"That might be the case, but you've put yourself in danger. I'd send you on your way right now, but it's not safe. Rodor and his men will be close by now."

Merwenna stared at him, trying not to show how hurt she was. "You could show some gratitude," she finally managed. "I only came to help you."

They stood there, gazes fused. Merwenna's breathing was coming in spasmodic gasps as she forced back tears. The last thing she wanted to do was cry before this man. His lack of thanks stung.

Suddenly, a man's cough intruded, followed by a voice outside the tent.

"Fy arglwydd!"

At the sound of one his men hailing him, Dylan's gaze shifted to the doorway.

"Beth?" he called back.

A short answer in Cymraeg followed and Dylan's face went taut as he listened.

"What is it?" Merwenna asked.

"We have a visitor," he replied, his exasperation clear. "Your father is here."

***

Wilfrid was standing next to the fire pit, awaiting them, when Dylan and Merwenna emerged from the tent.

Feeling as if her father had caught them in an illicit act, Merwenna's face burned. She cursed her blush, for it incriminated her even more. Yet when she saw the expression on her father's face, her embarrassment turned to dread.

Wil's narrow gaze, clenched jaw, and steely expression spoke volumes—he was furious.

"You ride fast, Merwenna," he greeted her. "I was sure I'd catch up with you before you reached the camp. However, you outran me."

"You taught me well," she replied with a wan smile that faded under his glare. He had not been complimenting her, and the force of his anger made her break eye contact and stare down at the ground.

"Good evening, Wilfrid," the Prince of Powys greeted Merwenna's father, his tone neutral.

"Greetings, Lord Cynddylan," Wil answered with a curt nod. However, his attention was still firmly fixed upon his daughter.

"So you felt compelled to warn the prince. Why is that?"

"Fæder, I'm sorry," Merwenna replied, still avoiding his gaze. "I had to warn him—he's in danger."

"And why does that matter to you?"

The tension between father and daughter stretched taut. Looking on, the prince remained silent. Around them a crowd of men gathered, watching the scene unfold.

"Because . . . it does. He deserves to know." Her response sounded feeble, even to her own ears. Yet it was the truth—why did no one believe her?

Wil let out a sigh and ran a hand over his tired face. "This is my fault. I married a headstrong woman, and I've indulged you all your life."

"Please fæder, I didn't intend to deceive you, or to do anything wrong," Merwenna replied, her voice trembling as tears threatened. "I didn't want to alarm you, so I said nothing."

"That's only the half of it," Wil replied, his grim expression returning. "Beorn's ashes are barely cold and here you are chasing after another man. You're in love with Cynddylan, aren't you? Why else would you ride here, as if pursued by demons, to warn him?"

Merwenna flinched. Humiliation coursed through her in a hot wave.

"No!" she croaked. "That's not true."

"Isn't it? By the look on your face I'd say you are lovers already."

"You're wrong!" she choked out—but her father had already dismissed her. He turned to Cynddylan, and their gazes locked.

The Prince of Powys exhaled slowly, plainly irritated that he had been dragged into this mess. He glanced around him at where his men worked to secure the camp for night. Clearly, he had more pressing issues to deal with.

"No, we are not lovers," he replied coolly. "Although I wouldn't wade in here hurling accusations if I were you—I'm not the one who can't control my daughter."

Wil glared at him, a nerve flickering in his jaw as he sought to control his temper. Merwenna shifted nervously. Her father was not a violent man, but he was fiercely protective of his family. There was no telling how he would react.

Moments passed before Cynddylan shattered the tension with an unexpected smile. "You can't be blamed entirely. After traveling with your daughter, I know how headstrong she is."

When Wil did not answer, the prince motioned to the crackling fire behind him, where his men were roasting a brace of conies.

"Come. Take a seat at my fire and fill your belly. We will speak later. Rodor and his men draw close. I need to prepare for them."

"I would speak of my daughter now," Wil insisted.

The prince's smile faded, and his face hardened. He was a man accustomed to giving orders, not receiving them.

"You forget yourself Wilfrid," he replied, his voice soft with an unspoken threat. "I have an attack to get ready for—your grievances will have to wait."

***

Merwenna and Wil had finished their meal, having picked their rabbit carcasses clean of meat, when Dylan and his men finally joined them at the fire.

A chill wind buffeted the camp, causing the flames to gutter in the fire pit. Dark purple clouds scudded across the night sky, obscuring the moon and stars intermittently.

Cynddylan had just sat down, when Owain brought him news.

"Madog has died," the slender young man crouched next to Cynddylan, his attention focused upon his lord. "He went peacefully in the end."

The prince nodded, his expression shuttered. "We shall build him a pyre before we move on from here—so that he may reach his forefathers without delay."

"Did you know him well?" Merwenna asked Owain. She and the warrior had become friends during the journey to Weyham, and she was used to conversing with him. However, under her father's baleful stare she wished she had not spoken.

In contrast, Owain did not seemed to mind.

"I did. We grew up together. He has a wife and five children awaiting him in Pengwern."

This sobering news caused a pall of melancholy to settle over the group. Unsettled, Merwenna looked down at the glowing embers. How many more children had lost their fathers at Maes Cogwy?

Silence fell around the fire, the mood subdued. Eventually, it was Gwyn who broke it. He turned his attention to Merwenna's father.

"How many men does Rodor bring with him?" Gwyn asked.

"I saw eight of them in the mead hall," Wil replied, "I know not if there are others."

"Do you know anything that might help us?" Gwyn pressed.

"Only that they are Penda's best fighters—handpicked by Rodor."

Across the fire, Cynddylan frowned at that warrior's name. "Traitorous bastard."

Wil regarded the prince, his brow creased in thought. "Will Rodor and his men attack in the night?"

Cynddylan nodded. "Near dawn, I'd say."

"Shall you lie in wait for them? Let them come to your tent before you act?"

Cynddylan shook his head. "Too risky. They will kill sentries in order to gain access to the camp. I'd rather not sacrifice more men for Mercian dogs."

"What then?"

Cynddylan favored Wil with an enigmatic smile. "We have a plan. It's not a traditional approach. Yet it might just work."

Chapter Twenty-five

A Lament for Cynddylan

In the quiet of pre-dawn, something stirred amongst the trees.

Men, moving like shadows up the hill, slipped from tree to tree. Although many of them were big men, they had stripped themselves of anything encumbering. The only weapons they carried were long bladed knives, easier to strike and kill with in the dark. Arrows, axes, spears, and swords would only hinder them.

Rodor moved near the front, his sharp gaze flicking from side to side, checking that the way was clear. He had expected to come across a sentry before now. The fact that they had not yet found anyone guarding the perimeter made Rodor wary. He raised a hand, signaling to his men to proceed cautiously.

They had traveled swiftly from Weyham, closing in quickly on their prey now that they knew Cynddylan's army traveled just a day ahead of them. They had left Weyham before the dawn and journeyed hard. Rodor had pushed his men mercilessly, allowing them only a short sleep before they continued on their way through the night.

Now they were all tired, but the excitement of the chase had sharpened their senses. Rodor could smell their bloodlust. Each man who followed Rodor was alert and ready to play the part their leader had spent days rehearsing.

The sky was just starting to lighten in the east, the faintest stain on the edge of the indigo blanket of night. They had to move quickly, before the camp awoke.

Despite the whispering wind, it was eerily quiet this morning. The lack of sentries now alarmed Rodor. They should have encountered at least two by now. Sensing a trap, he signaled to his men, motioning for them to follow him. He did not want to ruin his carefully considered plan; they would have to proceed carefully.

The camp was just before them now, he could see the outlines of tents and standards against the sky. Just a few yards more and they would be at the edge of it.

Rodor led his men up the final stretch, weaving in and out of the tightly-packed trees, till he came to a clump of broom that shielded them from the camp. It was a good spot to take stock of the layout of the encampment. He knew the prince's tent would stand at the heart of it but wanted to survey the camp first.

Rodor gently parted the broom before him and peered out.

Then he drew breath quickly, his body going still.

He had expected to see the encampment slumbering at this hour—a carpet of tents with smoking fires and huddled figures around them. Instead, he saw that the entire camp was awake, and that most of it was gathered around a great funeral pyre.

Confused, Rodor's gaze swept around the massed crowd of warriors. Torches flickered, illuminating grief-stricken faces. They were all strangely silent, as if some terrible weight lay upon them.

Then, Rodor saw four warriors carry a man out on a bier. The crowd parted before them, and Rodor stretched forward through the broom, peering to get a glimpse of the dead man's face.

It was hard to make out his features in the gloom, but Rodor could see he was a tall, lithe man with dark hair. And upon his head, he wore a silver circlet.

Rodor's breath hissed out between clenched teeth. No, it was not possible. He had never seen Cynddylan wear such a jewel, but he knew what a prince's circlet looked like. Penda's sons wore them on ceremonial occasions.

The warriors had reached the pyre. There, they lifted the bier onto the mass of branches and kindling, before stepping back. Among the men who had carried the bier, Rodor recognized the big, wild-haired man who was the prince's captain: Gwyn.

The warrior's face was crumpled in grief. He let go of the bier and stepped back from the funeral pyre.

Long moments of silence passed, and then Gwyn began to sing. His voice—strong, deep and tuneful—filled the clearing. And despite that he was not a man given to emotion, Rodor felt a chill prickle his skin.

It was a haunting lament, in Cymraeg, and although Rodor did not understand the words, he caught Cynddylan's name.

Ef cwynif oni fwyf i'm derwin fedd,
o leas Cynddylan yn ei fawredd.

"Caedmon," Rodor whispered to the lanky young man standing to his right, who was also listening attentively to the lament. "What's he saying?"

Caedmon, whose mother had been a slave from Powys, stirred uneasily, as if unwilling to reply, and fingered his stubbly blonde beard. After a few moments, he complied, his voice a low whisper.

I shall lament until I lie in my oaken coffin
for the slaying of Cynddylan in his grandeur.

Slain.

Rodor looked back at the pyre, where Gwyn had just finished his lament. Then he watched as the warrior took a torch and stepped forward to light the pyre.

Full of dry wood and twigs, it caught alight quickly.

Slain – but how?

The wind fanned the flames, and the sound of crackling wood and hiss of devouring flames filled the dawn. The pain-filled sound of men's sobs echoed across the clearing.

Rodor turned away—he had seen enough.

***

Rodor and his men traveled east without pause, until the sun cleared the tree tops and warmed their backs. Only then did he allow them to rest.

They collapsed under two ancient oaks, upon a bed of fallen leaves, and drank deeply from their water bladders. After a long, sleepless night, they were exhausted. The men spoke little amongst themselves, relieved to finally be able to stretch out their weary bodies.

Rodor sat, with his back against the trunk of one of the oaks, and took the first watch as his men stretched out to rest. Like them, his body cried out for sleep, but he fought it. Instead, he brooded over what they had witnessed at dawn.

Cynddylan was dead—slain, it seemed—and although Rodor's men had rejoiced to know it, their leader had been in an ill-mood ever since.

Whoever had killed the Prince of Powys had made things very easy for them. Even so, Rodor had been looking forward to watching Cynddylan's face as he died. He felt cheated.

Still, dead was dead.

Yet if only it were that simple.

Rodor had always trusted his instincts, and they told him that something was wrong. Who could have killed Cynddylan? The question gnawed at him, and he went round and round in circles trying to answer it.

He knew he had witnessed it with his own eyes; Cynddylan burning upon the pyre. And yet his gut told him that it was all a ruse, a lie. He had no evidence, just a conviction that grew stronger with every furlong they had traveled.

When we are rested, I will turn around and go back, Rodor promised himself. His men would not like it; they all thought their mission had come to a convenient, if slightly disappointing end.

I have to know if it was a trick, Rodor brooded. *I cannot return to Penda until I am absolutely sure.*

The warmth of the sun filtered through the branches and caressed Rodor's face. Despite that it was growing late in the year, the sun still had some heat to it.

He was exhausted. His muscles ached and his eyes stung from lack of sleep. Fatigue slowly pulled Rodor down into its embrace, and after a while he stopped trying to resist it. Sleep claimed him.

He eventually fell into a deep, dreamless slumber.

Rodor awoke, a while later, with a jolt.

Something was wrong.

He felt a cold blade at his throat, and his eyes flew open. He reached for his own blade, which lay across his lap, and found it missing.

Rage flooded through him—but it was too late for anger. He suddenly realized that he had been tricked. The Prince of Powys had played him like a lyre. He had known Rodor was coming, and instead of lying in wait in his encampment, had turned the tables—hunting Rodor, as he himself had been hunted. Cynddylan had thrown him off course, and waited till his enemy lowered their guard, before striking.

The last thing that Rodor of Tamworth witnessed before he died, was Cynddylan's face staring down at him.

He was smiling.

Chapter Twenty-six

Dylan Swears an Oath

The pyre had burned down to embers when Cynddylan and his most trusted warriors returned to camp. Nothing remained but hot coals and drifting smoke. Madog had left this world, both in body and in spirit, and was now with his forefathers.

Merwenna and her father awaited the returning warriors. She watched as the Prince of Powys strode across the clearing toward them. His purple cloak billowed out behind him as he walked. Gwyn followed close behind.

"Did you find them?" Wilfrid asked, when the prince stood before them.

Cynddylan nodded. "They are all dead."

Merwenna's rush of relief was mingled with an underlying horror. So much death. It seemed the whole world was awash with blood.

"What will you do now?" her father continued his questioning. "Return to Tamworth and demand answers?"

"And give Penda another chance to part my head from my shoulders?" Dylan gave a cool smile. "I think not. Vengeance is best delivered cold. Once I reach Pengwern, I will plot my reckoning—not before. We shall remain here for the rest of today and continue west at dawn."

"And what of my daughter?" Wil folded his arms over his chest. Merwenna recognized his stubborn expression and felt her fragile hopes dissolve. Her father had no intention of letting her get away with defying him.

"What of her?" the prince raised a dark eyebrow. "She's your responsibility, not mine."

"This is the second time she has run away, with no thought to the consequences. There will not be a third." Wil then turned to Merwenna, ignoring her horrified expression. "You are staying here. I'm not taking you home."

"Fæder!" Merwenna choked out, barely able to believe her ears. "You can't do that!"

"I can—once I can forgive, but not twice. I've had to leave your brother, mother, and sister behind to do backbreaking work while I chased after you. You told me you were sorry for running off to Tamworth. I see now that you didn't mean a word of it."

Merwenna stared at him, her stomach clenching sickeningly. She had never imagined her kind, loving father could be so cruel. She had forgotten that he was a warrior at heart and had the capacity to be ruthless when pushed.

"I gave you all," he continued, his hazel eyes deepening to green with the force of his anger, "and this is how you repay me. There is no longer a place for you under my roof. You seem so intent in following your own path—now is your chance. Go with your lover."

"Those are harsh words, Wilfrid," Cynddylan spoke up. "Yet you must realize that I owe you nothing. I don't have to take your daughter with me."

"You owe her your life," Wil rounded on the prince. "Take her back to Pengwern, make her a servant in your hall. You owe her that much."

"You would abandon her to people you do not even know?"

"You brought her home safely to Weyham. I know that you are not without honor."

Cynddylan's lip curled. "Thank you, I am humbled by your high opinion of me."

"But I don't want to go!" Merwenna found her tongue at last. Panic replaced numbing shock. "Please, fæder, don't do this!"

She stepped toward him, arms outstretched, but he raised a hand to ward her off. Wil's gaze was still fixed upon the prince.

"Will you take her into your hall?"

Cynddylan's mouth thinned slightly, and his gaze flicked from Wil's face to Merwenna's stricken one. "I suppose she can serve in my hall. My sister, Heledd, requires a hand-maid. Her cousin, who used to serve her, wed in the spring. Merwenna can replace her."

"Do you swear an oath on this?"

The prince's expression darkened. He glowered at Wil, but the older man's gaze did not waver.

"You want rid of your daughter," Cynddylan reminded him. "What does it matter if I swear an oath or not?"

"She dishonored her family and threw away her future for you."

"I never asked it of her."

"That matters not. She has chosen where her loyalties lie."

Cynddylan continued to hold Wil's gaze for a few moments longer. Then he glanced back at Merwenna, who watched the exchange with tears streaming down her face. Never had she felt so insignificant. She saw from the look on Dylan's face that he regretted ever setting eyes on her.

"Very well," Cynddylan replied, although he was clearly displeased. "I swear that I will take Merwenna with me, and that she will be my sister's hand-maid. I swear it upon my honor."

Wil nodded, satisfied at last. "And I shall hold you to it."

***

"How could you, fæder? You humiliated me!"

Merwenna faced her father in the small tent Cynddylan's men had erected for them. It was like looking into the face of a stranger. For the first time, she realized just how bitter betrayal tasted.

"It's no more than you deserve," he countered. "You have to learn there are consequences to your actions, Merwenna."

"But I haven't lain with him," Merwenna's throat was raw from shouting. "All I did was ride to warn him."

"A rash and ill-considered act," he replied, before sitting down on the furs beside the fire and beginning to unlace his boots. "You've made a fool of me again."

Merwenna glared at him, ignoring the tears that coursed down her cheeks. She could still not believe how harsh he was being. She kept thinking he would reconsider, but hours had passed since Cynddylan had sworn his oath, and her father showed no signs of relenting. If anything, he appeared more resolute.

Exhausted, Merwenna flopped down onto her furs. She shot her father a mutinous look and decided to try another approach.

"Mōder will be furious," she said. If her feelings did not matter, perhaps her mother's did. "She will never forgive you for leaving me here."

His gaze narrowed at that. "Perhaps, but she will be reassured when I tell her the Prince of Powys has sworn to look after you."

Merwenna buried her head in her hands, defeated. Never had she felt so alone. Her father had been her anchor, the one man whose love had been unquestioning. She had never known he was capable of dealing out such harsh punishment.

"You have an independent spirit, Merwenna," Wil spoke finally, shattering the weighty silence between them. "So much like your mother at the same age. But, like her, you have a lot to learn about life—and people."

Merwenna winced under his brutal appraisal of her character. Never had her father spoken so directly to her. It was true, he had always indulged her—but those days were clearly at an end.

"You don't belong in Weyham," he continued, his tone softening. "With Beorn gone, there is no future for you there. *Wyrd* is pushing you from the nest—now it's time to fly."

"But I don't belong in Pengwern either," Merwenna looked up, and her gaze met her father's once more. "What kind of future awaits me there?"

"Hand-maid to a princess is an honor," Wil pulled off his boots and tossed them into the corner of the tent. "The prince could have made you a lowly servant—shoveling night soil and scrubbing floors. Be grateful he did not."

Chapter Twenty-seven

A New Beginning

Merwenna watched her father ready his horses for departure, with a heavy ache in the center of her chest.

Despite that she was still furious with him, she did not want Wilfrid to leave.

Suddenly, she could not breathe. She wanted to be back home, in a world that was familiar to her. Instead, she was being forced to embark on a new life in a new land.

"Fæder," she began hoarsely. She had to ask him one last time. "Please reconsider."

Wil turned from where he had just finished fastening Huginn's bridle and regarded her. Unlike his sternness of the day before, his hazel-green eyes revealed a hint of sadness this morning.

"You know I won't do that."

"But I don't belong in Pengwern, in a king's hall."

"Your mother is an ealdorman's daughter," Wil reminded her. "Never forget that noble blood runs through your veins. You will not be out of place in Pengwern. It may even be the making of you."

"But will I never see you again?"

Wil held his daughter's gaze, and Merwenna saw the sadness there intensify. For the first time, she realized he was struggling to hide his own distress. This was not as easy for him as she had thought.

"Your mother and I will pay you a visit in early spring," he murmured. "As soon as the snow melts we will come, I promise you."

Merwenna blinked back tears and nodded. "Thank you."

Wil smiled gently in response. "Stay well, my daughter. Ride swiftly to Pengwern, and I shall see you in the spring—you have my word."

Her father's word was always one she knew she could depend upon, and so Merwenna nodded, brushing away a tear that had escaped and was trickling down her cheek. There was no point in weeping now. Her father's mind was made up. She would not be returning to Weyham.

She stepped back and watched Wil swing up onto Huginn's broad back. He held the reins in his right hand and led an irascible Muninn with his left.

Merwenna watched her father ride out of the clearing, past the last of the tents, and toward the tree line. He did not look back, and she could see from the set of his shoulders that he was upset. It took all her willpower not to run after him.

Instead, she remained there, rooted to the spot, watching until her father disappeared into the trees and was lost from sight.

***

The fire had a mesmerizing effect on Merwenna.

She sat staring, watching the flames dance, and listening to the lilting rise and fall of Cymraeg around her. She understood only the odd word and realized that would pose a problem in Pengwern. Language would provide another barrier between Merwenna and her new life.

I will have to learn their tongue, Merwenna resolved although her mood was such this evening that she could not dredge up any enthusiasm for it.

She felt worn out, a husk. After her father's departure, she had drifted around the camp like a ghost, eventually retiring to Dylan's tent where she had slept away the afternoon. The prince had decided to let his men rest for the day, after an exhausting, sleepless night. Merwenna had been grateful not to have to move on just yet.

Even so, she had awoken even more exhausted than before.

"You are tired, Merwenna," Dylan's voice interrupted her introspection. "Why don't you retire?"

Merwenna's eyes snapped open, and she glanced at the man seated beside her. Dylan had been quiet this evening. They had not spoken of the oath he had sworn her father, or what lay ahead. Like her, his gaze had turned inward.

"I'm exhausted," she admitted. "Yes, I think I shall go to bed."

Merwenna rose to her feet and brushed off her skirt, before bidding the men seated nearby goodnight in Cymraeg. "Nos da."

Most of them ignored her, while Gwyn gave a non-committal grunt. Only Owain dignified her with a faint smile. She was not surprised by the lukewarm reception; few of them wanted her here.

Discouraged, Merwenna turned and made her way toward Dylan's tent. Inside, she was surprised to find that Dylan had already made up their beds—two piles of furs on opposite sides of the fire pit.

That was a relief at least. She had feared that the prince would take his oath to mean she was his property to do with as he wished. The separate sleeping arrangements made it appear that Dylan would leave her be.

Merwenna sat down on the furs and unlaced her boots. She then undressed down to her long linen under-tunic and brushed out her hair, using her fingers to remove the tangles and knots. Yawning, she crawled into the furs and sank into their softness and warmth. Moments later, she fell into a deep sleep.

Dylan bade his men goodnight and made his way to his tent. It was late, and the prince longed to stretch out on his furs. They had an early start the next day, and if they made good time they would reach Lichfield—Powys' new eastern border—before nightfall.

Pushing aside the tent flap, Dylan ducked inside.

Merwenna was asleep, and the sight of her made his breath catch. She lay on her side, her mane of almond-colored hair cascading over the furs. It was warm inside the tent, and she had kicked the furs aside, revealing that she slept in the ankle length, sleeveless tunic she wore under her wealca. The tunic had ridden up, revealing her shapely legs.

Dylan paused there, his gaze drinking in the sight of her. He could see the outline of her nipples through the thin shift and the luscious swell of her breast. His mouth went dry and his loins started to ache. It took all his self-control not to join her on those furs and rip that tunic from her body.

Instead, he crossed to his own furs and started to undress.

Little witch.

Perhaps sharing a tent was not a wise idea. Tomorrow night, he would arrange for his men to erect one next to his for Merwenna for the remainder of the journey. She was too great a distraction to have sleeping next to him, night after night.

I cannot believe I swore that oath to her father.

Dylan lay down on his furs and stared up at the weather-stained hide roof of the tent.

Heledd will not like it.

His sister had a fiery temperament. He did not imagine she would take kindly to having a Mercian hand-maid. Many in his hall would not take kindly to having Merwenna amongst them; they would think he had made her his consort, or that she carried his child. It was likely they would turn on Merwenna and make her an outcast.

He hoped she had the spine to deal with it all, for he would not be able to look out for her.

Dylan rolled on to his side, and his gaze traveled over Merwenna's prone form to her face. She looked so young, so vulnerable. He understood her father's frustration with her; his need to teach her a lesson. He just hoped the price would not be too high.

Life in a king's hall was not for the faint-hearted.

Chapter Twenty-eight

Blood at Lichfield

"See that roof up ahead," Cynddylan pointed to the thatched, gabled roof poking up through trees to the west. "There lies the new border between Mercia and Powys."

Merwenna craned her neck and peered over the prince's shoulder. It looked to be the roof of an ealdorman's hall. Smoke wreathed from a hole in its center, staining the twilight sky. They rode through beautiful country; flat woodland of ash and elm with the purple outline of mountains beyond. The settlement of Lichfield lay at the heart of it.

"Lichfield," Merwenna murmured. "Do folk here know that it now belongs to Powys?"

"Not yet," Dylan answered. "But they will shortly."

Merwenna's mouth thinned at this news. She imagined how the folk of Weyham, herself included, would have reacted, if three hundred Cymry warriors had rode in and informed them that this land was no longer part of the Kingdom of Mercia and that they would pay taxes to a new lord.

Cynddylan and his men would not be welcome here although she thought better of telling him so.

Relations had been strained between them ever since her father had left. They had ridden together in silence, only conversing when it was absolutely necessary. Merwenna had little to say to the prince. She had been humiliated by her father's refusal to take her home and the way both he and Dylan had decided her future as if she were of no consequence. In turn, the prince's manner had cooled considerably toward her. He had been generous in swearing an oath to her father, but she could tell he was not pleased about it.

The prince drew his stallion up then and twisted in the saddle to speak to her.

"You'd better get down," he instructed her. "Things might get difficult up ahead. Stay with my spears until I give the army leave to enter Lichfield."

Merwenna did as she was bid, sliding off the stallion's back and landing lightly onto the leaf-strewn ground. She watched Dylan ride away, his purple cloak snapping in the wind. He rode up the column to join Gwyn at the front.

Merwenna was relieved to be staying behind. She walked alongside those warriors who traveled on foot, and breathed in the fresh evening air, laced with wood smoke and roasting mutton. Her stomach growled in protest, reminding her that she had eaten little since breaking her fast that morning.

The twilight deepened, the sky turning a deep indigo, and there was a deathly silence up ahead. The bulk of Cynddylan's army had now stopped, Merwenna with them, awaiting news from the front.

Night had almost fallen, before any word came.

Owain rode back, his thin, sharp-featured face solemn, and shouted orders to the men. With surprised looks and murmurs among them, the spears moved off.

Not understanding a word, Merwenna hurried up to Owain.

"What is it?" she called up to him. "Is it safe to enter Lichfield?"

"Safe enough, now," Owain replied. "The ealdorman met with Lord Cynddylan, and things got . . . heated."

Despite that she had told herself she cared not what happened to the prince, especially after his ingratitude toward her, Merwenna felt a chill go through her.

"Is he harmed?"

"Just one or two cuts," Owain replied with a grimace. "Although the ealdorman fared much worse—he's dead."

"Dead?"

"Aye, gutted. He didn't take kindly to the news that Lichfield now sits in Powys."

Listening to Owain's matter-of-fact account, Merwenna felt slightly queasy.

"Was it necessary to kill him?"

The warrior gave her a wry grin before answering. "When a man comes at you swinging an axe it is."

Merwenna stared at Owain, shocked.

"Climb up," Owain stretched out his hand toward her. "Lord Cynddylan has asked me to fetch you."

Merwenna took his hand and vaulted up onto the saddle behind him. The warrior urged his horse into a brisk canter, and they entered Lichfield along a road lined with elms. As they rode by the first houses, Merwenna noted that this settlement was much bigger and more prosperous than Weyham. Lichfield was not a town of Tamworth's dimensions, but the state of the wattle and daub cottages they passed on the way in revealed that Lichfield was a village that did well for itself. They passed a patchwork of arable fields, where cottars had been bringing in the last of the harvest, and clattered across a wooden bridge spanning the wide River Trente. The water's surface sparkled with the last rays of the setting sun.

Like in Weyham, the ealdorman's timbered hall sat at the heart of the village, on the edge of a wide green.

Cynddylan's men had filled the space and were erecting tents, unpacking supplies, and unsaddling horses, when Owain drew his horse up before the hall.

Merwenna dismounted and looked about her at the surrounding industry. In contrast, the village itself appeared deserted. The folk of Lichfield cowered from sight. Had it not been for the smoke rising from the thatched roofs, the glow of firelight from within, and the glimpses of frightened faces peering from doorways, Merwenna would have thought Lichfield's inhabitants had fled.

It's not right, she thought as she followed Owain toward the timbered hall, *to terrify folk so. This is their home.*

When she neared the wooden steps leading up to the oaken doors of the hall, Merwenna skirted the edge of a dark patch in the dirt.

Blood—a great pool of it. Owain had obviously told the truth. There had been a skirmish between Dylan and the ealdorman.

Merwenna's queasiness returned, and she wished she did not have to enter this dead man's hall. She would prefer to have remained outdoors and make use of herself by helping to prepare the evening meal. Judging from Owain's purposeful stride, there was no chance of that.

Inside the hall, it was dark and smoky. It reeked of unwashed bodies, stale sweat, and overcooked pottage. Dogs skulked in shadows, and a group of women huddled at one end of the hall, weeping. A single fire pit glowed in the center of the space, casting long shadows across the grimy interior.

"Merwenna." Cynddylan called out to her. He sat upon a stool near the fire, surrounded by his thegns. "Over here."

Merwenna did as bid. Yet as she neared him, she saw the reason he had called for her—he was injured. The leather arm guard covering his left wrist and forearm was slick with blood.

"You asked for me, Milord?" Merwenna stopped before him.

Her eyes had now adjusted to the dimness although the sounds of grief that echoed through the hall had stretched her nerves taut. Over the prince's shoulder, she saw the women were keening over a man's body.

The dead man lay upon a bier; a huge, broad warrior with a thick, black beard. They had covered his torso with a thick cloak although even at this distance Merwenna could see that it was soaked through with blood.

"I did," The prince sipped from a cup of mead. He seemed unconcerned that the man he had slain lay just a few yards away. "What say you of Lichfield so far, Merwenna?"

"It seems a prosperous village," she replied, cautious. "Although, I'm not seeing it at its best this eve."

The prince gave a humorless laugh in reply.

Merwenna bit the inside of her cheek to stop herself from saying what she really thought. Instead, she dropped her gaze and softened her manner. "You're injured, Milord."

"I need you to see to this, if you would," Dylan motioned to his blood-soaked arm, which he carefully rested across his knees.

"Murderer!" one of the women who had been weeping over the dead ealdorman interrupted them. She had risen to her feet and was pointing an accusing finger at the Prince of Powys. She was a matronly woman, dressed in fine linen with amber brooches in her greying blonde hair. Merwenna surmised that this was the ealdorman's wife.

"May the wound he gave you fester!" the woman shrieked. "May you suffer long and terribly before Nithhogg feasts upon your flesh!"

The woman's curses were an assault on the ears. Despite herself, Merwenna shrank back from the verbal assault. Yet Dylan appeared unmoved.

"This is a filthy, vile-smelling pit," he said before downing the dregs of his cup, "although I'll admit the mead's good."

He rose to his feet, ignoring the ealdorman's wife as she continued to shriek at him.

"Do you want me to silence her?" Gwyn growled, flexing his meaty hands as he savored the thought.

"No need—I think I shall leave the widow to her grief," Dylan replied. He then turned and fixed his gaze upon Merwenna once more. "I'd thought to spend the night here, but on second thoughts I'd be more comfortable in a tent. You can see to my wound there."

Chapter Twenty-nine

Healing Hands

Merwenna followed Cynddylan into his tent and waited for him to seat himself on a pile of furs by the hearth. Truthfully, she felt nervous about tending to his wounds. Like most women in her village, she knew how to clean and dress a wound. However, the sight of blood had always made her ill, a weakness that irritated her mother no end.

She only hoped she would not humiliate herself in front of the prince.

At her side, Merwenna carried a basket of healing herbs, unguents, and clean strips of linen from the ealdorman's hall. She had asked Owain to bring her some wine, for cleansing the wound, and awaited his return.

Merwenna hovered in the doorway and watched the prince attempt to unlace his leather arm guard with his opposite hand.

"Can you help me with this?" he asked finally.

"Of course, Milord," Merwenna knelt down at his side and placed the basket beside her. Then she reached out and began untying the guard with nimble fingers.

"Such formality," the prince teased. "Call me Dylan when we're alone."

Merwenna nodded but kept her gaze upon her task. She heard someone enter the tent behind them and looked up to see Owain place a jug of wine next to the basket.

"Do you need anything else?" he asked.

"That'll be all, thank you, Owain," Dylan replied. "You can leave us."

Alone with the prince once more, Merwenna focused upon removing the guard. She could see the sharp incision in the leather, where the axe blade had sliced through into his flesh. The blood covering it was starting to dry and was sticky under her fingers. Merwenna felt her bile rise as she peeled away the guard.

She heard Dylan's sharp intake of breath and knew she had hurt him.

"Woden," she murmured, peering at the deep cut that slashed across the prince's forearm. It was a nasty gash.

"There should be silk thread in that basket, if it needs stitching," the prince told her, his voice tight with pain.

Merwenna nodded and took a deep breath in an effort to settle her churning stomach. "I will need to clean it first."

She turned away from him and picked up the jug of wine. Then, without giving the prince any warning of her intention, she poured the red liquid onto his outstretched arm.

Dylan hissed a curse in Cymraeg through gritted teeth but, to his credit, did not yank his arm away. However, he had clenched his fist so tightly that his knuckles had turned white.

"Is that necessary?" he finally managed. Merwenna glanced at his face then and saw that he was ashen.

"I'm afraid so," she replied. "Wine will stop the cut from festering."

Merwenna doused the wound once more with wine, before cleaning around it with a scrap of clean linen. She was relieved to see that the blood had now been washed away. The wound was still bleeding slightly, but it was much easier to face when he was not coated, elbow to wrist, in blood.

Next, Merwenna took a bone needle and threaded it with silk.

"It's best if you look away while I do this," she told her patient. "I'm sorry, but it will hurt you."

He nodded and did as she bid. Merwenna worked quickly. She had been sewing all her life and wielded the needle with precision, sealing the wound shut with four neat stitches. As she worked, Merwenna tried to convince herself she was sewing a jute sack, not digging the bone needle through a man's flesh.

Even so, her mouth was full of saliva and her stomach lurched painfully. She felt light headed by the time she had finished. Still, she had completed the deed without embarrassing herself; her mother would have been proud. Perhaps events of late had toughened her up.

The prince's face was very pale, his skin coated with sweat. Yet he had not uttered one word of protest while Merwenna had stitched his arm, and that impressed her. She put aside the needle and thread and reached for a pot of honey that had been mixed with herbs. She then smeared the unguent over the wound and bound his forearm with clean linen.

When she was done, Merwenna sat back on her heels and washed her hands clean.

"Are you well?" she asked.

Dylan nodded, although he did not look it. "I could do with some fire in my belly though, to take my mind off my burning arm," he replied, his voice hoarse. "Could you fetch me some more of that wine?

Merwenna did as he bid, returning with a large cup full to the brim of wine. She passed it to the prince, who took a long, grateful draught. She then busied herself with tidying up the items she had used to tend his wound.

The silence between them was starting to become uncomfortable when Dylan broke it.

"Sit with me for a few moments," he bid her.

Hoping her reluctance did not show on her face, Merwenna sat down next to the glowing fire pit. After a few moments, she glanced at Dylan and saw that some of the color was returning to his cheeks.

He gave her a wry grin. "I thank you for your healing hands although the fact you no longer meet my eye is slightly discomforting. Have I offended you?"

Merwenna shook her head.

"Yet you still won't look at me."

She sighed and deliberately held his gaze to prove him wrong. "I never realized there was such a high price to pay for riding to warn you," she admitted, finally.

Dylan raised an eyebrow, as if he did not believe her. "Do you think your father harsh?"

Merwenna frowned and looked away. "I left him no choice."

"I swore him an oath to give you a place in my hall," the prince reminded her. "I intend to honor it."

"Thank you," she murmured, wishing he would change the subject. "You are most generous."

"My generosity isn't entirely selfless," Dylan replied, teasing her once more. She looked up and saw that he was gazing at her intently. There was a heat in his stare that made it suddenly feel uncomfortably warm inside the tent. "I've grown used to your company, and you are lovely to look upon."

Merwenna flushed hot but held his stare. Injured or not, he was looking at her as he had in the woods outside Weyham. She was aware of his nearness and the devastating effect it had upon her. Suddenly, she was desperate to steer their conversation away from its current path.

"What of Lichfield?" she asked lightly, deliberately changing topic. "Now that you command the village, what do you intend to do with it?"

"I will leave a garrison of fifty men here," he replied, leaning back on the furs and regarding her under hooded lids, "and continue on my way home."

Merwenna nodded but did not comment. She felt the prince's gaze upon her for a few moments longer before he spoke.

"What is it, Merwenna? You look displeased."

"Does this village really mean that much to you that you would slay its ealdorman to make it yours?" she accused.

"This village was already mine. I gave Aethelred the chance to speak with me. I did not ride in here looking for a fight. The ealdorman could have continued to oversee this village under my rule but he chose to come at me with an axe instead. That was his choice and he paid for it."

"But you'll be hated here now, don't you see that?"

Dylan shrugged, as if such things were of little importance to him. "A ruler doesn't concern himself with whether all his subjects love him. Lichfield is mine, by order of the King of Mercia, and the folk here now answer to Powys. That is all that matters."

Their gazes fused then, and Merwenna felt that same strange, irresistible pull as before. She felt as if she were drowning. Even so, his callous approach to the folk of Lichfield galled her. His arrogance was not that different to Penda's.

Merwenna finished tidying up and rose to her feet. She noted that Dylan was still watching her.

"May I go now, Milord?"

"You can, Merwenna. I've asked my men to put up a tent for you next to mine, so don't worry. You won't need to breathe the same air as this beast."

Merwenna's turned to him, surprised. "I didn't say you were . . ."

"You didn't need to—it's written all over your face."

The prince was glaring at her now. His expression was thunderous, and anger gleamed in the depths of his green eyes.

Cynddylan may have been a great lord, a ruler of men, but it appeared that her opinion of him mattered.

After the humiliation Merwenna had suffered at both his and her father's hands, the realization that she was capable of wounding Dylan gave her a grim sense of satisfaction. She was not sorry for what she had said, even if she might pay for her rashness later.

Without another word, she ducked out of the tent and left the Prince of Powys to nurse his wounded arm and his pride.

***

Mouthy wench.

Dylan drained the dregs of his cup and glared into the fire. What did a naïve girl know about ruling a kingdom?

She thinks me a monster.

Irritation surged through Dylan and he tossed his cup away. What did it matter what Merwenna thought of him. And yet, it did. When he had told her in the woods that evening that he was but a moth to her flame, he had meant it.

Wherever she went, his gaze tracked her.

Need for her burned like liquid fire through his veins. The lack of guile in her cerulean eyes, her frank, open nature coupled with her gentle spirit, made him yearn to spend time with her. Merwenna's soft voice was beguiling, even if often he did not like what she had to say.

He had never ached for a woman so. Merwenna's supple, lush body, evident even in the worn homespun wealca she wore, was slowly driving him mad. Had she not shrunk away from him that night outside Weyham, he would have had her already.

Had he not have been injured, he would have taken her tonight.

Enough, he told himself as he ran a tired hand over his face. *You can't go on like this.*

He should never have sworn an oath to her father. At the time, he had been secretly pleased that Merwenna would travel with him. Now, he realized she was a distraction he did not need—not now. There would be plenty to command his attention once he returned to Pengwern: a hall to rule, a crown to receive, an army to gather, and vengeance to be wreaked. The last thing he needed was to let his desire for a woman pull him away from what really mattered.

Long had he worked toward this moment. It had not been easy growing up in his father's hall. His uncles, his cousins, and his brother—they were all adversaries. The old king had told him to trust no one.

His father had spoken true, for Penda had betrayed him. Although he said little to his men on the subject, the betrayal galled Dylan more with each passing day. He would not let this lie—Penda would pay for his treachery.

Chapter Thirty

Survivor

The warrior stumbled the last furlong toward the gates of Tamworth. Dusk's long shadows stretched across the soft green hills and surrounding woodland; it would not be long before the guards drew those iron gates closed. He had to reach them first.

The young man's leather armor creaked as he ran, his lank blond hair plastered to his skull with sweat. Exhaustion pulled at his weary limbs, and his feet stumbled on the road, but he pressed on. His gaze was fixed upon the great stone tower that loomed over the town's thatched roofs—his destination.

Caedmon knew his life was forfeit, but he had no choice. He had to go before Penda and tell him what had transpired. He was a hardened warrior, his Cymry mother had once teased him that he had come out of the womb fighting, yet the thought of what awaited him made Caedmon's bowels cramp in fear. The King of Mercia had been clear before Rodor and his carefully chosen company left Tamworth, that failure had not been a possibility.

The assassination had not only failed, but Cynddylan had known of their plan to kill him.

Penda had to be warned, no matter the consequences.

It was only a twist of fate that had saved Caedmon from the same fate as Rodor and the others. Had he not stumbled off in the bushes to empty his bowels, he too would have been slaughtered under the trees where they had been resting.

Caedmon's guts had been paining him all day. The meal of salted pork and stale bread the night before had not agreed with him although the others seemed unaffected by it. He had been crouched in the bushes, around twenty yards from where his companions slept, cursing the pork, his breeches around his ankles, when the attack came.

He remained there, frozen to the spot, listening to the grunts, stifled cries—and the wet sound of iron biting flesh.

It would be death to venture from his hiding place, and so Caedmon had pulled up his breeches and hid himself in a growth of brambles. Later, when he was sure that Cynddylan and his men had gone, he returned to the camp and found all of his companions slaughtered.

Somehow, Cynddylan had learned of their plans.

Caedmon had stood over Rodor's body, staring down at the warrior's slit throat, and realized then that the funeral pyre and the lament for the dead prince had been a carefully planned ruse. Cynddylan would know Penda had betrayed him. Caedmon had taken off at a run then and had only rested when his body could go no further.

Now his exhausting journey was almost over.

"Wait!" Caedmon gasped.

He was just a couple of yards from the gates and could see that the guards were, indeed, pulling them closed.

"Let me in!"

He saw two figures, clad in boiled leather, appear in the gap between the gates. The guards glared into the gathering dusk.

"Who goes there!" one of them shouted, brandishing his spear.

"Caedmon, of Penda's guard," he called back, barely able to get the words out. His lungs burned and his breath now came in short, painful gasps. At the mention of their king, the guards smartly stepped aside and let him inside without another word.

A moment later, the great iron gates of Tamworth rumbled shut, sealing him inside.

***

"So you bungled it."

Penda leaned back in his carved wooden throne and regarded the warrior before him.

The young man looked fit to drop. His thin face was gaunt with hunger and exhaustion. He stank of sweat—and fear.

"Aye, Milord," the warrior's pale gaze met his. "Cynddylan knew we were coming and tricked us into thinking he was already dead."

"And yet you survived."

"I did, Milord."

Penda took a deep, measured breath and sought to control his temper. He had trusted Rodor to carry out this mission discreetly and efficiently. Instead, he had completely messed up. Worse still, this fool had—against Penda's instructions—returned to deliver the news.

The king had just finished eating and had retired to his throne upon the high seat with his wife, when the ragged warrior had burst into the hall. Caedmon's arrival had caused quite a stir. He was known to most of the residents here, and the sight of him in such a state caused activity to cease. Curious gazes had tracked Caedmon across the hall, to the high seat, leaving whispers in his wake.

Penda had sent his wife away, for he had no wish for anyone to hear what Caedmon had to say. The queen left obediently, joining her daughters next to one of the fire pits, where they were roasting chestnuts.

Penda glared at Caedmon, letting his fury kindle. To his credit, the young warrior knew the trouble he was in. Yet he stood before his king, unflinching, awaiting his punishment. He could have run away after the slaughter—instead he had returned to Tamworth to warn his king.

The news of Rodor's failure galled Penda terribly. He had hoped to rid himself of Cynddylan, but instead the Prince of Powys now had a grievance to nurse against him. Penda steepled his hands before him and viewed Caedmon under hooded lids.

"I wanted this done secretly," he said, finally. "Powys is a strong ally. Cynddylan was never supposed to return home, but no one was ever to suspect his death was by my hand."

"I understand, Milord," the young man swallowed hard. "Cynddylan will seek reckoning for this."

"He will, indeed—and that is likely to mean war between us."

Penda let this sentence hang in the air.

"If it comes to that, you would defeat him," Caedmon replied confidently. "Powys does not have the armies to best Mercia."

"Perhaps not," Penda mused, "but his army is large enough to cause us great damage. I have other plans for my fyrd. Going to war against Powys is not one of them."

Caedmon dropped his gaze then, while Penda silently fumed. It took all his willpower not to leap from his throne, seize *Aethelfrith's Bane* from where the sword hung on the wall behind him, and run the warrior through with it.

Incompetent, useless dolts. This is what happens when I leave important deeds in the hands of lesser men.

"Milord," Caedmon intruded upon his silent rage, his voice cowed. "I did not come here for forgiveness, but to warn you. I wholly take the blame, and any punishment, for this failure. If there is anything I can do to put things right, I will."

Penda clenched his fingers around the carved armrests of his throne and glowered at the young man. He had been one of Penda's best. Rodor had picked him for his quick, cunning mind and adder-like swiftness with a blade. It would be all too easy to kill Caedmon for failing him, but his satisfaction would be short-lived, and it would not ease his current predicament.

"I have a long memory, Caedmon," Penda rumbled eventually. "Those who fail me rarely live long enough to regret it. Yet, if you can prevent Powys from marching to war against us, I may show you mercy."

The young man's eyes widened. He had not expected this, and the knowledge that Caedmon had been prepared to die for his news, made Penda's fury lessen slightly. The lad was a fool, but an honest one. He had told the truth when he said he had not come here to bargain for his life.

"How may I assist you, Milord?"

"I will have to offer Cynddylan something to make him reconsider his vengeance. You will travel to Pengwern to deliver a *gift* in my stead."

"But you have already given him land," Caedmon's gaze narrowed. "Will you offer him more?"

"I have—and I cannot afford to relinquish any more of our territory to Powys. No, I will not offer him land. I have something else in mind."

Penda's gaze shifted then to the three females seated around the fire pit. Cyneswide was smiling at something her eldest daughter, Cyneburh had said. Her younger sister, Cyneswith, had just plucked a chestnut from the fire and was unpeeling its blackened skin with dainty fingers.

They were so much like their mother, his girls. Blonde, beautiful, and biddable. Cyneburh was approaching her seventeenth winter. The time was nearing for him to find her a husband.

Penda ground his teeth in frustration. He had plans for his eldest daughter—and none of them involved gifting her to a Celt. He had intended to wed Cyneburh to the new ruler of Northumbria, to help build an alliance between them, and he was loath to deviate from this plan. His gaze shifted then from his eldest daughter to his youngest.

Cyneswith was only eighteen months younger than her sister, and he had not yet made plans for her.

Sensing her father's gaze upon her, the princess looked up from where she had just finished peeling the chestnut and was about to take a bite of the sweet flesh. She smiled, and Penda felt a rare pang of remorse. She was so beautiful, so pure. His wife and daughters were his one weakness, his one indulgence. He did not want to share them.

Quelling his jealousy with his legendary iron will, Penda turned back to Caedmon, to find the warrior watching him expectantly.

"What will you offer him, Milord?"

Chapter Thirty-one

Pengwern

Merwenna peered over Dylan's shoulder, her gaze fixed upon the cascades of water that surged down the sheer cliffs up ahead. The thundering falls tumbled into a swiftly flowing river, filling the valley with a fine mist.

"Thunor's hammer!"

She felt the vibration of Dylan's soft laugh, in response to her outburst. "That, Merwenna, is the way into Pengwern."

"Really?"

Forgetting to be embarrassed, or to mind the fact that the pair of them had been largely silent traveling companions for the past five days, Merwenna craned her neck upwards. Her gaze followed the line of the rocky cliff face. There, she spied the high gabled roof of a great timbered hall, and the thatched roofs of surrounding houses spilling down the cliff beneath it.

"It's like something out of a dream," she whispered. "A hidden kingdom."

Pengwern perched high upon the rocky cliff-face like a hawk's eerie. The seat of the King of Powys sat at the end of a steep valley, at the head of the Hafren River, nestled amongst rocks and greenery. It was an enchanting spot.

"Don't let Pengwern's remoteness fool you," Dylan told her, his laughter fading. "It may appear as if it cannot be touched by the outside world, but let me assure you we are just as vulnerable as any other settlement in Britannia. War has reached us, even here."

Merwenna did not reply although the prince's response had dimmed her enthusiasm somewhat. Remaining silent, she turned her attention back to her surroundings. Despite the narrowness of the valley, there were a number of folk living here: small thatched huts sat on the lowest slopes, peasants worked fields of crops, and sheep and goats grazed alongside the river.

The sight of the approaching army caused quite a stir amongst the valley folk. Those working the land put down their tools and waved, huge smiles plastered on their faces. Folk emerged from their homes and made their way down to the road. There were grins and shouts of welcome. Merwenna witnessed tears of joy as one of Dylan's men broke free of the column and ran to his wife.

Watching their tearful reunion and the joy on their faces, Merwenna felt her chest constrict. A moment later, a wave of longing broke through her. The naked love on the man's face made her look away.

No man has ever looked at me like that—not even Beorn.

Of course, he might have, if his life had not been tragically cut short. Had he survived the battle and returned home to Weyham, there would have been plenty of time for the pair of them to become close and grow roots together, like two oaks planted side by side.

Dylan urged his stallion into a trot, jolting Merwenna out of her introspection. They had reached the end of the valley. She clung on around his waist as they began their climb up the steep, winding road to Pengwern.

Their arrival had caused a great clamor. Groups of folk appeared at the roadside as the army climbed higher, scrambling up the steep bank to catch a glimpse of their returning warriors.

Cynddylan's men called out to them. Although Merwenna did not understand the words, she judged from the look of joy and pride on the faces of the gathering crowd that they were spreading the news about their victory against Northumbria.

Wise not to tell them of Penda's treachery, Merwenna thought. *Let them enjoy this moment.*

Ahead, she spied the tall gates of Pengwern; hard wood and iron, looming before her. The gates drew open as they approached and Merwenna felt fear flutter up into her throat.

Suddenly, she railed against the man who had sent her here. Her father would have known Dylan's hall would not welcome her, but he had not cared. Mercia might have allied with Powys to fight a common enemy, but they were far from being on good terms. It was a cruel punishment to exile her to a foreign land.

I will be treated as a 'nithing'—a creature beneath notice—she thought, dread forming a heavy weight in her belly. *They will hate me.*

That was likely the truth, but this was her new life and she would not shrink from it. She had changed in the past weeks. The innocent girl who had so eagerly run off to find her betrothed seemed a stranger to her now; she now saw the world as a harsher place. The past weeks had made her tougher—or perhaps the strength had been in her all along, awaiting the chance to show itself.

Merwenna took a deep breath and squared her shoulders. Whatever awaited her beyond those gates, she had no choice but to face it.

Merwenna mounted the steps to the Great Hall and hurried to keep up with the long strides of Dylan, Gwyn and Owain. A retinue of warriors followed at her heels.

A cool, damp breeze feathered against her face and the muted roar of the waterfalls filled her ears. After a fearful start, it had been an exciting ride up to the Great Hall, through the narrow, twisting streets of Pengwern. The whole population had stopped work and lined the streets to welcome their prince and his men home. Their cheering and the joy was infectious, and although she'd had no part in it, Merwenna was caught up in the air of celebration. Children and women had thrown rose petals over the returning warriors, which floated down upon them like large, fragrant snowflakes.

Merwenna had felt the men's pride and a wave of sadness engulfed her. The warriors who returned to Weyham would have been given a similar welcome.

If only Beorn had lived to experience this.

They had left the crowds behind, upon riding into the yard below the Great Hall. Now that they approached the top of the steps, Merwenna wondered what welcome awaited within. Ahead, the carved wooden doors to the hall draw open to receive them. The prince reached the top of the wooden steps and strode to the doors. A moment later, they had stepped inside and were crossing the floor, rushes crunching underfoot.

Merwenna found it hard not to gape at the interior of the Great Hall of Pengwern.

She had hated the Great Tower of Tamworth—a place as cold and soulless as the man who ruled it—but this space was altogether different. It was like stepping into the ribcage of a slain beast—*Nithhogg* himself. The size of the great blackened beams overhead was such that Merwenna wondered at the size of the tree they had felled to construct them.

Axes and swords, spoils of battle, hung from some of the beams, and two massive fire pits dominated the space. Richly detailed tapestries hung from the walls. The most stunning one of all—depicting a wild-boar hunt in the forest—hung at the back of the hall, where it shielded the living quarters of Dylan and his kin from view of the rest of the hall.

Before this tapestry was the high seat, and upon it sat a man. At his back stood half a dozen older warriors, dressed in fine cloth, leather, and fur. Merwenna guessed that these were Dylan's kin.

At first glance, from afar, the seated man appeared Dylan's twin. Tall and lithe with curly dark hair, and dressed in dark leather, he cut a striking figure. However, as they drew nearer, making their way through the crowd of high born who resided inside the hall, Merwenna saw that the brothers were not as alike as she had first thought.

Merwenna watched the man rise from his ornately carved chair and step down from the high seat to meet them. He moved differently to Dylan, his walk lacking his brother's purpose. He had a handsome, finely sculpted face, and his features were a touch sharper than his brother's, his gaze more hooded.

The man's gaze never left Dylan's face.

"Cartref croeso, Cynddylan," he greeted Dylan with a cool smile. *Welcome home*, one of the few phrases of Cymraeg that Merwenna knew.

"Hello Morfael," his brother replied.

"I take it from the ruckus outside that you return home victorious?" Morfael commented.

"We do," Dylan replied, holding his brother's gaze. "And I see that you have grown comfortable in my throne, in my absence.

Morfael smirked in response. "Just keeping it warm for you, dear brother."

"Polishing it with your arse and hoping for my demise more like."

This caused laughter to ripple through the surrounding crowd although Morfael did not join them.

"Marching to war with the Mercians has sharpened your tongue," he observed.

"Aye, but that's a small price to pay. Penda has gifted us a considerable parcel of land. Powys now rules as far east as Lichfield."

Morfael's face lit with genuine pleasure for the first time since Dylan had entered the hall. "That is fine news indeed."

Dylan remained silent for a few moments, letting his brother, and his uncles and cousins behind Morfael, enjoy their moment of glory. He was not looking forward to spoiling things, yet the news of Penda's betrayal could not be kept from them for much longer.

"This warrants a great victory feast," Morfael stepped forward and slapped Dylan on the shoulder. "Of a scale that Powys has never known."

"Then it will be so," Dylan smiled back, "but before you break open the mead and begin the arrangements for a victory feast, there is something else I need to share with you."

Dylan was aware of the gazes of all present upon him as he continued. "I have news that will not be so welcome."

Chapter Thirty-two

Heledd

"Betrayer!" Morfael's face twisted. "We will have reckoning for this!"

Angry shouts and oaths of vengeance rang out across the hall.

"Indeed we will," Dylan agreed, once the noise had died down. "Penda's treachery will not go unanswered. Once the victory feasting is done, and after I have been crowned, I will gather another army. As soon as we have enough men, we shall march on Tamworth."

The prince's announcement brought bellows of support from around the hall.

Looking on, Merwenna had no need of translation. It was plain to see that Dylan had told his brother of Penda's plot to kill him.

The bloodlust in the eyes of those surrounding Merwenna, frightened her.

March on Tamworth? Was she the only one here who realized the folly of such an act? Dylan was letting his own anger, and that of those surrounding him, cloud his judgement; he could not see past his need for vengeance.

"Dylan!"

The commotion had just started to die down when a female's voice echoed across the hall.

Merwenna turned toward the voice, just in time to see a young woman, around her own age, fly across the rush-strewn floor toward the prince. She was breathtakingly beautiful: tall and slender with a mane of straight dark hair, chiseled cheekbones and piercing emerald eyes.

Ignoring everyone else present, the girl flung herself into Dylan's arms.

His reckoning momentarily forgotten, the prince laughed and swung her around, causing the fine blue linen of her skirts to billow.

Looking on, Merwenna felt jealousy slice into her like a blade, twisting cruelly just below the ribs.

Who was this beauty? Suddenly, she felt sick to her stomach.

He told me there was no betrothed waiting for him here.

Then she cursed herself. It should not matter to her anyway. And yet it did—it mattered very much.

Dylan hugged the young woman tight before gently releasing her and setting her back down upon the rush-matting. Smiling, he took hold of the woman's hands and gazed down at her.

"It's good to see you, Heledd."

Heledd—his sister.

Of course, now that the green-hued veil of jealousy had been lifted she could see it; the family resemblance was obvious. She had the same chiseled features as her two brothers, although hers were far more delicate, and the same moss-green eyes.

"You were gone far too long, Dylan," Heledd chided him, pouting. "And now you talk of leaving again, when you've just returned."

"I'm afraid, I must," her brother replied with an apologetic shake of his head. "However, I bring you a gift from Mercia."

"Really?" the girl's face lit up. "For me?"

Dylan nodded. "I might be dead now, if a kind young woman had not warned me of Penda's plan to murder me while I slept. In thanks, her father has gifted her to me, and I give her to you as your new hand-maid. Merwenna, come forward."

Merwenna hung back, flushing hot with embarrassment, and pretended she had not heard the prince. The moment she had been dreading had arrived.

"Merwenna," Dylan's voice hardened slightly. "Step forward."

Reluctantly, she did as bid, gaze downcast. Deathly silence followed.

Eventually, as the hush drew out, Merwenna raised her chin and dared a glance at her surroundings. Hundreds of pairs of eyes had fixed upon her. Merwenna's skin prickled and she fought the urge to stare down at her feet. She had promised herself she would not cower here, but the reality of matters overwhelmed her. The air suddenly crackled with hostility.

"This is a strange gift, brother," Heledd was staring at Merwenna, a scowl marring her pretty face. She spoke Englisc now, with a pleasant, lilting accent. "I do not want a Mercian woman to attend me."

"Ah, but this Mercian woman saved your brother's life," Dylan too changed to Merwenna's tongue, so that she could follow their conversation. "We owe her our thanks. She is sweet and biddable, and will make an excellent maid."

Merwenna ground her teeth. He made her sound spineless, mocking her for all to see.

"Have you lost your wits, brother?" Morfael interrupted, scowling. "I think—"

"Is she your whore?" demanded one of the older warriors, cutting Morfael off. He was a powerfully built man of around fifty winters. He spoke Englisc crudely, yet his meaning was painfully clear.

"No, she's not, uncle," Dylan answered, not appearing offended in the least by the man's rudeness. "Merwenna is still a maid and will make an ideal servant for my sister."

The Prince of Powys stretched his back then, stifling a yawn as he did so. It had been a long day—and the gesture signaled the matter was closed.

"Enough of this talk. Heledd—take Merwenna to your bower and show her where she shall sleep."

Dylan stepped away from the women, brushing past his frowning brother, and climbed up onto the high seat. Then he settled himself onto his carved wooden throne and stretched his long legs out before him. He glanced over at his uncle, who had not moved, and was regarding him, a scowl creasing his heavy features.

"It's good to be home, Elfan. Now, how about breaking open that mead?"

***

"You are not sharing my bower," Heledd's first words to Merwenna were hissed with ill-concealed venom. "I shall not sleep next to a Mercian."

They had just stepped behind the heavy tapestry that shielded them from view from the rest of the hall. Beyond, Merwenna could hear the rumble of men's voices. The princess' words stung but Merwenna did not answer. She had not expected a warm welcome here.

Instead, she cast her gaze around Heledd's tiny bower, taking in her surroundings. A pile of furs dominated the space; while a collection of tunics, wealcas and over-dresses, hung like brightly colored butterflies from the wall, either side of a tiny window. There was a small oak table in one corner, upon which were clay pots of creams and potions. The scent of rose, lavender, and rosemary reached Merwenna, and she inhaled deeply. It may have been small, but she could only dream of having a space like this all to herself.

"You will sleep outside," Heledd scooped up one of her furs and shoved it into Merwenna's arms. You can guard the way into my bower, like a dog."

Merwenna's lips compressed, but she continued to hold her tongue.

Frankly, it would be a relief to sleep apart from this nasty female. There were girls in her village like this, vain and spoiled with sharp tongues. She pushed her way out from behind the tapestry and spread out the fur on the narrow ledge outside. When she was done, she turned to find Heledd standing behind her. The princess watched her with a narrowed gaze.

"How may I assist you, Milady?" Merwenna asked. She hoped her respectful tone would sweeten that sour face. Although most of those inside the Great Hall were clustered around the high seat, passing around cups of frothy mead—she was aware that a few of the women were looking her way. Their gazes were not friendly.

"I don't want your help," Heledd sniffed. "This is not a gift but an insult. I will make sure my brother understands that by morning."

Merwenna cast her gaze down at the rushes. Suddenly, cleaning privies and shoveling muck seemed a far more pleasant chore than waiting upon this princess.

"The evening meal is almost upon us," Heledd continued. "You will help the servants and not rest for the night until the last one of them has finished their duties."

"Yes, Milady."

"Go on then. Don't just stand there. Are you dull-witted?"

Merwenna did not reply. Instead, she went gladly and joined the hive of bustling servants who were preparing the evening meal of baked pike, leek soup, and fresh bread, at the far end of the hall.

Unfortunately, the servants were no more welcoming than their mistress. To make matters even more difficult, none of them spoke a word of her tongue, and she was forced to communicate in broken Cymraeg. Her attempts caused an explosion of mirth. One of the serving girls rolled her eyes and muttered something to the woman kneading bread beside her. Whatever she had said must have been clever, for the pair of them doubled over, cackling.

Merwenna let out a long sigh and imagined she was far from here. She envisaged herself walking in the woods behind Weyham, listening to the evening chorus of birdsong. She imagined she was shelling peas with her little sister outside her home, watching the sun slip behind the trees.

Instead, a huge pile of leeks was roughly shoved into her arms by one of the servants— thrusting her back into reality. The woman barked an order at her. Merwenna did not understand a word of it, but knew nonetheless what was expected of her. She was to chop leeks for soup.

Glad to have a task that would take her mind off her unpleasant situation, Merwenna carried the leeks over to a bench and reached for a knife. Then she began to slice the vegetables.

As she worked, Merwenna cast a glance back toward the high seat. Dylan sat upon his throne, a cup of mead in one hand, while the warriors around him clamored for his attention. Although he sat at the center of the milling crowd, the prince seemed apart somehow. He listened to the raucous conversations of his uncles, brother, cousins and retainers, and nursed his own cup while the mead flowed around him.

This was what he wanted, Merwenna reminded herself, *to sit once more on his throne and focus on the glory of Powys.*

Yet if that was the case, surely he should have looked happier.

As if feeling her gaze upon him, the prince looked up, and their gazes met across the crowded hall. It was unexpected, for Merwenna had not realized he knew where she was. His emerald gaze held her fast, the intensity of it causing butterflies in her stomach.

Suddenly, it was as if only the two of them existed. Merwenna's breathing quickened. She should have looked away but could not summon the energy to do so. His gaze drew her in and stripped her naked before him.

Merwenna shivered and wrenched her gaze from his. Breathing fast, she looked down at the pile of leeks before her. If one of his kin spied him gazing at her like that, it would start no end of trouble. He should be more careful, for they were no longer traveling together, with only the likes of Gwyn and Owain to witness their lingering glances.

Things would be very different here. Her new life in Pengwern had begun—and it would take all she had to survive it.

Chapter Thirty-three

Servitude

The noise inside the Great Hall of Pengwern was deafening. The roar of drunken voices, interspersed with bursts of laughter echoed through the cavernous space. The din even drowned out the knot of musicians upon the high seat, who were playing a merry tune on their bone whistles.

Merwenna gritted her teeth under the weight of the cast iron pot she clutched and struggled to make her way between the long tables. Steaming leek soup filled the pot. She gripped the handle with one hand and a large wooden ladle with the other, spooning the thick soup into bread trenchers as she went.

The muscles in Merwenna's arms screamed in protest and sweat slid down her back under her tunic. Usually, a pair of servants would undertake this task, with one holding the pot while the other served. Tonight, the chore had been entrusted to her alone—perhaps in the hope she would spill the soup and be punished for it.

Yet Merwenna resisted; a stubbornness she had never known she had possessed coming to the fore.

They'll have to do better than this, she thought as she filled Gwyn's trencher. *I'm not a spoiled high born lady, afraid of getting callouses on her palms. I've worked hard my whole life.*

"Thanks, lass," Gwyn favored her with a smile. The warmth was unexpected but appreciated, after her frosty welcome here, and she smiled back.

Beside him, Owain also flashed her a grin. Warmth spread through her—she was grateful to them both. Suddenly, the Great Hall of Pengwern did not seem such a lonely place. She served Owain and moved on, inching her way down the table to where the lowest ranking members of the hall dined.

She had not been allowed to serve Cynddylan and his kin, for that was an honor given to one of the other servants. Dylan sat at the head of the longest table, flanked by his brother on one side, and his uncle Elfan on the other.

Heledd sat next to Morfael, delicately supping her leek soup with a wooden spoon. The girl's behavior reminded Merwenna of Penda's daughters. She had the same demure manner, downcast eyes, and coy smile as the Mercian princesses. Heledd did not join the conversation of her menfolk and only spoke when addressed directly.

Heledd may have a forked tongue, but before her menfolk she's nothing more than a pretty decoration, Merwenna thought, not without a trace of scorn.

She thought then, with a pang of homesickness, of her parents. Wilfrid and Cynewyn were equals. Her mother was beautiful and strong, not the kind of woman to sit in any man's shadow and simper like a fool.

Will I ever see her again?

Merwenna's gaze blurred with tears, and she was grateful that she had finally finished serving the last of the leek soup. She returned the pot to the serving tables and managed to compose herself.

The older female servant, who had instructed her to prepare the leeks, now barked out another order.

Merwenna stood there a moment, not understanding a word of the command. The woman shouted again, louder this time, as if Merwenna was deaf, not merely unable to speak her tongue. Then she pointed to a row of large trays of roasted pike.

Merwenna realized that she was to help carry the trays to the table. Muttering an apology in her stuttering Cymraeg, she moved to comply. Like the cauldron of soup, the tray was so heavy that the muscles in her arms screamed in protest when she picked it up. Merwenna clenched her jaw, fastened her fingers around the edge of the tray, and marched across the rush-strewn floor toward the tables.

Dylan sprinkled a little salt on the roasted carrots and onions that had been served with the pike. Then he broke off a piece of bread from his trencher. He chewed slowly, savoring the fine food.

He had forgotten just how good the cooks were in his hall. The food before him was peasant fare compared to the victory feast the cooks would prepare for three days' time; it would be a great spread in celebration of their win against Northumbria, his coronation, and the reckoning against Mercia that was to come. Such a feast had not taken place in Pengwern's Great Hall for many years, and his servants would be working night and day to ready themselves.

Dylan took a sip of wine from his golden feasting cup and leaned back in his chair. His gaze moved down the table, past the flushed faces of his kin, to the servants that bustled around the tables.

He spied Merwenna among them. Dylan had been surreptitiously watching her all evening. He had noted that she had been given the task of carrying the heaviest items, with no help from any of the other servants, and that she had done so without complaint.

Her cheeks were flushed now as she struggled under a massive platter of roast pike. She placed the tray on the table, in-between two of his men, heaving a sigh of relief, before returning to the servant's galley to collect another. She was a hard worker, but that did not surprise him. She had grown up toiling alongside her family.

Still, this could not continue.

He had told himself that he would not interfere once they arrived here. He had promised himself that he would let Heledd order Merwenna around as she saw fit. Now he realized he could not. She deserved better.

Try as he might to think on other things, Merwenna now plagued his thoughts night and day. His body ached for her, need raging through his veins like a fever that increased with each passing day. He had tried ignoring her, but it only made his craving for her worse.

This evening should have been one of the happiest of his life, but he felt hollow. His brother and uncles spoke of war against Mercia, and he joined them—but his heart was not in it. Instead, his gaze kept roving around the hall, seeking out the winsome face of the young Mercian woman who had ridden to warn him and been cast out from her family for doing so.

Her father had accused her of being in love with him, which she had hotly denied. She had made it plain to Dylan, on many occasions, she still grieved from Beorn. But she must have cared for Dylan a little to have risked exile from her family.

And how did he repay her? He had consigned her to a life of servitude in his hall. He had seen his sister's treatment of Merwenna earlier, and tomorrow he would put a stop to it.

"Milord," one of the serving wenches appeared at his elbow bearing a bronze jug. "More apple wine?"

Dylan shook his head and waved her away. Now that his thoughts had fastened upon Merwenna, he was not in the mood for drinking.

"You look pensive for a man with much to celebrate," Elfan noted shrewdly, to his right. "What ails you this eve?"

Dylan gave his uncle a laconic smile and helped himself to another piece of bread. "Just weary after a long journey home," he replied. "I'm looking forward to sleeping in my own bed again."

Elfan nodded, appearing unconvinced. "You are changed."

Dylan raised an eyebrow. "How so?"

"You appear distracted. When we speak of war against Penda, you say the right words, but it's as if your mind is somewhere else."

The prince gave a derisive snort although secretly it alarmed him that his uncle had seen the truth. "There's no need to worry that I have no thirst for vengeance," he smiled, showing his teeth. "Penda will taste my blade soon enough."

Chapter Thirty-four

Jealous of a Dead Man

Merwenna looked up at the full moon and let out a long sigh.

If only I could stay out here.

She basked in its silver light for a few moments, enjoying the peace.

Merwenna crouched next to the stone well in the stable yard. She had just finished scrubbing the huge pot that had contained the leek soup and was taking a breather before hauling the cauldron back up to the hall.

A brace of torches, hanging from the wall of the nearby storehouse, cast enough light her way so she could complete her task. Still, it had taken a while to scour the pot clean and her back ached from bending over it. Every fiber of her body screamed for rest.

Yawning, she got to her feet. Then she cast a farewell glance at the friendly moon, picked up the pot, and climbed the steep stairs back up to the Great Hall.

Inside, most of the inhabitants were bedding down for the night. The light was dim; only the glow of the fire pits illuminated the space. Merwenna picked her way across the floor, stepping over men, women, children, and dogs and set the clean pot down on the freshly scrubbed table in the servants' galley.

The other servants had all finished their chores for the evening and were laying out cloaks and furs around the far wall to sleep on. Merwenna did not bid any of them goodnight, and none of them favored her with a glance either. Instead, she crossed the hall, carefully stepping over prone bodies as she went.

At the far end, she stepped up onto the raised platform and made her way toward Heledd's bower and the small fur she had laid out before it. There was no sign of the princess, for she had already retired behind the tapestry for the night.

Merwenna sank down onto her fur with a groan of exhaustion, her limbs sinking into its softness. Another evening like that and she would be bent over like a crone. However, she was too tired to even feel sorry for herself.

She closed her eyes and immediately felt herself start to doze off. Sleep had almost claimed her when a voice jerked her back into wakefulness.

"Merwenna. Are you awake?"

She scrambled upright, heart pounding. Disoriented and blinking like an owl, she peered up at Dylan's shadowed face. "I am now," she whispered. "What do you want?"

"I need you to take a look at the wound on my arm."

"Now?"

"The stitches are starting to itch. I think they need to come out."

"Don't you have a healer in your hall who can do that?"

"I do," he hunkered down so their gazes were level. His green eyes gleamed in the dim light, and Merwenna saw that he was smiling, "but he stinks like a goat and kills more folk than he cures. I'd rather have your tender hands administer me."

The intimacy of his tone made Merwenna flush, and she was glad that the darkness hid it. Suddenly, her fatigue lifted, and she was painfully aware of how close he was.

"Very well," she replied breathlessly, a strange excitement coiling in the pit of her belly. The rational part of her told Merwenna she should refuse him. Now that they resided in Dylan's hall, she should not be alone with him—but a surge of recklessness obliterated her reason.

"Good," he rose to his feet. "Follow me."

Merwenna got up and cast a glance about her to see if anyone was watching.

Not a soul amongst the carpet of sleeping bodies below stirred. Relieved, she followed the prince to the back of the platform, where another tapestry blocked his quarters from view. Dylan pushed the heavy material aside and held it there so that she could enter.

Merwenna accidently brushed against him as she ducked inside and caught the warm, masculine scent of him. To her shame, she breathed it in deeply, all her senses keenly aware of his nearness.

There was no doubt about it, this man had an extraordinary effect upon her. She loved Beorn, but even his most passionate kisses had not been able to rouse the excitement that one glance from Dylan could.

Her father was wrong—she had not ridden to warn the prince because she was in love with him. And yet she had not done it out of altruism either. The Prince of Powys had ensnared her, and she had not thought twice about riding to warn him.

Seeing Dylan again had confirmed what she had already suspected—whenever she was in his presence, she felt truly alive.

The prince's quarters were a warm, inviting space, twice the size of Princess Heledd's bower. As *her* space was colorful, feminine, scented with flowers and herbs, her brother's was pleasantly masculine. Plush, dark fur hangings formed the walls, and a fire pit burned in the center of the space. Dylan's quarters were unfurnished, save the luxurious pile of furs a few feet from the fire pit and a large wicker chest sitting against the exterior wall. Above it hung a huge war axe. The weapon was well-worn with chips out of its iron blade, an intimidating sight.

Near the fire pit, Merwenna spotted a healer's basket awaiting her arrival. She turned to Dylan and found him right behind her.

"Let me take a look at your arm," she instructed him. She needed to keep her thoughts focused on the reason she had been summoned here.

They sat down upon a large fur near the fire, and Merwenna gently removed the bandages around the prince's injured forearm. Nearly a week had passed since Lichfield, and she had dressed the wound and changed his bandages a few times since then.

"What say you?" Dylan asked. "Is it healing well?"

"It is," Merwenna replied, flashing him a smile. She was proud of her handiwork. "I was worried it would fester, but it has completely scabbed over and is mending well. However, those stitches do need to come out."

The prince nodded, their gazes meeting for a moment. The heat she had seen there, outside his bower, had increased, and he gave her that slow, sensual smile that she recognized from their first meeting in Tamworth.

It was a smile that needed no words.

Merwenna broke eye contact and turned to the basket, retrieving a small knife and pair of iron pincers. She then passed them both through the flickering flames of the fire, as her mother had taught her. Doing so helped prevent wounds from festering.

It only took a few moments to snip the stitches and pluck them from Dylan's skin. The wound started to bleed slightly, so she dabbed it with a clean cloth soaked in an herbal tincture.

"You are very able at this," Dylan said, finally. "Is your mother the village healer?"

"No," Merwenna replied with a rueful smile. "Weyham has no healer, so all the women in my village must learn healing skills. Truthfully, I have done little healing myself, but I have always assisted my mother. Her knowledge of herb lore is the best in Weyham."

"You look a lot like her, you know."

Merwenna looked up from wrapping his forearm in a fresh bandage, her gaze meeting his. "I am like her in many ways. My father has always sworn we are both too stubborn and willful for our own good," she replied.

Dylan smiled. "Some men like a woman with spirit."

"And some prefer a woman who does as she's bid."

The prince laughed softly. "And where's the fun in that?"

He was doing it again, looking at her with that melting gaze that stripped away all her defenses. "Such a woman would bore me soon enough."

Merwenna swallowed, holding his gaze. Her heart was beating so hard it felt as if it would break free from her ribcage.

Gently, Dylan took hold of her right hand, which had just finished securing the bandage, and placed it on his chest. Merwenna's palm pressed against the soft wool tunic he wore, the heat of his body seeping through it into her skin.

She also felt the thundering of his heart.

Her stomach pitched, as if she had just fallen off the edge of a precipice.

"Do you see what your nearness does to me?" His smile had faded now, leaving intensity in its place. "I'm sick with longing for you. Food and drink have lost their taste. When you stand close to me I cannot breathe."

Merwenna stared at him, shocked into silence by the prince's admission.

“I thought I could ignore it,” Dylan continued. “I thought being back here would make me focus on other matters—but all I can think of is you. Merwenna, you are slowly driving me mad.”

“Don’t say that,” she whispered, her fingers curling into a fist against his chest. “You shouldn’t . . . we shouldn’t . . .”

“It’s him, isn’t it?” The bitterness in Dylan’s voice made her draw back slightly. “I never thought I’d be jealous of a dead man—but I am. Will he have your heart forever?"

Chapter Thirty-five

Want

"I love Beorn," Merwenna whispered, "and time will not change that."

She saw disappointment flare in Dylan's eyes but pressed on nonetheless.

"He died only a few weeks ago. All of this has happened too soon."

"I didn't plan this either," he replied with a wry smile. "But keeping away from me isn't going to bring him back."

"I know that," she replied, holding his gaze. "Beorn and I were bonded by promises and dreams, but what I feel for you is different."

"And what is that?" Dylan asked. The bitterness had disappeared. He reached out and stroked her cheek. The sensation caused a shiver to ripple down her spine.

If only she had the courage to tell Dylan how she burned for him. Yet she had never lain with a man, what did she know of such things?

"I . . ." she began, staring at him helplessly, struggling for the words that eluded her. "I want . . ."

She did not have the chance to say anything more, for Dylan pulled her into his arms.

His mouth claimed hers.

She let out a groan and surrendered to him. The smell of him, the taste of him, unlocked something deep within her. Merwenna lost all sense of where she was. She was conscious only of his tongue, which slid between her lips and explored her mouth, and his hands that tangled in her hair.

This was what she had been afraid of. This lack of control; this need that once surrendered to, was all-consuming.

Merwenna's limbs grew weak, her body molten. Instinctively, she reached up and tangled her fingers in his curly, dark hair. Dylan groaned and pulled her onto his lap. His hands ran down her back. He then clasped each buttock tightly, pulling her firmly against him. She felt the hard column of his arousal against her belly and gasped. She had always imagined this moment would frighten her—instead she ached to reach out and touch him there.

She angled her hips even further toward him and slowly ground herself against him.

"Merwenna," he groaned into her mouth. "Do you have any idea what you do to me?"

Not awaiting a response, he pulled her with him so that they lay stretched out on the fur mat. Then he rolled over so that she was under him and kissed her again, his tongue teasing hers, and his hands cupping her face.

Merwenna went limp and pliable in his arms. She could not have resisted him even if she had wanted to. Her mind was nothing more than a whirlpool of need. Her senses ached for him; she could think of nothing else except having his naked skin against hers.

Dylan eventually ended the kiss. He propped himself up on his elbows, breathing heavily, as if he had been running. He stared down at her face—his eyes dark and luminous in the firelight.

"The gods help me, I won't be able to stop myself soon," he told her, his voice rough. "Go now, if you don't want me to touch you. But if you stay, you're mine."

Merwenna gazed up at him, her pulse throbbing through her body. She would surely die if he stopped touching her.

"I'm yours," she whispered.

That was all he needed. He kissed her again, all restraint gone. His hands were everywhere, hiking up her skirts and stroking the skin of her thighs. Merwenna clutched at him, desperate to touch his skin.

Realizing her frustration, Dylan released her, climbed lithely to his feet and began to take his clothes off—his gaze never leaving hers. Merwenna watched him, entranced. There was something incredibly sensual about watching him undress for her. His wool tunic dropped to the ground and Dylan unlaced his breeches. Merwenna's mouth went dry as he stripped them off. He stood before her, naked, clad only in the gold and silver arm rings he wore on his right bicep. His desire for her was evident.

Seeing the direction of her gaze, Dylan smiled.

"It is your turn, cariad."

Trembling, Merwenna climbed to her feet to face him. She stood there as he reached out and undid the girdle around her waist. Knowing what he was about to do next, Merwenna lifted her arms and allowed him to pull her wealca and tunic over her head, so that she too stood naked.

The cool night air brushed against her heated skin and prickled as his gaze raked her from head to toe. Finally his gaze rested upon her breasts, and she heard him give a low groan. Then he was on his knees before her. He drew her left nipple deep into his mouth as he suckled her.

Merwenna arched her back and stifled a cry. The pleasure was so intense she felt her knees buckle beneath her. Together, they sank onto the ground. Underneath his lean, finely muscled body, her own hands roamed at will. She wanted to touch every inch of him.

He started to suckle her other breast, while he parted her thighs. When he stroked her gently between them, Merwenna gasped his name. A few moments later, he inserted a finger deep inside her, and the trembling grew violent; she whimpered against his shoulder.

Dylan pulled her up against him so their bodies were pressed together from chest to hip. His mouth devoured hers. Merwenna grew bolder. As they kissed, she gently bit his lower lip; her hands traveling down the hard planes of his chest, across his belly, to his shaft. Her finger tips lightly traced it, exploring.

Dylan groaned as her explorations grew bolder. She ran her fingers up the long, hard length of it to the swollen head. When she stroked him there, Dylan gasped something in his own tongue. Then he parted her thighs wide.

Despite that she was a maid and knew what was to follow would bring her pain, Merwenna welcomed the touch of him. He slid into her, slowly. His body trembled with the effort he was making to control himself. Merwenna arched herself up against him, impatient to have him inside her.

When Dylan was half-way inside her, a sharp, tearing pain knifed through Merwenna, causing her to whimper, her nails biting into his back. However, Dylan was too far inside to stop now. With a groan, he thrust deep, seating himself fully.

She remained rigid, slowly releasing the breath she had been holding. The pain faded, replaced with a glorious, aching fullness.

Dylan began to move inside her in slow, deep thrusts.

Merwenna was lost.

She had no idea that it could be like this between a man and a woman. All that mattered was this hunger for him, this deep ache inside her, and this fire he was slowly stoking. Dylan reached down between them and stroked her as he thrust. Merwenna gasped his name once more, her body quivering—and her reaction drove him over the edge.

With a hoarse cry, he thrust hard into her and found his release.

In the aftermath, they clung together, sweat-soaked and breathing hard. Merwenna lay against Dylan's chest, listening to the thunder of his heart—and wished that she could stop time.

There could be no more perfect moment than this one. She did not want it to slip away.

***

Merwenna traced her fingertips across Dylan's chest, following the whorls of crisp, dark hair. She inhaled the warm, musky scent of his skin and propped herself up on one elbow, so she could look at him. He was dozing—in that dreamless state between sleeping and wakefulness—and she was loath to disturb him.

"Dylan," she said softly, tracing the line of his jaw with her fingertips. "I should go."

Dylan's eyes opened and their gazes met. Merwenna felt the same fire as earlier kindle in the pit of her belly. This man had cast a powerful spell over her. She could not look at him without being stripped of reason and will.

"Why?" he murmured. "Stay here with me tonight."

"But folk will notice my absence—they will talk."

"Let them, I care not."

Merwenna gazed at him, taking in the chiseled lines of his face. "You don't?"

"No," he gave her that slow smile that made her tingle all over and reached up to stroke her face. "What good is it being the ruler of Powys, if you cannot do as you wish under your own roof? This hurts no one."

"I'm not sure your kin see it that way."

"They will see it as I tell them to," Dylan's smile turned cocky, and he ran the pad of his thumb along her lower lip. "Your mouth is like a rosebud," he murmured, making it clear he wished to focus on other matters.

Merwenna smiled, aware of the heat rising between her and Dylan again. She was not difficult to convince. There was no place she would rather be than lying naked on the furs with this man. Their limbs were still entwined, and she felt his manhood stiffen against her belly. The sensitive flesh between her thighs began to ache in anticipation of what was to come.

Dylan answered her smile with a kiss. His fingers tangled in her hair, pulling her down to him. Moments later, all thoughts of leaving the prince's bower and returning to her bed outside Heledd's bower were a distant memory.

Chapter Thirty-six

Tainted

Cynddylan, Prince of Powys, greeted the day with a spring in his stride. He had slept little and would pay the price later for it. Yet right at this moment, he had never felt so alive. He strode across the hall to where a great wheel of cheese, fresh bread, and an earthen pitcher of milk sat awaiting him. He helped himself to a hearty portion.

A night bedding the beautiful Merwenna had given him an appetite.

He caught sight of his brother, who also approached the table to break his fast, and greeted him with a grin.

"Morning, Morfael."

His brother gave him a sidelong glance and poured himself a cup of milk. "You're in high spirits."

"I'm back under my own roof, in the company of my friends and kin. Why wouldn't I be?"

Morfael took a sip from his cup. "You told uncle that girl wasn't your whore—why did you lie to him?"

Dylan swallowed a mouthful of bread and cheese and gave his brother a measured look. It had taken less time than he had thought for news of Merwenna spending the night in his bower to circulate the hall. Tongues were, indeed, flapping.

"I didn't," he replied. "Until last night, we had never lain together."

"Why did you bring her here, Dylan?"

"I told you, she saved my life. I swore an oath to her father that I would take her with me and protect her."

"That is a strange oath," Morfael was frowning now. "There must be more to it than that."

"I admit, her loveliness made it easy to agree to it. Merwenna and I formed a bond in the time we have traveled together. I first met her in Tamworth. She had gone there looking for her betrothed—a warrior who died at Maes Cogwy."

"So you've taken her as your consort?"

"I have—what of it?"

"You are about to receive the crown of Powys; the same that graced the heads of our forebears, our father. You need to start looking for a high born wife of Cymry blood—not a Mercian peasant. What if she breeds your bastard?"

The brothers' gazes locked, and Dylan felt his sunny mood dim slightly. Morfael had crossed the line.

"Who I bed, and who I wed, are my business—and mine alone." Dylan growled. "And, I'd warn you against continuing along this vein."

Out of the corner of his eye, Dylan caught a flutter of movement.

He turned from Morfael to see Heledd marching toward him across the rushes. Her pretty face was creased in a murderous scowl.

Dylan let out a slow breath. Not Heledd as well—Merwenna had warned him of this.

Merwenna.

He had left her, bathing in a cast-iron tub he'd had brought into his quarters at first light. The memory of her naked, supple body, beaded with moisture as she bathed, made him wish he had not ventured outside to break his fast. It was too early in the day for arguments.

However, seeing the fury in his sister's eyes, he realized that he would have to nip these rumblings of discontent in the bud.

"Heledd," he greeted her. "You're up early this morning."

"I could not lie abed," she replied crisply. "Not when there is your coronation and victory feast to organize."

"And I appreciate your efforts," Dylan smiled.

Heledd's gaze narrowed. They both knew she had not approached him to speak of such matters.

"Is that *girl* still in your bed?"

"She is."

The princess's face paled and her mouth thinned. "I do not want her to attend me."

"Why not?" Dylan replied, feigning a lack of understanding. "She will serve you well, and will make a gracious hand-maid."

"But she is your . . ." Heledd's voice trailed off, and her face flamed.

"She is my lover," Dylan finished his sister's sentence, "but that does not make her tainted."

"She was already tainted," Heledd pointed out, lifting her chin haughtily. "She's Mercian. She doesn't belong here."

"I decide that, Heledd," Dylan replied, ensnaring her gaze with his, "and I also decide who serves you as your hand-maid. You will accept her assistance, and you will gentle your manner toward her from this day forward. She is your maid, not a kitchen skivvy. Is that clear?"

The princess's eyes glistened with tears, and her mouth had set in a stubborn line, but she nodded, nonetheless.

"You will pick out one of your old tunics for her this morning, and you will kindly take her through her new duties," Dylan continued. He kept his tone gentle but he knew his sister could hear the iron just beneath. "Is that clear?"

"Yes, Milord," she whispered.

Dylan watched his sister give a brief curtsey before she turned on her heel and fled across the hall back to her bower. Her back was stiff with outrage, but she would obey him.

The prince turned back to his meal to find Morfael still standing beside him. Dylan cast aside the bread and cheese he had been enjoying. His siblings had both succeeded in ruining his appetite.

"Not another word, brother," Dylan ground out. "I warn you."

Morfael nodded, minding him this time. He moved away and left Dylan alone at the table.

***

Merwenna squeezed out the cloth and inhaled the scent of rose, lavender, and rosemary. To bathe in a tub, in complete privacy, was a delight. The water was cooling now, but she was loath to leave it. She had washed her hair, using an herb-scented lotion, and it now hung over one shoulder in a damp curtain. Afterwards, she had lain back against the smooth edge of the cast iron tub, enjoying the heat that flooded through her limbs.

Is this what it's like to be high born?

Outside, she could hear the rumble of voices, clang of pots, and the thump of wood, as the Great Hall awoke. Merwenna stirred restlessly, sloshing water over the side of the tub. She should join them, for Dylan had told her that she would continue to serve his sister today. She would win no friends here by lying around when there was work to be done.

Yet it was difficult to leave this bath. Such moments of pleasure were rare enough to be cherished.

Like last night.

Even now, the memory of what had passed between her and Dylan made Merwenna's toes curl and heat flush across her body. She may well come to regret it soon enough, but at this moment the magic of their coupling still thrilled her. Merwenna closed her eyes, letting sensual images from last night play before her.

"You'll turn into a fish, if you stay in there any longer."

Her eyes flew open to see that Dylan had returned. He let the fur hanging fall behind him and stood there for a moment, his gaze making a frank appraisal of her.

"Although, I'd say you were a siren already," he advanced on her, a smile tugging at the corner of his mouth, "whose beauty would lure a man into treacherous waters."

"Is that what I've done?" Merwenna asked. Her heart had started to race at the sight of him, and her nakedness suddenly made her feel vulnerable.

"You have," he replied, "although, there's no other place I'd rather drown."

With that, he took hold of her hands and pulled her to her feet in the tub. More water sloshed over the side, wetting the rushes beneath, but neither of them paid it any mind.

Dylan's mouth came down fiercely over Merwenna's, and he pulled her hard against him. Merwenna gave an answering groan. She reached up, entwined her arms around his neck, and pressed her slick breasts against his chest, wetting his thin linen tunic through.

Last night's fire returned, with a sharper hunger for them both. Now they had both been given a taste, they wanted more. With an animal growl, Dylan picked Merwenna up and carried her across to the furs. He then threw her down upon them and tore off his wet clothes.

Suddenly, all thoughts of the day's chores, or what the future held for her, dissolved from Merwenna's mind. This man, magnificent in his nakedness, was all that mattered.

With a smile full of heat and promise, she held out her arms to him.

Chapter Thirty-seven

Different Worlds

"Thank you for the dress—it's beautiful."

"It's old and drab, but it'll suit you."

Despite herself, Merwenna flinched under Heledd's spite. She did not reply, instead smoothing out the butter-soft wool tunic beneath her fingers. Heledd had only said that to hurt her, for they both knew it was a lovely dress, made of soft, fine wool, and dyed grey-blue. Merwenna had never worn a garment like this before; it made her old wealca and the homespun tunics she had grown up in look like mere rags. She was used to wearing sleeveless garments, even in winter, but this dress had long, bell-like sleeves.

She felt like a princess wearing it although, clearly, she was not.

"If you are to serve me, I cannot have you looking like a peasant," Heledd sniffed. "Come, I shall show you the clothes I need washing. I also have a pile of mending for you."

Merwenna followed the princess to the wicker basket on the other side of her furs. It was stuffed full of under-tunics and a collection of brightly colored over-dresses.

"They must all be washed separately, or the dye will bleed and ruin them," Heledd instructed. "There is a special block of lye soap for the task. You must ask the servants for it."

Merwenna nodded, not relishing the thought of attempting to ask for such a thing in her broken Cymraeg.

"How do I say 'soap' in your tongue," she asked.

"*Sebon*," the princess snapped. "Now, over here there are the clothes that need to be mended." Heledd motioned to the pile of items hanging over a wooden chest. "You will need to ask for a needle and the right color thread from the other women."

Merwenna nodded once more. Heledd must be referring to the high born ladies who spent most of their day sitting at their distaffs or looms. None of them had viewed her with a friendly eye the day before, and Merwenna was wary of approaching them today.

"How do I say . . ." she began, hoping that Heledd would give her some more useful vocabulary in order to communicate without making a fool of herself, but the princess had clearly run out of patience with her.

"Enough," Heledd shoved the wicker basket full of dirty clothes into Merwenna's arms. "Learn it for yourself."

Merwenna took that as her signal to quit Heledd's bower. The princess only barely tolerated her. Yet Dylan had obviously made his authority felt, for she had not been ordered to scrub pots today.

Balancing the basket against her hip, Merwenna emerged from Heledd's bower and made her way down from the platform into the main area of the hall. It was nearing time for the noon meal, and the servants were hard at work, pummeling dough for griddle bread and adding the finishing touches to the venison stew.

One of the servants, the harridan who had barked orders at her all last evening, met Merwenna's eye as she walked toward them. The woman scowled at her but Merwenna smiled back and made straight for her.

She would ask this woman for the soap.

It was time she developed a thicker hide; she had to learn how to weather these folks' scorn, instead of shrinking from it. She could not let the servants make her cower, or she would forever slink around the Great Hall like a cur.

***

The stone furnace roared like a Yule bonfire.

Dylan stepped inside the smith's forge, drawing back slightly at the intense heat that struck him across the face. The acrid odor of molten iron stung his nostrils, and the thick pall of smoke hanging in the air made his eyes water.

A low, dimly lit building housed the smith's forge—and Dylan had never seen it so busy.

His gaze shifted around the space, traveling from where the smith—a huge fellow with arms like tree-trunks—gripped the beginnings of a sword-blade with pincers upon a heavy iron anvil, while a young man struck the blade repeatedly with a hammer. It was grueling work and sweat poured off the lad's brow, running in rivulets down his bare arms. Nearby, four other lads were hard at work, beating glowing lumps of iron into spearheads.

The noise was deafening.

"My Lord Cynddylan," the smithy bellowed, acknowledging the prince with a wide smile.

"Good morning, Bryn, how goes it?"

"Well enough."

The smithy gestured to the young man to stop striking the blade. Then he rubbed a beefy forearm across his sweaty brow.

"I've got the lads working night and day—but it'll depend on how many weapons you need."

"I'm gathering a mighty army," Dylan replied. "Word has gone out. Warriors will start arriving from all corners of Powys, a few days from now. We'll need a thousand spear heads and as many axes and sword blades as you can manage."

The smithy sucked his teeth at this news, while the lad next to him visibly blanched.

"We will do our best, Milord," he replied, although Dylan saw the concern in his eyes, "although it'll take two moons, at least, to make it all."

Dylan frowned. He had hoped to be ready before then.

"Surely you don't plan to march on Tamworth so soon?" the smithy asked. "The leaves are starting to fall, it will not be long before winter is upon us. Begging your pardon, Milord, but only a fool goes to war in winter."

The smith's apprentice grew even paler at this comment and flicked Bryn a look of mute panic.

No one spoke to the Lord of Powys thus.

"I thank you for the reminder," Dylan growled. "Although I'm well aware of that fact."

Bryn had been his family's smithy for decades and served his father loyally. As such, Dylan let the comment pass. Silence stretched out between them, and Bryn broke eye contact, suddenly fascinated by the dirt floor of the forge—he knew he had over-stepped the mark.

"So it will be in the spring then, Milord?" the smithy finally asked.

"It may well have to be," Dylan replied. In truth, he was disappointed. He chafed at having to wait so long; he would have to organize housing and food for the coming months, for all the men he was rallying to him. Yet the last thing they needed was to be waylaid by snow and bitter cold.

As Bryn had pointed out, waging war in the midst of winter was a madman's quest.

***

Outside, it was a dazzlingly bright morning. The air was crisp and laced with the resin-scent of wood smoke. Merwenna hummed to herself as she carried the basket and soap down the steep wooden steps to the stone well in the stable yard below.

The view from this height was mesmerizing, and Merwenna paused half-way down the steps to admire it. The thatch roofs of Pengwern fell away beneath her, amid a riot of autumn colors, into the rocky valley. The roar of the nearby falls filled her ears, as did the rise and fall of men's voices in the yard below.

Her gaze shifted from the view and fastened upon Dylan. He was talking with a small group of warriors in the center of the yard. Men moved around him, carrying battered weapons and shields toward the smithy. The forge lay behind the stables, and the clang of iron against iron drew her attention.

Merwenna winced at the noise, her gaze traveling around the yard, taking in the industry going on there.

Is he preparing himself for war already?

The prince had only been home a day, and it appeared he was hard at work readying himself to leave again.

Anxiety curled itself into a tight knot in Merwenna's belly. Beorn's loss had been terrible enough, but she could not bear the thought of losing Dylan as well.

He's not yours to lose, a cruel voice reminded her. *You are not his wife.*

Merwenna took a deep breath to quell her rising panic. Life here would only be bearable with Dylan at her side. If he left, she would be reviled once more. And if he never returned, she would be cast out, or worse.

Her light mood gone, Merwenna continued down the steps. Once she reached the bottom, she made her way to the well and filled a wooden pail with water in preparation for washing the princess's soiled clothes.

It was then she felt someone's gaze upon her and glanced up from her task. Across the yard, despite the fact that he was still deep in conversation with his men, Dylan stared at her. His gaze seared hers, and the intensity of it took her breath away. This man's sensuality and appetite thrilled her; she could hardly wait till they were alone once more.

Yet the prospect of war had now cast its dark shadow over her fragile happiness. The unfairness of matters choked Merwenna, and she turned back to her chore, her emotions in turmoil.

It truly was a man's world. Warriors lived and died by the sword while women stayed behind and picked up the broken pieces.

"We will need at least a thousand men. Perhaps even double that, if we wish to beat Penda."

Owain spoke quietly, his lean face uncharacteristically tense this morning. Dylan had just emerged from the smithy and had stopped to exchange a few words with Gwyn and Owain. As soon as Owain began to speak, he noted that something was worrying the warrior.

It had also not escaped Dylan that they would need a formidable army to take on Penda. Like Owain, he had witnessed the Mercian fyrd with Penda at the helm. He had once reflected that he had been relieved to be on Penda's side, not opposing him. Here he was planning to do just that.

"You fear them," Dylan observed, "and rightly so."

He clapped Owain on the shoulder and met the younger man's gaze steadily. "Yet matched with the same numbers, we can beat them. We will not go into battle until we are ready. I want reckoning for our people—I have no intention of sending my men to senseless slaughter."

Owain nodded, although Dylan saw the flicker of doubt in his eyes. It seemed the warrior, who had fought so bravely at Maes Cogwy, had lost his stomach for battle. Dylan knew Owain had a young family here and that he was loath to leave them again so soon, but that was the sacrifice a warrior must make—one they would all have to make.

Dylan glanced in Merwenna's direction. He had seen her make her way down to the well, where she now knelt, scrubbing wet clothes. She was a vision in that woolen dress; its color matched her eyes. Unlike the wealca she had worn till now, this garment hugged her curves—making her seem older, more womanly.

She caught him staring and boldly returned his gaze. Her lips had parted slightly, and he saw the rise and fall of her breast quicken.

He too would be leaving someone behind.

Suddenly Dylan understood Owain's reluctance. Until now, he'd had no ties here beyond kin. Now there was Merwenna, and although their passion was still fresh, he knew that when the time came, it would be a wrench to leave her.

Merwenna looked away then, her gaze shuttered. He could see that she brooded upon something. He wished to know what it was, but she had distracted him from his conversation long enough.

Regretfully, Dylan turned his own attention back to his men and to talk of war.

Chapter Thirty-eight

The Prince's Consort

Merwenna carried an earthen jug of plum wine from table to table, filling cups as they emptied.

Tonight, she served the Prince of Powys, his kin and retainers. This time, she was not hauling pots and platters around. None of the servants appeared to be happy with this arrangement, but all of them minded their lord and did not voice their discontent. Even so, Merwenna caught the sour looks and muttered comments directed at her, whenever she returned to the servants' galley to refill the jug.

After a while, she became deaf and blind to their resentment. She only hoped that in time they would grow to accept her presence here.

Tonight's evening meal was considerably less lavish than the night before, consisting of a simple pottage and dumplings. The cooks had their hands full preparing for the great feast, in just two days, which would celebrate both their victory against the Northumbrians and Dylan's coronation.

Wagons laden with meat, produce, grains, cheeses, and nuts had been trundling in all afternoon, and the store houses beneath the Great Hall were now packed to the rafters with food. Inside the hall itself, work had begun in earnest in preparing the array of rich dishes for the celebrations. Merwenna had lent a hand in the afternoon; plucking geese that would be stuffed with bread, onions, and chestnuts and roasted for the feast. Despite that no one was talking to her, Merwenna had enjoyed the industry inside the hall and the gathering excitement for a celebration that would involve, not just the Great Hall, but all of Pengwern.

Merwenna refilled the cup of an ealdorman's wife and glanced wistfully up the table, her gaze resting upon Dylan. Although she was grateful not to be lugging an iron cauldron of boiling soup around the table, she wished she could have been seated there, at Dylan's side.

That's what a night in a prince's bed does to a woman, she chided herself. *Next, you'll be demanding he wed you.*

All the same, she longed to be at his side.

Dylan caught her eye then and motioned for her to draw near. Ignoring the warrior next to her, who had just held out his cup to be filled, Merwenna went. As she neared the prince, she saw that Dylan was speaking to his uncle and brother. They broke off their conversation upon her arrival.

"Wine, Milord?" she asked Dylan in Cymraeg.

"Aye, just a drop," he replied, his eyes smiling at her.

"Fill mine up too, wench," Morfael held his own cup to her. Merwenna dropped her own gaze demurely and obeyed him. It was not wise to appear too bold around Dylan's kin. She moved to also refill Dylan's uncle's cup, but Elfan warned her off with a scowl. Merwenna's gaze moved across the table to where Heledd sat, to find the princess frowning at her.

"Wine, Milady?"

"No," Heledd responded flatly.

Merwenna took that as her cue to move on. She turned to make her way back down the table and cast a glance back at Dylan as she did so—he was watching her.

They shared a secret smile.

"It will not be borne," Heledd muttered between clenched teeth, just loud enough for those surrounding her to catch her words—Dylan among them.

"What won't, dear sister?" The prince dragged his gaze from where Merwenna leaned over to refill one of his men's cups. That gown hugged her curves indecently; he did not want her serving other men. Instead, he wanted Merwenna here, sitting at his side.

"That girl," Heledd replied, her emerald gaze snapping. "You parade her in front of us."

Dylan leaned back in his carved chair. He took a sip of tart, plum wine, regarding his sister over the rim of his cup. "Do I need to ask your permission, Heledd?"

The princess flushed and looked down at her pottage. Yet Dylan could see the fury that vibrated from her slender body.

"Your sister is too well-bred to say it, but she merely voices what we all think," Elfan growled. "We don't want your Mercian whore here. She's leading you around by your cock, and making a fool of you. Send her back to the peasant's hovel from whence she came and find yourself a consort worthy of the ruler of Powys."

The conversation around them died. His uncle's gruff voice echoed through the hall.

A heartbeat of silence followed before Dylan acted. One moment the prince had been lounging in his chair, cup in hand—the next, he moved—so quickly that Elfan never even saw him coming.

Dylan leaped across the table and slammed his fist into his uncle's mouth.

Elfan toppled backward off the benches onto the rushes, his cup flying in one direction, his meal in the other.

Dylan stood over him, fist clenched. Around him, a hush filled the hall. He knew its residents had witnessed plenty of scenes similar to this in the past between Dylan and Morfael, when the brothers were younger and more hot-headed. However, it had been a while since anyone had seen him lose his temper with one of his uncles.

Elfan had left Dylan no other choice.

His uncle stared up at him, blood trickling down his chin. Dylan saw the outrage in his eyes but also the shadow of fear.

"Do you have anything else to say, uncle?" the prince asked, the softness of his voice belying the rage that pulsed through him. He felt angry enough to kill the man if he uttered another word against Merwenna. Perhaps Elfan sensed this, for he shook his head.

"No, Milord," he replied thickly, through bloodied lips.

"Good," Dylan straightened up and cast a glance over the faces of his silent brother and sister. "Let that be a warning to you all. My patience is at an end."

His gaze met Merwenna's then. She was standing at the end of the table, grasping the jug of wine to her breast. Her blue eyes were huge on her heart-shaped face, and he saw her alarm, her fear.

She knows that was about her.

Dylan looked away from Merwenna and back down at his uncle. To everyone present, it would seem he had overreacted. Yet he felt a fierce protectiveness over the young Mercian woman he had made his lover. He would not tolerate another word against her.

***

Merwenna carefully brushed out Heledd's hair, gently untangling the knots in her dark, wavy hair with a bone comb. They were in the princess's bower. Heledd sat upon a low stool and Merwenna stood behind her. A clay cresset burned against one wall, casting a golden light across the tiny space. Outside, the gentle rise and fall of voices could be heard, quietening now as the hall's residents bedded down for the night.

"Merwenna," Heledd broke the lengthy silence between them, surprising her hand-maid, for this was the first time the princess had addressed her directly, using her name.

"Yes, Milady," she replied cautiously.

"How did you meet my brother?"

Merwenna gave a pained smile, glad the princess could not see her face. She read the hidden meaning behind the question.

How did two people from such two different worlds come together?

"In Tamworth," she replied, finally. "I had traveled there to look for my betrothed. A warrior named Beorn who rode off to Maes Cogwy with Penda's fyrd. I had gone before King Penda, for I could not find Beorn amongst the men returning from war, and asked him of my betrothed. Penda did not recall him, but Lord Cynddylan did. He confirmed that Beorn had perished in battle."

Heledd had gone very still.

Merwenna concentrated on combing through the last section of her hair, before she set the comb aside and stepped back.

"There, Milady. I'm finished. You have lovely hair." It was the truth, Heledd's hair shone like liquid silk in the soft light.

"Thank you." Heledd swiveled round on the stool to regard her. The princess's gaze was not hostile, as it had been earlier. Neither was it friendly.

"I've never seen Dylan like this," she admitted. "He has spent his life preparing himself to rule, to be the king his father was. He knows he will have to take a wife one day but women have never swayed him—till now."

Merwenna gazed back at the princess, not sure how to respond. There was an accusing note to Heledd's voice that warned Merwenna against lowering her guard.

"No one is more surprised by all of this than me," Merwenna replied. "My life was in Weyham, with my family and the man I was to wed. Fate has played a cruel trick in bringing me here. This is not the future I would have chosen."

Heledd's gaze narrowed. "Do you love him?"

The question took Merwenna's breath away. She really wished Heledd had not asked that—for it was the subject that she had made a point of avoiding of late.

Love. She once thought she knew exactly what that meant, but these days the meaning had blurred. These days, such feelings were complicated by guilt, by duty. The truth of matters could not be hidden from—it had been staring her in the face for days now. Heledd had made her confront it.

Silence stretched between the two young women, and Heledd frowned. Merwenna's lack of response damned her.

"Well, do you?"

"Yes," Merwenna replied, her voice barely above a whisper. "I do."

The princess's frown eased, and a glimmer of warmth flickered in the depths of those green eyes, so similar to Dylan's. She nodded and rose to her feet, signaling that their conversation was at an end.

Merwenna backed away, toward the tapestry. She had just grasped hold of it and was about to slip outside, when the princess spoke once more.

"Since our mother died there has been so little happiness in this hall," she murmured. "So little laughter. Just the voices of men; talking of war, of borders, pacts, and promises—and now, reckoning. It is good to see my brother smile, to see him care for more than waging war on our neighbors. Could you not soften him, convince him to cast his need for vengeance aside?"

Merwenna paused and her gaze met the princess's once more. "If only I could turn him from this course," she replied with a sad smile. "Happiness is hard won and easily lost—but your brother may come to learn that too late."

Chapter Thirty-nine

Last Words

Dylan lay on his back, staring up at the rafters, and gently stroked his lover's back. Merwenna faced him, tucked into his side. The warmth of her breath tickled his skin. The sweet scent of her wrapped him in a silken curtain. He was aware that she also drowsed, enjoying the languor that had followed their passion.

He had never felt so relaxed, so at peace with the world as he did at that moment. It was as if nothing else mattered.

He had never known a woman like Merwenna. The sight of her, the touch of her, the smell and taste of her, branded him like fire. Each time they came together, the aftermath left him laid bare. He was just recalling how she had ridden him tonight—firelight playing across her beautiful breasts, her head thrown back as she groaned in pleasure—when Merwenna's voice, edged with sleepiness, intruded.

"That axe—is it yours?"

Dylan's gaze followed hers, across his quarters to where the great war-axe hung from the wall.

"No," he murmured. "It was my father's. He took it from his enemy—a chieftain who tried to seize power from him, and paid for his treachery with his life. The weapon saw many battles before my father hung it on the wall for the last time a few years ago."

"You've never fought with it?"

"No—the axe isn't my weapon of choice. I'm not built for it. I prefer to fight with my father's sword in my hand."

Merwenna propped herself up on her elbow and gazed down at him, her eyes dark and troubled.

"Do you love to fight?"

Dylan gave a soft chuckle, surprised by the question. "I wouldn't call it 'love' exactly. It's the life I was born to. I do it because I must—it's all I know."

"But what if you stopped?"

"Then Pengwern would fall. Kingdoms sit upon a knife-edge—it takes little to topple them. I fight to keep everything I hold dear safe."

Merwenna stared down at him, but he could tell she was not appeased.

"What is it?" he asked, finally. "You are chewing over something, are you not?"

"I don't want you to ride against Penda," she replied, her face the most serious he had ever seen it. "I don't want to lose you."

Dylan stared back at Merwenna. Frankly, he was torn between being irritated at her interference and being touched by her candor.

"I told you why I must go to war," he replied, his voice hardening slightly. "A king cannot betray another—as Penda did—and go unpunished."

"But you could die, do you not ever think on it?"

Dylan sighed and resisted the urge to roll his eyes. Why did women look upon war in such simplistic terms?

"I could . . . but then I could choke on a piece of meat in my own hall. What valor is there in such an end? There is no greater death for a warrior than in battle—you know that."

"You would rather have songs written about you than live?" she accused him, anger kindling in her gaze. "What good are songs to those who mourn you? Beorn thought as you, but he had never experienced battle. He'd never seen what it does to those who are left behind. I expected better of a man who knows the truth of what he faces."

Merwenna gazed into Dylan's eyes and knew that she had angered him.

She had not meant the conversation to travel this far. She had been luxuriating in the aftermath of their lovemaking, when her gaze had alighted upon that war-axe. The menacing weapon cast a gloomy shadow over the whole space. She had wondered at the axe's significance and had wanted to ask him of it.

Now, she wished she had not.

They were now discussing the very matter that had been tormenting her. After her conversation with Heledd, she had not been able to think of anything else. The more she spoke, the less he seemed to understand

Dylan's face had tensed, and his gaze had narrowed dangerously. Her last comment had clearly offended his pride. A man's pride was a fragile thing—and she wished she had chosen her words more carefully.

Watching him, Merwenna felt her pulse start to quicken. She had not meant to anger him; she had only wanted to make him comprehend. But she had not told him what was in her heart—the real reason she did want him to go.

"You speak of what you do not understand," he said, his voice cold now. He moved away, so they were no longer touching. He then sat up and frowned down at her.

"I understand enough," she countered, her own anger rising. Did he think her a fool?

“No, you don’t. This is the life of a ruler. If a man will not go to war to protect his people, then he has no right being king.”

“You’re not going to war to protect them,” Merwenna sat up and faced him. “Vengeance is about your vanity and nothing else.”

He stared at her, his gaze narrowing dangerously. Merwenna knew now that she had gone too far. It was too late to turn back. She had better say all of it.

Trembling with the force of her anger, Merwenna rose to her feet and reached for her clothes. All the while, Dylan watched her.

“My vanity?” he echoed, as if unable to believe she had insulted him thus.

“If you go to war against Mercia, I cannot stay here,” she told him, tying her girdle about her waist. “The folk here hate me already. Having one of the enemy living under their own roof will be more than they can bear. Without your protection, my life will be in danger.”

“No one here will harm you,” he ground out, rising to his feet to face her.

“You can’t promise that,” she replied. “Once you’re gone, they can do what they want. And if you never return they can stone me to death, if it pleases them.”

“So that’s what’s bothering you.” Dylan folded his arms across his bare chest and glared at her. “You’re not worried about my welfare—it’s your own that concerns you.”

Merwenna gasped. His accusation was cruel and unfair—how could he think so badly of her? This was all going wrong. He misunderstood her at every turn.

“You know that’s not true,” she choked out. “Are you so arrogant that you cannot see past your own nose? Do as you please, for I see my words mean nothing to you—but know this—if you go to march on Mercia, I will leave Pengwern.”

“And where will you go?”

He was taunting her now, the look in his eyes making her feel small and silly, like a child throwing a tantrum.

"You are no longer welcome in Weyham," he reminded her. "Your father won't be pleased to see you darken his door."

"That's no concern of yours," she snarled at him. "I'll go where I please."

"That's where you're wrong," he stepped toward her, intimidating in his nakedness. "I swore an oath to your father, remember?"

"I release you from it."

"That's not your decision but your father's."

"*Nithhogg* take you both," Merwenna spat at him. "I belong to neither of you. To think I have given my body, and my heart, to a conceited churl who disregards everything I say and turns my own words against me. Can't you see why I wouldn't want you to die in battle? Are you that blind?"

Dylan stared at her, clearly rendered speechless by her outburst. Yet Merwenna ploughed on, heedless to the consequences.

"Go then, wreak your vengeance upon Penda. But if you do return to Pengwern, I won't be here waiting for you."

She was so angry that she could have lashed out and struck him. Instead, Merwenna whirled and fled from Dylan's quarters so that he would not see the tears that had obscured her vision.

Stunned silence followed her.

Chapter Forty

The Peace-maker

Caedmon rode up the steep slope toward the gates of Pengwern and craned his neck upwards to catch a glimpse of the Great Hall. The magnificent timbered building perched high upon a rocky outcrop above a sea of thatched roofs, a sentinel over the surrounding lands.

The warrior had not imagined that Pengwern sat in such an isolated spot, or in such a lofty position. The views of the valley below were so vertiginous that the ride up to the gates had made him queasy. Whenever he glanced away from the road, the horizon had whirled, making him feel as if he would topple from the saddle at any moment.

The sight of the gates ahead brought relief, for their journey's end lay close at hand. Glancing back at the small company that rode with him, the reason for his arrival cast a shadow over his relief.

It was a small price to pay for his life, yet not a task he wanted.

There was nothing to say that the Prince of Powys would not reject Penda's gift outright. He could easily send them back whence they came—and if he did,

Caedmon's execution upon his return to Tamworth was certain.

Caedmon gritted his teeth and pushed down his cowl so that the guards at the gate could see his face. This was a humiliating errand, to supplicate himself on behalf of the King of Mercia stuck in his craw.

He had been one of the first to agree to Rodor's call when he had received orders from Penda to assassinate Cynddylan. It mattered not that his mother was one of the Cymry—he felt no sense of allegiance to these people. The fact that his mixed blood had made him a victim of bullies as a child had made him hate his mother's people all the more. Cynddylan's arrogance had grated upon him, and he had hungered to see Cynddylan brought low.

Only now wyrd had turned against him, and it was Caedmon who would have to beg for his life.

"Halt!" a helmeted guard blocked Caedmon's way before the gates. "State your name and business here."

"I come from Tamworth," Caedmon replied in fluent Cymraeg. "I bring a gift from King Penda of Mercia for Lord Cynddylan."

"A gift?" the guard regarded him skeptically. "And what might that be? We need no gift from that traitorous whoreson!"

Caedmon ignored the insult and turned in the saddle. He focused his attention on the small cloaked figure in the midst of his men.

"My lady," he commanded, "come forth."

The figure urged its mount forward and drew level with Caedmon. Then a pale, slender hand reached up and pushed back the cowl shielding the rider's identity. The girl, as fair as summer blossom despite the fear shadowing her eyes and the pallor of her cheeks, stared back at him.

"This is Penda's gift," Caedmon informed the guard coolly. "His youngest daughter—Princess Cyneswith."

***

A hush had descended upon the Great Hall, and all gazes riveted upon the newcomers.

Merwenna had been sitting near one of the hearths, mending one of Heledd's gowns while the princess worked at her distaff beside her, when the party entered. She had been focused upon her task, trying to distract herself from the misery that gripped her innards in a vice, when the hall went still.

Now, her gaze also tracked the small group that crossed the rush-strewn floor toward the high seat.

For once, the inhabitants of the hall were not glaring at her but at the tall, spare man with greasy blond hair and a sparse beard who led the way. Encased in boiled leather, he walked with a warrior's arrogance, his travel-stained cloak rippling behind him. At his side walked a small, blonde girl wearing a fur-lined cloak. Four more warriors brought up the rear.

Even from a distance, Merwenna knew they were not from Powys. Her breath hitched in her throat as the party passed by.

That's Penda's daughter!

The girl did not glance her way; her blue-eyes were fixed ahead, her chin trembling as she sought to control her fear. She was the younger of the two. Although neither of the princesses had shown any warmth to Merwenna during her time in the Great Tower of Tamworth, she felt a stab of pity for the girl. She was plainly terrified.

The party halted before the high seat, where Dylan waited.

Around them, the Great Hall bore the signs of the coming celebration. Garlands of late blooms hung from the rafters. Servants had been busy removing the soiled rushes and replacing them with clean ones, and the aroma of baking pies and cakes mingled with the smell of lye and rosemary from their cleaning.

The blond warrior who led the newcomers paid no heed to what surrounded him. His gaze was fastened upon the Prince of Powys. Dylan reclined in his chair, darkly handsome in a dark blue, sleeveless tunic, and leather breeches. His brother flanked him to his right, his uncle Elfan to his left.

The sight of Dylan made Merwenna's chest ache.

He had not come after her last night, had not tried to mend things between them. But then, why would he? He was the ruler of Powys, and she was nothing but a foolish girl who had made a grave error in judgement. Merwenna had lain on the fur outside Heledd's bower for the rest of the night, trying to stifle her sobs. Never had she felt so alone—so foolish, so lost.

"I hear that Penda has a gift for me," the prince spoke, intruding upon Merwenna's thoughts. His face was impassive, his gaze watchful as it rested, first upon the warrior's face, and then upon the girl's.

"Yes, Milord," the blond warrior rumbled. "He offers you Princess Cyneswith, to atone for the treacherous behavior of his men."

Dylan frowned at that. "His men? So Penda does not claim responsibility for sending them to slay me?"

"No, he does not," the warrior replied flatly. "Those men took the decision to hunt you by their own accord and not with his blessing."

The man then bent his head and lowered himself onto one knee. Looking on, Merwenna noted the tension in his body. She could see he was hating every moment of this but forced himself on nonetheless.

"You are the loyal ally of Mercia. Lord Penda would not wish to jeopardize the trust between our kingdoms."

"Yet his men did," Dylan replied. His gaze had narrowed, and it was plain from his expression, and from those of the men who flanked him, that he did not believe a word.

"Those men betrayed Penda," the warrior replied, his gaze downcast, "but he understands your anger."

"Does he?" Dylan steepled his hands before him, his gaze narrowing further. "I wonder, if that is the truth."

"He does," the man insisted, glancing up. Merwenna caught a note of desperation in his tone. "He wishes to mend things between our kingdoms—and for that reason he offers you his beloved daughter, Cyneswith."

All gazes shifted to the young woman who stood silent next to the kneeling warrior.

She stood, her back ramrod straight, her eyes glistening with tears. Her long, blonde hair, as pale as sea-foam, fell unbound over her shoulders. Watching her, Merwenna could not help but feel a stab of jealousy at the princess's regal beauty. And, at the same time, the misery within her turned to desolation.

No matter what Dylan's decision, whether he made peace or went to war, she would lose him.

"A peace-maker," Dylan mused, with a cold smile.

The man kneeling before him was a poor liar and was not the type to kneel so readily. Dylan wondered what he had done to warrant such humiliation.

"He would sacrifice his tender daughter to prevent war between us?"

"He would, Milord."

Dylan leaned back in his throne and inhaled slowly. This was an interesting development although he was in no mood for it. It was clearly a ruse. Penda had discovered what had happened to his men and sought to avoid war between them. Still, it was unexpected.

The prince's gaze left the two figures before him and traveled over the faces of those observing the meeting. Most of them did not speak, nor understand, Englisc, but he wagered they had guessed the meaning of their words well enough. Dylan's gaze then fell upon Merwenna, and although he had told himself he would not seek her out, it rested there.

She stood by one of the fire pits next to his sister, the garment she had been mending clutched in her hands. Her face was pale and strained. Her gaze met his for a moment, and he felt his breath leave him.

Damn her.

Merwenna of Weyham had bewitched him. Even now, when he should be focusing on other matters, she drew him to her, disarmed him. She had angered him last night. Some of her words had struck a nerve, and try as he might he could not cast them aside.

Clenching his jaw, Dylan looked away from Merwenna, his gaze returning to the pale beauty before him. She looked barely old enough to be handfasted. Penda was a heartless bastard for sending her here.

"Penda asks much," Dylan finally answered, "and I am not sure I wish to grant him this favor. However, you have traveled far and will be hungry and weary. You will be my guests tonight."

"Thank you, Milord," the warrior looked up, his gaze meeting Dylan's. In his eyes, Dylan saw no gratitude, only emptiness.

"Tomorrow I will be crowned," Dylan continued. "Once I am king, I shall give you my answer. Now, get to your feet man. You'll wear out the knees of your breeches prostrating yourself before me."

***

"One Mercian among us was hard to accept—but two of you." Heledd led the way up to her bower, not bothering to hide the exasperation in her voice. "Soon we will be overrun."

Yet, despite Heledd's indignation, Merwenna also sensed resignation there as well; the princess was clearly a survivor and adapted quickly to new circumstances.

Princess Cyneswith said nothing, looking at neither Heledd nor Merwenna. Instead, she followed them into Heledd's bower meekly, her gaze downcast. In contrast to Merwenna's reaction, the small but comfortably furnished space did not make her gawk with envy. Merwenna remembered the princesses' lovely bower in Tamworth's Great Tower and knew why.

"There is little space here, but Merwenna will make up a bed for you next to mine."

Cyneswith stirred then, her gaze shifting to Merwenna—as if seeing her for the first time.

"I remember you," she said, her voice as flat as her eyes, "from Tamworth."

Merwenna nodded.

"What are you doing here?"

"It's a long tale," Merwenna replied, forcing a wry smile.

"One that she won't bore you with," Heledd cut in. "Merwenna, take some of my furs and make up a bed for Cyneswith over there. After you've done that, organize the servants to bring a tub in here for the princess to bathe."

Merwenna nodded, although she could not help feel a tug of resentment.

Heledd had not welcomed Merwenna in such a fashion. The unfairness of it should not have stung her, but it did nonetheless. She left Heledd's bower without another word and went to do her bidding.

Chapter Forty-one

No Friendship between Kings

Dylan took a seat upon a low bench, next to his brother and uncle. They were playing *Gwyddbwyll*, a game in which the two players moved carved figurines across a wooden board that had been inlaid with squares of gold. As usual, Morfael was winning—and was just moves away from taking Elfan's king. Elfan was looking none too pleased about it.

Dylan stretched his legs out in front of the fire, grateful that their attention was drawn by the game. It was getting late, and he was not in the mood for another discussion.

It had been a wearying day. As soon as Penda's emissary, Caedmon, was out of earshot, his kin had made it clear they thought Penda's gift contemptuous.

He was inclined to agree with them.

He had not refused the gift outright and would sleep upon it. Unlike his kin, who were keen to see Penda's daughter and her entourage ejected from the hall, he had decided to wait before taking action. Dylan needed to reflect on what the King of Mercia's generous gift really signified.

"You're pensive this eve, brother," Morfael said, taking his uncle's king, and sitting back with a grin of triumph. "Surely, you're not considering Penda's offer?"

"Of course he isn't," Elfan cut in with a scowl. His lips were still swollen from where Dylan had struck him.

"The thought of wedding Penda's daughter does not thrill me," Dylan admitted, "but I am curious as to why he made the offer. He needs me."

"He sought to kill you," Morfael reminded him. "It makes no sense to pacify you now."

"Yes, but he values our allegiance," Dylan replied with a cool smile. "Penda still has many battles left to fight, much territory to conquer. He would call upon Powys again and does not want to make an enemy of us just yet."

His uncle made a rude noise at that, his gaze shifting to the other side of the hall where Heledd, Cyneswith and Merwenna worked at a large loom, upon a tapestry.

"Mercians will always be my enemy," he growled, "and there are too many of them under this roof for my liking. When will we be rid of them?"

Dylan and Morfael's gazes followed Elfan's.

Dylan could not help but notice that his brother's gaze lingered upon Cyneswith.

"The Mercian princess is fair, is she not?" he asked Morfael lightly.

His brother gave a sly smile although his gaze did not shift from where the Mercian princess delicately wound thread onto a spindle. "Very," he replied.

Elfan spat on the ground and rose to his feet. Without bidding either nephew good night, he strode off, evidently disgusted by the turn the conversation had taken.

"He's in a foul mood this eve," Dylan observed. "Who pissed in his pottage?"

"You did," Morfael replied, shifting his gaze from the winsome Cyneswith to his brother. "He doesn't understand why you didn't send them away this morning."

"Elfan sees the world as it was, not as it is," Dylan countered. "He lives in the past and has never been able to accept that Mercia and Powys are now allies."

"Only we're not really friends. Penda would betray you again in a heartbeat."

"As would any ruler I allied myself with," Dylan reminded him. "It's no different to Gwyddbwyll, even if we pretend otherwise. The moment one of us has the upper hand, we take it. There is no friendship between kings."

Letting this sobering fact lie between them, Dylan's gaze shifted from the dancing flames of the fire pit. His gaze settled upon where Merwenna worked, her head bent over her task. He had avoided her all day. They had not spoken since she had fled from his quarters last night, and he wished to mend things between them. His bed was lonely without her. He missed her more than he would have liked to admit. Yet, with the arrival of Penda's daughter, and the possibility he might wed her, Dylan suspected that Merwenna would not welcome him.

Even so, his gaze lingered upon her, willing her to look his way.

"You're in over your head with that girl."

Dylan glanced back at his brother and frowned. He thought about denying it. He and Morfael had been rivals for so long, he did not like his brother to see any vulnerability that he could exploit to his own ends. Morfael had seen the direction of his gaze, and the naked longing in his eyes. Was there any point in lying to him?

"Aye," he murmured. "I should have seen it coming, but I thought she wouldn't get the best of me."

Morfael raised a dark eyebrow and poured himself a cup of mead. "That's unlike you."

"No, I'm usually a lot more careful. Merwenna took me by surprise."

"She doesn't belong here—any more than Penda's daughter."

Dylan gave his brother a dark look. "That's only because she has been ostracized from the moment she set foot in Pengwern."

Morfael shrugged and placed his cup down beside the Gwyddbwyll board.

Dylan watched his brother rearrange the wooden figurines on the board before him and realized Morfael was preparing himself for another game.

"I'm not in the mood to play again," Dylan growled. "Don't you ever tire of beating me at it?"

"Come, brother," Morfael flashed him a disarming smile. "It has been months since we played last. Let me best you in one thing, at least."

***

Merwenna could not sleep.

She lay on her back, on the fur outside Heledd's bower, and stared up into the darkness. There were no tears tonight—her despair went deeper than that. The unfairness of it all choked her. If Dylan wed Cyneswith, he would not march to war, and yet he would be lost to her all the same. She had grieved when she lost Beorn and thought no pain could surpass that. But she had been wrong. This actually felt worse.

Merwenna and Dylan would be living under the same roof. She would be forced to see him and his queen every day. She would see Cyneswith's belly swell with his babe. The thought caused her to curl up like a wounded animal and clutch her own stomach. How would she bear it?

She could run away, as she had already planned to if Dylan went to war. He would be keeping watch on her, expecting her to do something foolish. No, she would be made to stay—to suffer.

"Merwenna," Dylan's whisper, near her ear, catapulted her out of her misery.

His presence here was a painful reminder of two days earlier, just before they had lain together for the first time. So much had happened since then—so much had changed.

She sat up, glad that she had not been weeping. Not that he could see if she had, for the light was only dim enough for her to make out his silhouette crouched before her.

"What is it?" she whispered coolly. Surely, he did not assume she would return to his bed? Not after what had passed between them last night. Not after today.

"Will you walk with me?" he whispered back. "I would speak with you awhile."

Merwenna hesitated. Her first impulse was to refuse him, for hurt still burned within her. However, there was a gentleness to his voice, a humility that she had never heard before. It would be their last chance to speak before he was crowned tomorrow.

"Very well," she murmured, rising to her feet. "I will need to fetch a cloak."

"I have one for you," Dylan replied. Before she could reply, he had settled a thick fur about her shoulders. It was much thicker and warmer than the woolen cloak she usually wore. Merwenna wordlessly accepted it.

"Come." He took hold of her hand and led her through the darkness. They stepped off the platform and skirted the edge of the Great Hall, picking their way around and across sleeping bodies as they went. The only light was the faint glow of embers from the two fire pits. Dylan moved with the confidence of a man who had often crept away from the hall under the cover of darkness as a youth.

They reached the oaken doors and slipped outside. It was cold, and a chill breeze feathered across Merwenna's cheeks. Dylan paused a moment and retrieved a pitch torch from where it burned in a bracket against the wall. Now that she could see him, Merwenna noted that Dylan too wore a thick fur cloak about his shoulders.

"Pengwern is magical at night," Dylan told her as they descended the wooden steps. "Bathed in moonlight."

Merwenna did not reply. He was in an odd, pensive, mood. Yet she liked it and was loath to shatter the moment. Indeed, it was lovely outside, despite the chill. From the stairs she could see the glow of fires in the valley below, lighting the darkness like fireflies.

They crossed the yard and passed through the gate beneath. Dylan greeted the guards there before leading the way into the streets beyond. Pengwern was deserted at this hour. They walked alone through the narrow dirt streets lined by squat wattle and daub dwellings. Overhead, the moon lit their way. Like in Weyham, folk here worked hard from dawn till dusk. Few lingered outdoors after nightfall, preferring to stretch out in front of their fire pits and rest their weary limbs.

Dylan and Merwenna walked in silence for a short while, before he wordlessly took her arm and tucked it through his.

"I spent my childhood playing in these streets," Dylan told her, "when our father wasn't teaching us to hunt and fight, Morfael and I would play hide and seek here until fæder would send someone out to look for us. We'd get our arses tanned for that."

Merwenna imagined Dylan as a small boy and, despite the misery that churned her up inside, fought a smile. "You were full of mischief?"

"I was."

They continued walking through the tangle of narrow lanes till the way widened and the houses drew back. Here, they stepped out onto a wide ledge of rock surrounded by thick green foliage. Moonlight cast a silver veil out across the valley. The thundering waterfalls sparkled as if alive, and the magnificence of the view made Merwenna catch her breath.

"It's enchanting."

"This is my favorite corner of Pengwern," Dylan admitted quietly.

Merwenna gave him a quick look and found him watching her. The light from the flickering torch he carried cast his face in gold, threw his eyes into shadow and highlighted the sharp angles of his cheekbones—making him look every bit the battle lord he was.

As always, his nearness made it difficult for her to breathe.

"Why did you bring me here?" she asked.

Dylan stared back at her, a wistful smile curving his lips. "My hall is full of flapping ears and wagging tongues. I wanted to speak with you, alone."

Merwenna nodded, not trusting herself to speak then, for a lump had wedged itself in her throat.

"Tomorrow will change many things." Dylan had stepped closer to her so that they stood just a hand span apart. The heat and scent of his skin made her limbs weaken. Then, he reached out and gently stroked her face. "A battle or a bride—what should I do, cariad?"

"You . . . w . . . want me to tell you?" Merwenna stuttered, distracted by his sensual touch.

"I want to know what you would advise, yes."

Merwenna took a deep, trembling breath. "I would have you choose the path that will not lead you to war."

"You would see me wed Penda's daughter?" The surprise in Dylan's voice was evident.

"If it means you stay safe, yes."

Dylan's smile twisted into something darker. "Ah, Merwenna. You wouldn't keep me safe forever—there will always be other battles, other enemies."

"But I would from this one."

Silence stretched between them for a few moments before Dylan spoke once more.

"Last night, you said that you had given me your heart. Is that the truth?"

Merwenna swallowed. She had regretted being so open with him, as soon as the words were out of her mouth—but, she could not undo them. "Yes," she whispered.

"So pure, so beautiful, so proud," Dylan murmured, stepping closer still. "I do not want to lose you."

Merwenna's throat closed and tears stung her eyes. Had she heard right—did he care for her? Would he fight for her?

"We could still be together, even if I wed Cyneswith," Dylan continued, his voice smooth as honey. "Why can't a king can have a wife, *and* a lover?"

Merwenna inhaled sharply. Suddenly, winter descended upon their lofty ledge. She abruptly stepped back from the prince, so they were no longer touching, and pulled the fur cloak tightly about her shaking body.

"That may be your plan," she bit off the words, breathless in the rage that suddenly consumed her, "but I will have no part of it."

She sensed Dylan's shock. He dropped his hand and stared at her.

He was offering her a life many women would grasp with both hands—and here she was throwing it back in his face.

I will not share him with another woman.

She would rather lose him forever than travel such a road.

"You are too proud," he said, finally, his voice rough with hurt. "I cannot give you what you want."

Merwenna stared back at him, disappointment bitter gall in her mouth. "Then I shall have nothing at all," she replied.

Chapter Forty-two

The Crowning of Cynddylan

The morning of the coronation dawned bright and fresh. Yet, even before the first rays of sun warmed the edge of the Great Hall of Pengwern, its inhabitants were already hard at work.

Servants hurried to and fro, making the final preparations for the celebration and the great feast that was to follow. They hung the last of the garlands and scattered fragrant bunches of rosemary, thyme, and sage over the clean rushes. Then they cleared the space for all those who would cram themselves inside the Great Hall to catch a glimpse of the crowning of Cynddylan.

Merwenna took a cup of hot broth and made her way past where the cooks were rolling out pastry for the apple and blackberry pies for the feast. She had just finished helping both Heledd and Cyneswith dress and had paused to break her fast before she would brush and braid their hair.

None of the servants looked up as Merwenna walked by. Reaching the end of the hall, she stepped out onto the platform outside and paused there to look out across the valley.

A brisk breeze caught at her unbound hair, whipping it around her face. Below, she could see that all of

Pengwern bore signs of the day's celebration. Garlands and streamers hung between the streets, and the smell of roasting mutton drifted up from where folk prepared a feast in the town's market square. This was a rare day of rest for those who spent their lives toiling in the fields or tending the livestock that fed Pengwern. Once the celebrations began, the reveling would go on long into the night.

Merwenna tightened her chill fingers around the cup, drawing in its warmth. Unlike those of Pengwern, this day brought her no joy. She had not thought she could feel any worse than she had upon Cyneswith's arrival.

Dylan's offer had completely crushed her. Her disappointment, both in him for thinking she merited such an arrangement, and in her for giving her heart so carelessly, made it hard to breathe. Sun warmed her face and the clouds scudded across the sky. Merriment surrounded her—but this morning, Merwenna felt nothing but despair.

Voices reached her, and Merwenna's gaze shifted from the view across Pengwern's thatched roofs to where a company of riders thundered into the yard below. They were warriors clad in leather, with lime shields on their backs and spears at their sides, astride stocky horses. The first of Dylan's chiefs had arrived, and many more would come before the crowning of Powys' new king at noon.

Merwenna sighed.

Enough wallowing in self-pity, she told herself. *You cannot fight fate. This is my life now.*

Like many things in life, knowing the truth, and accepting it, were entirely different matters.

***

Dylan slid on the last of his arm rings and held out his arm so Morfael could buckle on his arm guards. Unlike the leather guards he usually wore, which were battle-scarred and scuffed with use, these ones were made of embossed leather. They had been his father's, made for Cyndrwyn's own coronation many years earlier.

It felt strange to have his brother help dress him, for it served to highlight their difference in rank. Morfael had long chafed at being the younger brother, the one who never mattered to their father.

For years, Dylan had been sure Morfael had been plotting against him—and the sight of him reclining on the high seat like a lord upon Dylan's return to Pengwern had only made him more suspicious. Yet, over the last couple of days, Morfael's behavior toward him had become far less antagonistic. He had openly criticized Dylan for bringing Merwenna to Pengwern, but since then their rapport had been almost . . . brotherly.

"Nearly done," Morfael announced. He then reached for two gold clasps, stepped behind his brother, and fastened Dylan's long, purple cloak to his shoulders. Meanwhile, Dylan buckled his sword about his waist.

"I feel as if I'm going into battle," Dylan observed with a grim smile, glancing down at his mail shirt.

"In a way, you are," Morfael replied. "The people of Powys look to their king to guide them. You will receive the council of the gods. They will love you, and judge you, like never before."

"Thank you for the reminder," Dylan cast his brother a dark look.

Morfael grinned back, enjoying his own cleverness. "My pleasure."

Dylan bit back a cutting remark and slid jewel encrusted rings onto his fingers. It was not Morfael's fault he was bad tempered this morning. He should be jubilant; he had been waiting for this moment all his life.

A shadow now lay upon him.

Merwenna was to blame. Before meeting her, his life had been simple, his choices and purpose clear. She had turned all the things that had once mattered to him to dust. Now all he cared about was that he had upset her. He had made her a crass offer that had caused her to hate him.

I've been a fool.

The noise inside the Great Hall was deafening. It reached the brothers, even beyond the tapestry that shielded them from view. Folk had crammed inside, shoulder to shoulder—and now they were awaiting him. It was time for him to go before them. Dylan hesitated.

"What's wrong?" Morfael's gaze searched his face. "Not sure you want the crown after all?"

Dylan snorted rudely in response. The crown was what he had been born to wear. If Morfael thought that was the reason for his hesitation, then he really did not know him at all.

"Right then," Morfael gestured toward the tapestry, the gesture mocking. "Your loyal subjects await."

Dylan nodded and moved toward it. However, he was half-way there when he paused and swiveled round to face his brother.

"Morfael, I have something to ask you," he began, his gaze meeting his brother's squarely.

"Go on," Morfael quirked an eyebrow, intrigued.

"I would make you an offer," Dylan continued. "Much depends upon your answer."

***

Merwenna's gaze never left Dylan throughout the entire ceremony.

The prince—soon to be king—stood upon the high seat, which was now draped in plush purple, resplendent in his finery. Behind him hung the flag of Powys—a blood-red lion rampant against a field of gold.

Merwenna's gaze remained upon him while his uncle Elfan recited a long list of oaths that the new king would have to swear to, which Dylan then repeated. Although she understood little of what was spoken, her attention did not waver from him. She could tell from the timbre of Dylan's voice that he took none of the oaths lightly.

Dylan then knelt before his uncle. Elfan placed an iron crown upon his nephew's head. The new King of Powys rose to his feet, a wide smile on his face. A great roar went up inside the hall, the sheer force of it causing the timber structure to vibrate.

The cheering continued as Dylan's most trusted warriors, Gwyn and Owain among them, pushed their way through the crowd, bearing a great oaken shield. Morfael and Elfan joined them, and Dylan seated himself upon it.

Together the group hoisted Dylan high into the air. He grinned from ear to ear, as he clung on to the edge of the shield. It was a symbolic gesture in which they showed their new king to the gods. Merwenna had heard of this ritual but had never realized the effect it would have on those gathered.

The crowd roared. They stamped their feet, and clapped their hands—and for one brief moment Merwenna forgot her unhappiness. She forgot that she did not belong here, for the joy and devotion inside the hall momentarily transported her with them. Her skin prickled and for the first time she truly understood the power a king wielded. A man had to be strong, indeed, to shoulder such responsibility.

Merwenna kept her gaze riveted upon Dylan's face. She loved him. He was arrogant, stubborn and proud—but she ached to be with him all the same. On the journey here, and in the private moments they had shared, she had come to know the Prince of Powys. Dylan was so much more than he appeared. His sharp mind, dry sense of humor, passion, and strength had stolen her heart.

Her love for him just made his unfeeling offer last night hurt all the more.

He knew she would never agree to such an arrangement. It was almost as if he had done it to push her away. They had walked back to the Great Hall in silence, a chasm between them that could not be breached—and had not spoken since.

Cynddylan, King of Powys, sat back down upon his carved wooden throne to thunderous applause, an enigmatic smile curving his lips. Pain constricted Merwenna's ribs, as if an iron band crushed her. Tears blurred her gaze and she looked down at her feet.

That smile would always be her undoing.

Chapter Forty-three

The Feast

It was said that Pengwern had never seen such a feast. Long tables lined the Great Hall either side of the fire pits, groaning under the weight of all the food: platters of roast sweet onions and carrots, pies, breads, cheeses, tureens of rich venison stew, goose stuffed with chestnuts and apples, and duck stuffed with plums.

Men carried in the carcasses of two spit-roasted wild-boar. Mead, ale, and wine flowed freely. The smoke from cooking cast a haze over the cavernous interior; and the rumble of laughter, conversation, and the strains of a bone whistle and a harp echoed high into the rafters.

Dylan sat upon his carved chair at the head of one of the tables.

Upon seeing Merwenna approach, bearing a jug of wine, he held out his gold, jeweled cup for her to fill. She did so obediently although she avoided his gaze all the while. She was pale, even in the golden light of the torches lining the walls, and her expression was solemn. Yet she had never looked lovelier to Dylan.

"Thank you, Merwenna."

She ignored him, and moved off to fill his brother's cup.

Morfael barely noticed his cup being filled, for his gaze was on the pretty blonde maid seated beside him. Cyneswith had just answered his question. Her gaze was downcast, but Dylan noted the blush that crept up her neck. Despite her timidity, the girl was succumbing to his brother's charm. Like Dylan, he spoke her tongue fluently. Morfael said something else, and the girl ventured a smile, her gaze darting up to shyly meet his.

Dylan's gaze shifted further down the table, to where the rest of his kin and retainers sat helping themselves to the mountain of food before them. Heledd sat next to Cyneswith. His sister was dressed in a fine emerald gown with gold trim, her dark hair bound in intricate coils about her crown. She was listening demurely to her uncle, Elfan, who sat opposite her. Watching Heledd a moment, Dylan gave a wry smile—his sister's fiery nature made it difficult to maintain the façade of a modest maid although she did her best.

His uncle, who was already red-faced from the four cups of mead he had consumed thus far, was lecturing his niece on the responsibilities of kingship. Next to him sat Caedmon, Penda's emissary. The young man said nothing although the twist of his mouth hinted at his thoughts on Elfan's discourse.

Caedmon looked like he would rather be somewhere else.

His expression was sullen and not even the sumptuous spread before him seemed to warm his countenance. Dylan could hardly blame him; a Mercian warrior did not belong here. Gwyn, Owain, and a handful of Dylan's most loyal retainers sat to the emissary's left, but Caedmon ignored them, and they did the same. Gwyn and his friends were already well into their cups and getting rowdier by the moment.

"So, how does it feel to be king?" Elfan asked, raising his cup to Dylan.

“Ask me tomorrow, when my wits aren’t addled by good food and wine,” Dylan grinned back and raised his own cup.

“Your father always complained of that crown,” Elfan continued. “Said it was uncomfortable and made his scalp bleed.”

“He wasn’t wrong,” Dylan agreed. “It feels as if it’s made of thorns.”

“Such is the burden of kingship,” Morfael cut in. He had managed to tear his gaze from the comely Cyneswith long enough to follow their conversation. “Although you don’t look like you’re suffering to me.”

Dylan laughed and helped himself to a piece of mutton and rosemary pie. “Fret not,” he replied, meeting his brother’s eye, “I don’t need assistance wearing it.”

“My Lord, Cynddylan,” Caedmon’s voice interrupted the banter between the brothers. “You said you would tell me your answer, after your crowning. Will you accept Lord Penda’s gift or not? I must know your answer.”

The chatter of conversation at the table round them died away. Gazes swiveled toward the Mercian.

Not for the first time, Dylan noted the fluency with which Caedmon spoke his tongue. The warrior’s tone, however, was bordering on insolent, as was his demand for an answer so early into the feasting.

Dylan had planned to announce his decision later, but Caedmon had forced this moment upon him. He shifted his gaze from Caedmon and noted that Merwenna had made her way up the other side of the table. She now stood near enough to hear all that was spoken.

He took a deep, measured breath. He might as well say this now.

“I have thought upon it,” he replied, regarding Caedmon over the rim of his cup, “and I have made my decision.”

Caedmon nodded. The warrior’s impatience emanated off him in waves. “And what will it be?”

"I accept Penda's gift."

Dylan's admission brought gasps from around the table, but he held out his hand to still them.

"Wait—I have not yet finished. Cyneswith will remain in Powys, and we will have peace. However, she will not wed me but my brother."

Stunned silence reverberated around the table. The only person present who did not appear shocked was Morfael. His brother sat quietly, a knowing smile playing on his lips. Beside him, Cyneswith looked bewildered. She glanced from Caedmon's face to Dylan's, and then to Morfael's. She did not understand the words that had passed between them—but clearly realized that they discussed her fate.

Caedmon stared at Dylan, his mouth gaping. "What?"

"You heard me," Dylan replied, ignoring the warrior's rudeness for the moment. "I declare Morfael, 'Steward of the East'. He will govern the new lands recently gifted to Powys by Mercia. My brother will take up residence in Lichfield, and his new bride will make peace between our kingdoms."

Merwenna stood still, clutching the jug of wine so tightly that she worried the clay might crumble beneath her fingers.

Had she heard right? Her understanding of Cymraeg had improved of late, but she worried that she had misheard the words that had just passed between Dylan and Penda's emissary.

Dylan's gaze shifted from Caedmon to where she stood at the envoy's shoulder. She had been about to refill his cup when the conversation had taken a turn.

As if sensing her confusion, Dylan then repeated his last sentence, this time in Englisc.

Cyneswith's gasp of surprise only confirmed the truth.

Merwenna had, indeed, understood. Shock warred with burgeoning hope.

What does this mean?

She stared at Dylan and saw the warmth in his eyes, the quirk of his smile—an endearing blend of cocky and hopeful. Perhaps fate had not turned against her after all?

Merwenna looked down, trying to keep her emotions under control, and moved to refill Caedmon's cup. However, upon seeing Merwenna at his elbow, the warrior snarled and shoved her away.

"Get back from me, bitch!"

The jug flew from Merwenna's hands and crashed onto the table, dousing the feasters in rich, plum wine.

"I want no more Cymry hospitality," Caedmon shouted. "I piss on you all!"

Caedmon had not come to the feast planning to kill Cynddylan.

He had merely donned a mail shirt under his tunic as a precaution, for he did not trust Cynddylan, or any who served him. The tunic he wore was loose, and long, reaching to mid-thigh. It had been easy to conceal a knife under its hem.

Every moment under this roof galled him. He hated these people, loathed breathing the same air as them. He would never have guessed that the new King of Powys would agree to peace in one breath and insult Penda's generosity in the next.

Treacherous dog.

Caedmon could not go back to Penda with news that Cyneswith had wed Cynddylan's younger brother. He would live only long enough to deliver the news before Penda gutted him in a rage. Penda had not sacrificed his precious daughter so that the King of Powys could cast her aside like a peasant.

He could not prevent it. He was one Mercian in a sea of Cymry. Cynddylan had the upper hand. Whether it happened now, or later, Caedmon was a dead man—but before he drew his last breath he intended to slay the cur who had been the source of all his misery.

Caedmon cursed them all and unsheathed the knife, with the lightning speed that had won him a place among Penda's best. Unlike the rest of the feasters, he had drunk and eaten sparingly. The rest of them were slow to react, their minds fogged by wine, their stomachs heavy with rich food.

With a roar, Caedmon launched himself across the table toward the king, scattering food and cups of wine.

Merwenna's scream saved Dylan from having his throat cut open by Caedmon's blade.

Never, had Dylan seen a man move so fast. The warrior's gawky, rawboned appearance hid a lethal skill. Penda had sent a killer to treat with him.

The flash of his attacker's blade filled Dylan's vision as he toppled back off the bench onto the rushes. His crown flew off and rolled away across the floor. Had he been seated on his throne when Caedmon attacked, its carved armrests and high back would have trapped him like a cage, leaving him unable to escape. As it was, he did not have time to roll to his feet, before Caedmon was upon him.

The blade sliced toward Dylan's throat. His fist curled around Caedmon's sinewy wrist, holding it fast. He strained against his attacker in an attempt to keep the Mercian's blade from biting. He was stronger than his opponent. Yet Caedmon was on top of him and had the advantage.

Dylan looked into Caedmon's eyes and saw a killing rage. He had seen wrath like this on the battlefield, had felt it himself when bloodlust ignited in his veins. He knew that when a man entered such a state, he cared not for his own life. All that mattered was dealing out death. He saw the man's desperation, his hate.

Slowly, the blade inched toward Dylan's exposed throat. He was losing the battle for his life. Any moment now, the blade would bite into his flesh. Sweat beaded Dylan's face. He fought Caedmon with every inch of his strength but still the knife moved closer.

A shadow fell across them—and a booted foot lashed out, connecting with Caedmon's ribs.

Morfael, his handsome face twisted in fury, drew back his leg and kicked the Mercian once more. This time, he aimed for just under the armpit, putting all his force into the blow. With a grunt of pain, Caedmon fell off his quarry, his grip on the knife loosening for an instant.

An instant was all Dylan needed.

He drove his knee up into Caedmon's stomach and shoved his arm upwards. A moment later, he was on top of his attacker, pinning him to the ground.

Caedmon writhed like a landed trout, his teeth bared, and his eyes bulging. Dylan was barely able to keep him down. He would not be able to subdue the warrior—the only way Caedmon would stop fighting was when he ceased to draw breath.

Dylan had wanted to keep this man alive, to find out whether this attack had been another one of Penda's tricks. However, Caedmon was a man with nothing left to lose.

Dylan had to end it.

He smashed his fist into Caedmon's face, dazing his opponent. Then he wrested the blade from Caedmon's grappling fingers and plunged it into the base of his opponent's neck. Caedmon made a choked, gurgling noise and abruptly stopped struggling. His eyes widened in surprise, as if he could not believe his time had come. He grappled for the blade, his fingers curving around the bone handle.

Blood gushed from his neck and soaked into the rushes, flowering into a crimson lake around them.

Chapter Forty-four

Truths

Dylan pushed himself up off Caedmon. His gaze fastened upon the warrior's face, watching as he choked to death. When Caedmon finally lay still, his pale eyes gazing sightlessly at the rafters, the king rose to his feet.

For the first time since he had been attacked, Dylan became aware of his surroundings.

All feasting and merriment had ceased. His brother, uncles, and warriors surrounded him, their gazes baleful. Caedmon had done the unthinkable.

"Filthy betrayer," Morfael's expression was murderous. He spat on the Mercian's corpse, glaring down at him as if he wished to tear him apart with his bare hands.

"No good telling him that now," Dylan gasped, still breathless from the brief struggle. The skin of his throat still tingled from anticipating the bite of Caedmon's blade, and he rubbed at it. "He can't hear you."

Morfael knelt beside Caedmon and pulled down the dead man's blood-soaked collar.

"The villain wears a mail shirt," he muttered. "He planned this."

A shocked hush reverberated around them.

No man wore a mail shirt, or carried a weapon, at feasts. These celebrations were rare moments when a warrior could let his guard down and relax in the knowledge no harm would befall him. To do so was to insult his host and breach an unspoken rule.

Dylan's gaze shifted from his brother to the table behind them. The feasters were no longer seated. They stood, ashen and shocked, staring at the king and the man who had tried to slay him. Dylan's gaze eventually paused upon Cyneswith's taut face and there it stayed.

"Did you know of Caedmon's plans?" he rasped.

She shook her head, her blue eyes growing huge.

"Speak girl!" Elfan roared. He stood by Dylan's side, his face puce with outrage. His meaty hands flexed and looked ready to snap Princess Cyneswith's delicate neck. "Has treachery turned you mute?"

"I did not know!" she cried, her voice shrill with panic. Her gaze darted around the faces of those she had been feasting with, pleading for their understanding. Dylan saw the terror in her eyes and despite the anger that pulsed through him, he felt a twinge of pity for her.

"Who is this man?" he demanded, gesturing to the dead Mercian at his feet.

"One of my father's guard," she gasped. "I know very little of him, only that his mother was from Powys. My father choose him to escort me because he spoke your tongue. I swear on Woden and Thor that I, and my father, had nothing to do with his actions."

"Your father did not plan to have me murdered at my own coronation then?"

"No!" the princess cried, tears streaming down her face. "He wants peace. He would never have sent me otherwise. Do you think he would put me in danger?"

"I think Penda of Mercia would throw his own mother to the wolves, if it served his purpose," Dylan growled, advancing on the girl. "I think you would lie to protect him—even if it cost you your life."

"I wouldn't!" Cyneswith insisted, swallowing a sob. Despite her obvious terror, she did not back down. "But my father would never have sent me here with an assassin. He would know I would be harmed."

"Cyneswith is right."

Merwenna stepped up beside the princess. Cyneswith jumped, startled, but Merwenna linked her arm through hers in a silent show of solidarity.

"Penda is cruel and ruthless," she continued, her gaze meeting Dylan's, "but he is protective of his wife and daughters. I saw them together, as did you. He would not send her here with a man ordered to kill you."

Dylan halted mid-step. Merwenna's intervention disarmed him.

"Why do you speak up for her?" he asked, frowning. "This girl would not do the same for you?"

Merwenna held his gaze and smiled. Her blue eyes were luminous, her cheeks flushed. Her unbound almond-colored hair rippled around her shoulders in silken waves.

He had never seen a woman so beautiful.

"Perhaps not," she replied, her voice low and firm, "but I cannot stand by and let her be blamed for this."

"The girl speaks true," Morfael murmured, stepping up behind Dylan. "Cyneswith is guiltless. Look into her eyes, Dylan, and tell me she knew of Caedmon's treachery."

Dylan did as his brother bid and stared deep into the princess's guileless blue eyes. He saw no deceit there—only sincerity. Such a sheltered, innocent young woman could not have kept up the pretense of a lie this long, he realized.

"Very well," he stepped back and raked a hand through his hair. "I believe you."

Cyneswith sagged slightly against Merwenna and looked about to faint.

Heledd stepped up then, her face pale and taut in the aftermath of nearly seeing her brother murdered.

"Will you still have peace, Milord?" she asked. "Now that you know Penda had no part in this."

"Surely not?" Elfan exploded, unable to hold his tongue any longer. Their uncle strode forward, shouldered Morfael aside, and faced Dylan. "We must have vengeance."

"The man to blame is dead," Dylan replied. "Who would you have your reckoning upon?"

Dylan could see the fury in Elfan's eyes, and knew his uncle would not let this lie. Yet Dylan now saw things with startling clarity—it was as if he had spent the last days traveling through fog, and now the mist had cleared. Suddenly, he knew what path he would take.

"Cyneswith will wed Morfael," he told his uncle, emphasizing each word for Elfan's benefit, "and we shall have peace."

"A 'peacemaker'," Elfan's mouth twisted, and he spat at Cyneswith's feet. She shrank back against Merwenna, terrified. "All I see before me is a whey faced Mercian slut."

"Mind your tongue, uncle," Morfael growled, inserting himself between Elfan and Cyneswith.

"You would taint our blood-line!" Elfan roared, turning on the prince. "You would forget that Penda sent killers to slit your brother's throat. You would forget the reckoning you vowed—just to wed this bitch!"

"Enough!"

Dylan's command fell like the blow of a war axe, his voice echoing in the silence of his hall. He fixed Elfan in a cold, hard stare. "You forget your place, uncle. Don't make me remind you again."

Elfan's already high coloring had darkened from puce to purple. He glared back at Dylan, the muscles in his jaw working furiously. He held his tongue.

"The time has come for Powys to forge a new path," Dylan continued, his gaze never leaving his uncle's. "We must bend with change, or we will break. It's true I wanted reckoning against the King of Mercia, and I would have sought it—but Penda showed good will in offering his daughter as a 'peacemaker'. I will not wage war at all costs, when peace would serve us better."

Dylan's gaze swiveled then to Merwenna. She stood, still bracing the trembling Cyneswith. However, her focus was entirely upon him.

A lump rose in Dylan's throat, and he found he was nervous about what he would say next. He had been building up to this moment before Caedmon had attacked him—but he would leave it no longer.

"I could not accept Penda's gift for myself, for I intend to wed another," he began, his gaze never leaving Merwenna's face. He saw a blush stain her cheeks and noted that her eyes gleamed with unshed tears, but he pressed on lest she misunderstand him. "I would be handfasted to you, Merwenna, if you will have me."

Merwenna stared at Dylan, breathless with shock. Her heart was pounding so loudly, she was surprised all present could not hear it.

Suddenly, it was as if they were alone. She forgot the gazes that pressed against her from all sides, forgot that she was a low born girl from a village in Mercia, and that many here would never accept her.

All that mattered was Dylan, the words he had just spoken—and the love she saw in his eyes.

"Of course I'll have you," she whispered. The tears that had been brimming in her eyes spilled over, but she paid them no mind. Instead, she stepped away from Cyneswith, releasing her arm as she went, and covered the two paces that separated her from Dylan.

She flew into his arms, laughing as he swung her round.

Dylan squeezed her against him in a crushing embrace. When he set her down upon the rushes, he cupped her face with his hands and kissed her, not caring who bore witness to it.

"Cariad," he whispered against her mouth. "You stole my heart that night in the woods outside Weyham—and I've loved you ever since."

Merwenna stifled a sob, not sure whether to laugh or cry. "You do?"

"Aye—I'm just sorry it took me so long to say it. I can be block-headed at times."

"I thought I had lost you," she gasped.

She was aware then that, around them, folk were smiling. Some were even wiping away surreptitious tears. But not Elfan, who had stormed off in disgust the moment Dylan declared his love for her.

Morfael was grinning, while next to him Cyneswith smiled and brushed tears from her cheeks. Even Heledd was beaming, her eyes sparkling with emotion. Gwyn and Owain roared their approval and called for cups of mead all round.

Merwenna looked back at Dylan and found that he was staring at her, his gaze devouring her openly. He gave her a private, sensual smile and Merwenna felt her innards melt like candle wax.

He is mine.

If this was a dream, she never wanted to wake from it. Fate had taken her on a journey that had truly tested her. Summer had turned to autumn, and the woman who stood here in the King of Powys' arms, was not the girl who had run away to Tamworth. She had loved, and lost—and then discovered something magical lay on the other side of despair.

She had found Cynddylan, and she would remain at his side for as long as she breathed.

Epilogue

The Spring Visit

Six months later . . .

Merwenna took the bunch of wild flowers from the small girl and pressed a thrymsa into her palm. Barefoot, dirty, and dressed in threadbare homespun, the waif gasped at the wealth the Queen of Powys had just bestowed upon her. Her thin fingers tightened around the gold coin, as if she feared it might vanish.

"Thank you, M'lady!"

Merwenna smiled and glanced down at the flowers the girl had collected from the meadows in the Hafren Valley below; they smelled sweet and reminded Merwenna that, despite the chill in the air this morning, spring had arrived.

"Off you go," she ruffled the girl's dark curls. "Buy your family some meat with that gold."

The girl nodded clutching her basket of flowers in one hand, her precious thrymsa in the other. Merwenna watched the urchin race off through the crowd, and her smile widened.

It was a princely payment for something so simple, but she felt in a generous mood. Wyrd had smiled upon her. Why should others not benefit from her good fortune? On this early spring morning, with the sun warming her face, and the sound of laughter and industry around her, she was very glad she had made Pengwern her home.

Yet there were times when she thought of Weyham and her family, and at those moments a veil of sadness would descend upon her. As happy as she was with Dylan, she missed her parents and her siblings. She wondered now, how they had fared over the long, harsh winter.

Still, the beauty of the morning chased away any homesickness. Merwenna stood in the market square, just off the tangle of streets below the Great Hall. A throng of folk bustled around her, bartering for the first of the spring greens, salted pork, fowl, cheeses, eggs, and grains. One farmer had brought in a mob of goats to sell, their plaintive bleats rising above the chatter of voices.

The aroma of fresh bread attracted Merwenna to where a baker sold loaves off the back of a small cart. She bought herself a roll and ate it while she continued her meandering path through the bustling market. The bread was delicious, and she finished it quickly. She was constantly hungry these days, especially now that the early days of sickness were over.

Merwenna's hand moved down to the swell of her belly beneath her fur cloak and felt something kick against her hand. Her womb had quickened shortly after she and Dylan were handfasted. Their babe grew quickly and strong—and was due shortly before Beltaine.

Merwenna finished her circuit and left the market square behind. She took the lane back toward the Great Hall. She was around ten yards from the gates when she spied a tall, dark-haired man. A purple cloak rippled behind him as he strode toward her.

As always, her stomach fluttered at the sight of her husband.

"Good morning, Milord," she greeted Dylan with a playful smile. "Would some spring flowers please you?"

"Perhaps," he replied, pretending to look cross. "Is that where you've been? I've looked everywhere for you."

"The morning is too beautiful to be spent indoors," Merwenna chided him. She gazed up into his eyes and felt the familiar tug at her heart. She would never tire of looking upon this man, nor of listening to him—or touching him. Despite the sternness of his voice, the languid softness of Dylan's gaze told her he felt the same way.

"What did you want me for?" Merwenna asked, suddenly breathless.

"You have visitors," he smiled, gesturing behind him. "All the way from Weyham."

Merwenna gasped and peered around her husband. Up ahead, she caught sight of a man and a woman wearing thick fur cloaks, their cheeks ruddy with cold. The travelers stood by their horses before the gates of the Great Hall. She recognized their black, shaggy mounts immediately—Huginn and Muninn.

Joy flowered in Merwenna's breast. She knew her father had promised her a spring visit, but she had long believed he would not come. Yet Wil had kept his word, and he had brought Cynewyn with him.

Dylan took Merwenna's hand and squeezed gently, his gaze never leaving her face.

"Will you not come and meet them?" he asked.

Merwenna tore her own gaze away from where her mother had started to wave frantically and looked back at her husband. He was grinning at her. She smiled back and gave his hand an answering squeeze.

"Lead the way, my love."

And he did.

The End

Historical Note

As with all my novels set in 7th century Anglo Saxon England, *The Breaking Dawn* is based on actual historical figures and events. This time around, we also visit 7th century Wales.

Cynddylan ap Cyndrwyn—the Prince of Powys (Wales)—was a well-known historical figure of the time, who ruled from around 641—655 AD

The alliance between Mercia and Powys did exist, and historians have learned a bit about Cynddylan from two famous poems: *Marwnad Cynddylan* (The Death song of Cynddylan) and the *Canu Heledd* (Heledd's lament), a 9th century poem in which his sister sings of her brother's death. Both are hauntingly beautiful, if grim, poems.

In a nutshell, here's what my research unearthed about Cynddylan:

- He wore a mail shirt and purple cloak

- He was fiery, stubborn, brave and ruthless—a great warrior

- He went to battle alongside King Penda of Mercia, against the Northumbrian King, Oswald, bringing 700 warriors with him. They fought together in the Battle of Maserfield (Maes Cogwy in Welsh), in the summer of 641 AD The battle ended with Oswald's defeat, death and dismemberment

- He died fairly young and never married (I ignore this detail—it's a romance after all!)

- He had 9 sisters and 12 brothers (I also ignore this detail—for the sake of the story —preferring to shrink the family to one sister, Heledd, and one brother, Morfael)

- After the Battle of Maes Cogwy, Cynddylan appears to have fallen out with Penda

Details around Cynddylan's death are hazy. There is debate about whether Cynddylan was killed alongside Penda in 655 A.D. at the Battle of Winwæd, or whether he and his family perished the next year when Oswy destroyed his 'court' at Pengwern (we don't get this far in the novel—I prefer to leave Dylan's future open, for the reader to decide).

Jayne Castel

About the Author

Award-winning author Jayne Castel writes Historical Romance set in Dark Ages Britain and Scotland, and Epic Fantasy Romance. Her vibrant characters, richly researched historical settings and action-packed adventure romance transport readers to forgotten times and imaginary worlds.

Jayne lives in New Zealand's South Island, although you can frequently find her in Europe and the UK researching her books! When she's not writing, Jayne is reading (and re-reading) her favorite authors, learning French, cooking Italian, and taking her dog, Juno, for walks.

Jayne won the 2017 RWNZ Koru Award (Short, Sexy Category) for her novel, ITALIAN UNDERCOVER AFFAIR.

Connect with Jayne online:
www.jaynecastel.com